THE LAST INHERITOR

By the same author

The Silk Project
The Cats of Benares
(published by Heinemann)

The Cobra Kite
The Voice of the Crab
The Last Summer of the Men Shortage

THE LAST INHERITOR

a novel by
Geraldine Halls

St. Martin's Press
New York

c, 1

Copyright © 1979 by Geraldine Halls
For information, write: St. Martin's Press,
175 Fifth Avenue, New York, N.Y. 10010
Manufactured in the United States of America

Library of Congress Cataloging in Publication Data

Halls, Geraldine.
    The last inheritor.

    First published in 1979 under title: The felling of Thawle.
    I. Title.
PR9619.3.H29F4   1980   823   80-22071
ISBN 0-312-47087-8

13L

FEB 25 '81

FOR SHIRLEY MOULDEN
because of our long friendship
and because you gave me the idea

PART I
Thawle

Lord Guy, last heir to the crumbling family estate, Thawle, evades the ruthless and wily schemes of antique dealers anxious to get hold of the priceless collections in the old mansion.

Lady Evelyn Buys a Cup and Saucer

'I'm sorry, Lady Evelyn,' said Magnolia Tree, 'but it's
Trade Only on Saturdays.'

Magnolia's soft Somerset accent mitigated to some degree
the severity of this pronouncement on the conditions where-
by she conducted her professional life, so that Lady Evelyn
de Boissy felt free to wander about the premises of Magnolia
Tree Antiques, inspecting at her leisure the blue and white
plates displayed on a dresser, an 'end of day' glass basket, a
Parian hand vase and a collection of Staffordshire dogs
arranged according to size. But always returning to the
window to stare, yet again, at the pink lustre cup and
saucer.

'As if I haven't told her a dozen times, Syd,' said Magnolia,
not bothering to moderate her voice, 'and there's my notice
staring at her outside, as large as life. I'm in bulk, Syd, and
I haven't got time to waste on ignorant amateurs with
nothing to do on a Saturday afternoon.' Raising meanwhile
her pale blue, pink-lashed eyes to the gloomy face of Sydney
Meyer, Bristol dealer in furniture and general bric-à-brac,
who, Magnolia had noted as soon as he set foot in her shop,
invariably stank of beer at three o'clock every Saturday
afternoon, but nevertheless she put up with him because he
was Trade, hadn't tried to handle her yet and spent at least
five quid a week on junk sheer junk, flogging her for two
bob a time antique ginger-ale bottles that were selling for a
dollar fifty in the States.

'I would just like to see the pink cup and saucer,' said
Lady Evelyn, stretching into the window a fragile hand
which threatened not only the lustre cup and saucer but a
Marie Gregory ruby glass jug, the finest that Magnolia had

come by in the eighteen years of her trading life.

Lady Evelyn was known to be over eighty and made no secret of the matter. Old age had done away with most of her flesh and reduced her bones, never very robust, to the appearance of hazel twigs in mid-winter. It was generally agreed, however, that neither time nor age had impaired her famous beauty – in fact by some were said to have enhanced it by eliminating irrelevant details. Magnolia did not share these views and it would never have occurred to her to concede to Lady Evelyn a vestige of beauty, but she did accord her a small measure of admiration for having the stamina to continue driving a car, if only a Mini.

Said Magnolia, bursting with the blood and muscle provided by an ample diet of pies and cream buns, 'Lady Evelyn, if you *must* – please allow me.'

Casting a glance at Syd, whom she suspected to be light-fingered (because why else on a warm spring day would he be wearing as he invariably did that ample black coat flapping well below his knees, and nosing around in her blue and white), Magnolia rose to her feet and to divest herself of a deposit of pie crumbs that had accumulated in her lap, shook out her chintz skirt with the bunches of violets, long to the ground – two years ahead of the fashion designers – which she had run up last night from the bedroom curtains of Rose Cottage, Castle Cary. Alfie Middle had cleared that slum three weeks after some local dogs had discovered the owner dead in the Brussels sprouts, keeping the junk for himself and letting Magnolia loose on the quality stuff which was out of his line : these chintz curtains and several other pairs which she was in the process of converting into cushion covers and pot holders for her stall at the Crewkerne market; a shelf of books on theology, good for sixpence a time; two soap dishes; a china jug and basin; two chamber pots and bulbs from the garden : all as well-deserved payment for her inventory. Alfie not being able to read so well as he put it. Or write.

Alfie, Magnolia's thoughts roamed about him as she shoved

Lady Evelyn from her window and leaned forward for the lustre cup and saucer, was proving invaluable and up to date had kept his hands off her.

Sydney Meyer

'WHY ON earth would she want that cup and saucer?' Magnolia demanded to be told when Lady Evelyn had departed. 'Reggie says that barn of a place is stacked with Chinese armorial, goose tureens, jade, silver, pictures, you name it, the lot.'

Reggie Thring's status as one of the premier antique dealers in an area roughly comprising five counties derived, not from the magnitude of his turnover, for in this matter there were several bulk shippers whose trading figures – if anyone, even their accountants, let alone the Inspector of Taxes, had been able to find out what they were – would have outdistanced Reggie at least tenfold, but from the impeccable quality of his stock – English furniture, jewellery, silver, glass – and the impeccable purity of his reputation. It was said that he had never exploited the ignorance of destitute gentlewomen, who in that area abounded, and had never sold a piece of furniture without at first meticulously describing its defects. Being human, he had made mistakes, but had always been the first to admit to them.

Magnolia felt herself to be on intimate terms with Reggie, a claim pronounced to all and sundry with such confidence that Reginald Thring, gentleman, ex-Charterhouse, ex-Cambridge, found himself unable to refute it.

'I suppose she's going to give it to the maid or some other menial for a wedding present. Mean as Jews,' smoothly concluded Miss Tree, well aware of what she was saying.

'Broke as Jews,' sadly replied Mr Meyer. 'I saw that son of hers the other day having a beer at The Red Lion in Wells.

Had his poor little feet on the bottom rung of the bar stool, all turned up so you could see the soles. Two big holes stuffed with newspaper.'

'Affectation,' Magnolia declared, producing a snorting sound from the back of her nose, unlovely, but effective when expressing contempt, and as much that brushed against Magnolia's life was contemptible, an integral part of her conversation. 'If they're so broke why don't they flog that armorial and all those paintings?'

'Suppose they like them, and feel they're in the family. They've got their pride,' said Sydney, 'like the rest of us. Moreover,' he continued, after a pause during which he hoped that Magnolia might devote some thought to the subject of pride, 'I don't suppose that Reggie Thring has set foot in that house since Lord Charles died which must be all of fifteen years ago, so who is he or anyone else to know what's gone and what's there, because otherwise why can't poor Lord Guy afford to buy a new pair of shoes? Reggie likes to advertise his connections and I for one take anything he's got to say with a grain of salt. I'll take these three. And this one for the bottles.'

Fishing into the interior of his overcoat, which contrary to Magnolia's suspicions he used as a bank, depositing and withdrawing every day, Sydney produced a roll of notes, pulled off three, flicked through them twice with thumb and finger equipped with a rubber ring designed for this purpose and laid them on Magnolia's desk, his hand suddenly beginning to shake uncontrollably as it always did when he found himself in the position of having to part with money.

Wrapping up the four blue and white plates in last week's *Somerset Gazette*, Magnolia regretted the first period Spode with the impressed mark on the back. An Indian hunting scene depicting an elephant, trunk upraised, under a palm tree in the left-hand top corner, sahibs in solar topees on its back, other sahibs on horses assisted by a pack of white dogs pursuing a boar, unbotanical trees and bushes disposed about and tigers rushing around the rim. She had hoped that no one would buy it, reminding her as it did of her Indian heritage, her grandparents having gone there to be missionaries and to produce her father, who along with her mother, also missionaries, had fallen to the Mau-Mau in Africa.

But if you wanted to get on, which Magnolia did, you couldn't be sentimental in this business, and Magnolia swiftly repelled an advancing wave of sentiment by calculating that the first period Spode plate she had bought from an ignorant Cornish native for ten bob was a more than adequate exchange for a dozen ginger-ale bottles, marbles rattling around in their squashed necks, screw tops complete, which when shipped to the States would show her on the present rate of exchange a gross profit of three pounds. Labour costs, comprising Magnolia's time and one shilling an hour to the Staff – Mrs Carter's ten-year-old, mentally retarded kid, Timmy – running costs on the car, rates, taxes, electricity, telephone, the answering service and other sundries deducted, probably around one quid, showing a net profit on the deal of two pounds on a ten-bob outlay. Not bad.

'I still can't imagine,' said Magnolia, as Sydney, his body having absorbed its midday quota of beer, was moving thirstily to the door, 'what she wanted with that lustre cup and saucer. She's been here every Saturday afternoon for the past four weeks, staring at it with that goofy look, they're all inbred.'

Sydney halted, arrested by this remark. A vast Semitic sorrow derived from ancestral memories of exile in Egypt and persecutions in the souks of Damascus invaded his eyes and for a moment threatened a number of Magnolia's most prized convictions.

'There's people,' he said, 'as buys things because they want to use them. Like that Australian I had last week. Show me something you can sit on, he says, or put things in, or eat off or eat out of or eat with. That's all they think of. No traditions. Unless it comes to Moore china. They'll always buy a bit of Moore. But no confidence in their own judgement. Sell them something with a BADA sticker and they'll hang on to that sticker for ever more irrespective of what its doing to the veneer. They'd rather have that sticker than what it's on. And then there's the Americans who only want things for flowers. Chamber pots, spittoons, copper coal-scuttles. Or something to put the bottles in or the TV set. Sell them a Queen Anne bureau and they'll chuck away the drawers or use them for flowers, rip out the guts and fill it up with the TV or a dozen bottles of Bourbon and Scotch. Sell them a pair of ribbon-back Chippendale chairs and they'll put a glass top on the legs and make a trellis out of the backs for their indoor plants.'

'And there's others,' said Sydney Meyer, 'who only wants to show off. Mirrors with cherubs, Louis Fourteenth gilt-wood suites and it doesn't matter if they happen to have been knocked up in 1890 providing they look like money. Blackamoors holding out little trays for visiting cards. Not that I'm not partial myself to a quality blackamoor. Then you come to the few, the very few, Magnolia Tree, that has taste, really refined. That wants good simple English, and an oriental rug that's been made out in the desert by a family – mother and father and little children all with loving care. And a bit of old Chelsea or oriental. And there's some,' concluded Sydney Meyer, 'that sees something that strikes a chord. It's my guess that when somebody like Lady Evelyn with all she's got or had, because we don't know if it's there or not, in spite of Reggie Thring and his aristocratic connec-tions, when, as I was saying, Lady Evelyn sets her heart on a lustre cup and saucer the reason will be that it strikes a chord.'

Having said which, Sydney remembered his thirst and easing through the door his bulky overcoat with its abundant upholstery of English currency, emerged on to the pavement outside that now quite famous shop in a quiet Somerset town and made his way to his preferred pub to fortify him-self before returning to Bristol and the forever recurring and unsolvable problem of his mother.

Magnolia Tree

MAGNOLIA HAD dressed the window of her shop with a display of English blue and white and a notice declaring that she specialised in fairings, books, postcards and theatre programmes, and that she dealt with Trade Only on Saturdays. To the right of this announcement, mounted and framed, was the *pièce de résistance* of her postcard collection depicting the plane in which Louis Blériot had crossed the Channel in 1909, signed by the man himself, and, to the left, the *pièce de résistance* of her theatre programmes, Graham Robertson's 'Pinkie and the Fairies', opening at His Majesty's with Ellen Terry, which she wasn't going to part with under five quid, particularly not to that Portobello spiv Ozzie David, who shook with frustrated desire every time he set eyes on it, but had dug his toes in at three pounds ten.

For apart from her Indian and African connexions, Magnolia, during a series of researches leading her back through a wavering line of uncles, aunts and cousins much removed, had established to her own satisfaction a remote blood connexion with the family of Beerbohm Tree, a discovery which had seized her imagination and launched her in her sixteenth year into the beginnings of her theatre programme collection. Considering her situation in an environment by no means culturally inclined – pigs, cows, sheep, horses, dogs, cider, beer, the big annual event being the Shepton Mallet Agricultural Show – Magnolia was remarkably well informed on the theatrical productions of the second half of the nineteenth century up until 1930, because if you wanted to be a specialist you had to set yourself limits and after 1930 the golden age was over, with Oscar, Sarah, Ellen, Henry, Beerbohm, Gordon and the rest either dead or past their prime and the rot had set in.

At five-thirty Magnolia prepared to close her shop, first taking in from the pavement, which was becoming obstreperous with the kids, all illegitimate, from Mrs Carter's slum down the road, her 6d. book tray, her 1/– book tray and the 'Everything for 3d.' tray, comprising odd cups, odd saucers, a broken fan, a thimble, buttons, beads and a pottery model of 'Bonzo' with a broken ear. A perfect gold-mine. As the church clock struck six she watered her potted herbs and the magnolia tree in the cut-down keg, a likeness of which appeared on her business cards and on the top of her note-paper.

This tree was not the Japanese sort bursting out in spring into big pink cups in Queen's Square, Bath, but *Magnolia grandiflora*, a species which in its maturity could achieve a height of seventy feet. Magnolia planned to sell it off when it outgrew its pot and replace it with a smaller one, and so on. Although it flourished in Great Britain, it had not attracted her attention until that last disastrous summer when she had frizzled in southern Spain. The tour disorganised, the food inedible and the heat unendurable. When, along with twenty-five English, Australian and American sheep, she had been herded into the gardens adjacent to the Alcazar in Seville, she had learned from a guide-book given to romantic hyperbole that the first magnolia tree to put down its roots in Europe had been planted on that very spot by Christopher Columbus from seeds brought back on his return from the New World. Magnolia, at all times sceptical, did not wholeheartedly accept this assertion, but an aroma seeping not only from the pages of the guide-book but from the very stones and skies of Seville, and comprising a spicy stew of history, blood and beauty all ripened and fermented by hot weather, worked on her imagination. Touring neighbouring Andalusian towns, she had observed, lining the streets, these same migrant trees with their fleshy white flowers blooming in luxuriant leaves and had seized upon them to turn to her advantage what had previously seemed to be a rather poor joke on the part of her parents.

Having attended to herbs and tree, Magnolia retired to her Export Department, which, along with Textiles, was accommodated in a shed behind her living quarters at the back of the shop. She set in motion her pebble-polishing machines, left them turning away converting last week's Cornish pebbles into polished eggs – beautifully marked with red, white and green flecks of quartz – completed the inventory of twelve chamber pots, five jugs and basins, seventeen soap dishes and three dozen ginger-ale bottles waiting to be packed in the cartons she collected every Tuesday afternoon from the off-licence, and despatched to the States on Monday afternoon as soon as the Staff got out of school.

This task accomplished, she composed a letter to the local press complaining of the inadequacy and inefficiency of postal services, and consumed her supper of a pork pie, two cream buns and a bottle of Coca-Cola.

The late light flushed the ancient stones of that Somerset town which, forever responsive to the changing skies, smiled, frowned and meditated. The daisies on the Abbey lawn, before closing for the night, glowed with a last impulse of brightness. The air throbbed and crashed to the beat of the Hi-Fi in the Youth Club at the Church Hall. And up in the moist hills on the road to Bradford-on-Avon, Lord Guy de Boissy, youngest and only surviving son of Lady Evelyn, wondering what it was that had set the spaniels barking, hurried from the kitchen where he had been preparing an Irish stew, to discover the unconscious body of his mother sprawled at the top of the steps leading to the front door of Thawle, the de Boissy ancestral home.

Her head was turned to one side, her cheek pressed to a clump of aubretia that had thrust between the cracks of the terrace stones.

Guy turned her body over and called to her. 'Mummy, dearest Mummy!' Lady Evelyn smiled, clutching to her breast a bunch of buttercups and a parcel wrapped in the *Somerset Gazette*.

Lady Evelyn Goes Home

WHEN MAGNOLIA had wrapped the pink lustre cup and saucer in the pages of the *Somerset Gazette* and had secured the parcel with rubber bands, Lady Evelyn placed it in her shopping basket on top of a pound of Cheddar cheese, two bottles of Guinness and a packet of Twinings Earl Grey tea, and set off home in her Mini.

Taking the old road from Wells to Shepton Mallet, she stopped on the ridge overlooking the Vale of Avalon where the hedges were low and the steeply descending fields, animated with the dancing tails of spring lambs, afforded a view of Glastonbury Tor, standing like a monument in a lake of mist. The cow parsley was beginning to break into flower.

Lady Evelyn picked a posy of buttercups for her poor little cousin, Alice, only six years old and in bed with 'flu. Returning to the Mini, she put the flowers carefully on the seat beside her, spreading them out so that they wouldn't be crushed and would still be fresh when she reached home.

Having driven out of Shepton Mallet under the railway bridge and up past the cottages where the aubretias hung in pink and purple loops over walls that still caught the sun, and up to the top of the hill where the snow banked up in winter, Lady Evelyn took the right-hand turn to Bath.

On the stretch of road following the Fosse Way out of Oakhill, the new leaves on the beeches were so thin and translucent that all beneath was water in a rock pool where you splashed barefoot with your knickers tucked up, chasing, but never catching, tiny darting fishes and closing sea anemones with your finger.

Passing a gypsy caravan parked in a layby and turning right off the Fosse Way towards Bradford-on-Avon, Lady Evelyn shivered excitedly under the impact of dark eyes imbued with the mysteries of Egypt and absorbed into her very soul authoritative predictions concerning her destiny. Lady Evelyn had since wondered whether that old gypsy woman, trailing her skirts over the grubby scorched grass of Hampstead Heath on Bank Holiday, had foretold her future, or whether, recognising incipient ambitions in the eyes of an eight-year-old child, she had simply prescribed directions that Lady Evelyn had submissively followed. Presumably she had pursued the life she wanted. Or had she? Lady Evelyn was not sure.

On the quiet road to Bradford-on-Avon, she drew up by a gate beyond which black and white cows were big gentle toys displayed on a green carpet in Hamleys, that Christmas when she and Alice had been taken to Regent Street to see the decorations. Or had it been thirty-five years later when as the wife of Lord Charles de Boissy and looking for a Christmas present for her little son Guy, a tall, thin man with grey hair had helped her choose between two rocking horses. A pony with a real fur coat, and a dappled grey with a painted coat but a horsehair mane and tail. Still up in the attic over the kitchens in Thawle.

The tall thin man had lifted Guy and put him on each of the horses so that he could see which one he liked best, but never changing his expression even to smile at the child, and moving always in a solemn jerky way. It had amused Lady Evelyn to think of him as one of the mechanical toys, though rather large, with a key in his side that someone had recently wound up to set him in motion. She had turned her cheek into the fur collar of her coat to hide a smile. At the same time, remembering that other visit to Hamleys, so many years before, with her aunt and Alice.

Eight years old, ten years old, fifty years old, eighty years old. Roaming back and forth over her life Lady Evelyn gazed from the window of her Mini at the toy cows in Hamleys, scooping up in their long blue tongues bunches of buttercups, or raising their heads with daisies dropping from their lips.

Ever since she had seen the cup and saucer in Magnolia's window, she had arrived at a disconcerting though not unpleasing sense that Time had got out of hand. She had always regarded Time as respectably controlled. But the image her mind had projected of a well-behaved river rising in mountains, flowing through calm, comfortable plains and spilling itself into a peaceful sea, was no longer appropriate. Time had become a display of fireworks, a carnival of lights that flashed and failed, eluding in their transience any attempt to hold and regard them. Tossed back and forth through the years and vividly confronted by episodes that had seemed trivial at the time and had long been forgotten, Lady Evelyn found herself clinging to her recollections of the many remarkable events that had made her, which, jumbled about with fantasies and dreams, seemed to have lost their substance, so that she wondered if they had ever taken place and whether the splendid people who had paraded through her life had ever existed.

She looked about her. The sky was dark; the fields stroked by the shadows of tall, solemn trees. It might have been midnight under a full moon. Only the buttercups still harboured their gold. The daisies had retired. Lady Evelyn became aware of a stillness that was cold, petrified, and bereft of peace or mercy. It closed about her, threatening to immobilise her for ever. She struggled to escape.

An eight-year-old child started up the Mini and found her way back home. The Princess in the goblin mine feeling through the dark, her hand on her grandmother's silken thread.

Thawle

THAWLE, the de Boissy ancestral home, was not regarded by those who considered themselves equipped to decide such matters to be of much architectural consequence. The sturdy Tudor structure of the original building had been all but obliterated by a series of frivolous additions comprising wings, galleries, balconies and porticos added over a period of some three hundred years. But Thawle was situated amongst woods of great beauty, the river Rustle, a modest tributary of the Avon, flowing beyond and below its once formal terraced gardens, and with the passage of time the whims of the lords of Thawle had come to terms with one another. Sun, rain, the mists coming down from the northern hills, mould, ivy, lichen, moss and small plants producing flowers through cracks in walls, pulled the house together and soothed its argumentative factions. Even purists who attacked the mansard roof added in the nineteenth century, and the four towers reminiscent of the Château of Carcassonne, were obliged to admit that the makers of Thawle had, if only by accident, managed to pull it off. One wouldn't want it otherwise, monument as it was to human folly and to that obstinate Gallic refusal to forget about France, no matter how remote one's connections with that country might be.

There wasn't a fault to be found with the stables. Solidly English down to the last brick.

Throughout the four hundred years of its history, the house had witnessed four murders and harboured three ghosts, not, as most would have expected, the murderers or their victims, but wistful creatures of little account who wandered disconsolately and ignoring one another along halls and stairways lit successively by torchlight, candlelight, gaslight and electricity. With the approach of the twentieth century these apparitions became more and more diaphanous. During the First World War they lost their feet and when in 1943 a German bomber crashed in the orchard they disappeared and were said to have been shocked back to their graves.

Throughout the eighteenth and nineteenth centuries, the male members of the de Boissy family divided their time between England and France, indulging a taste for painting and *objets de vertu* in the one country and for healthy young women of low birth in the other. But the departure of the ghosts precipitated a decline following the improvident

21

spending of Lord Edward who had extended the de Boissy cultural horizons to Russia and China and was responsible for the famous collection of Fabergé and the jades and ceramics in the Oriental Room. His son, Lord Philip, contributed little to the enhancement of the estate or to the family legend in the way of romantic escapades, but his grandson, Lord Charles, enjoyed both notoriety and prosperity achieved by a succession of pretty women and a stable of race-horses. On his death the estate shrank almost to the orchard walls and the racing stable was reduced to a promising three-year-old, Rolling Home, whose shoulders never felt the grip of a jockey's knees.

In the years following the death of Lord Charles, Thawle became darker and colder. The central heating, at all times an economic disaster, was abandoned. Hundred-watt light bulbs were replaced by twenty-five watt. Members of the staff who had died of old age were not replaced, and although no one was dismissed, most departed to escape discomfort and rheumatism.

Lord Guy

LADY EVELYN had produced three sons. The eldest, Wilfred, had died after having been mauled by the cheetah he had established in the Aviary behind the stables. The second child, prematurely born, had lived for only two weeks. Guy, the only surviving son, had been born when Lady Evelyn was forty-two.

Guy passed his time combining the pursuits of a leisured country gentleman and an underpaid farm labourer. He woke and rose with the birds, donned riding breeches and descended to the kitchens for a lump of sugar. Rolling Home awaited him outside the stables, attended by Giles Malley, Lord Charles's senior groom, who had stayed on after the break-up of the stable, on the basis of board and keep. After Rolling Home had eaten the sugar and licked the taste from the palm of Guy's hand, Giles gave Guy a hitch into the saddle, a service that was unnecessary, but which Guy enjoyed because it had persisted since his childhood and which Giles enjoyed because it invested his existence with a sense of purpose it might otherwise have lacked.

In winter it was barely light when Guy and his horse set forth together, making their way through the few remaining acres of the once extensive woods and meadows of Thawle. The main path through the woods was old and so deeply sunk that horse and rider were almost hidden from the view of anyone standing in the woods above. When the path became sloshy after rain, or in winter hard with ice, Guy rode through the higher woods where the paths were firm. He liked the winter best. Rolling Home cantered slowly with the regular monotonous motion of a rocking horse, his hooves, lightly placed, barely making a sound on the toffee-coloured paths padded with fallen leaves. Bare branches, clotted with the nests of rooks, let in the sky.

But in summer he kept to the Saxon road, riding straight through the woods to the meadows beyond and stopping at a white gate which led to Lord Charles's racing paddock where three Derby winners, Traveller, Redbreast and Aucassin, had been trained to form. All now – horses and paddock – belonging to someone else. He felt little regret for the loss of his property. He had enough to deal with as it was. But when they came to the gate Rolling Home lifted his head and pricked his ears as though the long green fields were calling him and reminding him of his youth. Sometimes he stood obstinately firm and shook his head, fighting the reins, as Guy turned him back to the woods.

After he had returned Rolling Home to the care of Giles, Guy cooked and ate his breakfast of bacon and eggs alone in the kitchen. Having made it plain to Irene that he did not want to have anything to say to her in the morning. When he had finished, he prepared breakfast for his mother. Kippers, smoked haddock, herrings or fish roes on toast, which along with more toast, marmalade and a pot of tea he arranged on a tray, decorated with a rose in summer, primroses in spring, acorns in winter or, when he happened to find one, a feather. He carried the tray to her room, lit her fire, and sitting on her bed as she drank her tea told her about his projects for the day and about anything that might have happened, such as the appearance of a squirrel or pheasant, during his ride in the woods.

'Rolling Home doesn't like the woods,' he once said to her. 'He goes to the gate and pricks his ears because he wants to be back in the paddock. When I turn his head he tells me that he doesn't want to go. He wants to stand and look over the gate at the paddock.'

Lady Evelyn stretched out her hand to brush back from his brow a dark lock of hair, identical in her recollection to the lock of hair that had forever dangled over the brow of Lord Charles and provoked the inquisitive fingers of so many pretty women.

'My darling, you are too sensitive. What are we going to do about you when you worry so about the feelings of a horse?'

'Why,' said Guy, 'should his feelings be less important than ours?'

After he had taken his mother's tray back to the kitchen he changed into his working clothes and his working life. He picked and bottled the orchard fruit, shared the cooking with Irene, raised ducks and chickens and saw to most of the minor repairs. Larger repairs, such as the roof, were ignored as being beyond the realms of possibility. But most of his time was spent in an extensive vegetable garden which produced a surplus for Giles to take to the weekly markets in Bradford-on-Avon and Frome.

Giles and Irene

GILES SHARED the stables with Rolling Home. Here, in the three most luxurious stalls which had housed Traveller, Aucassin and Redbreast, he had established his living quarters. The partitions between the stalls had been knocked down and the area achieved was sufficiently spacious to accommodate a table, three chairs, a cupboard for his clothes, twenty-four saddles, thirty-six bridles and sundry straps, girths, stirrups and spurs, hanging from pegs on the northern wall. Jockeys' caps and silks – the green and white of the de Boissy stables – displayed above added a splash of colour to an otherwise leathery-looking room.

Giles had knocked up some shelves on the southern wall for Lord Charles's trophies which were arranged according to importance and size. On the southern wall more shelves displayed brushes, curry combs, bottles of linseed oil, tar and saddle soap. Giles, with a religious fervour which he carried back with him from ten o'clock Mass at the Catholic church in Thawle-on-Rustle, soaped and oiled the leather and polished the bits and spurs every Sunday morning with the same care he would have devoted to them had there been horses to justify their existence. As Rolling Home never ventured from the soft turf of Thawle's fields he had no need for shoes, but Giles, after he had groomed him and cleaned his teeth, attended to his hooves which were trimmed with a blacksmith's knife and painted with tar.

When he could spare the time Giles also helped clean the house, a task that was not arduous for there were now few inhabited rooms. The really big job was the main hall which was paved with tiles ordered by Lord Edward in 1880 from the factory of Sèvres. The huge Persian carpet and the two smaller Ghiordes rugs had to be rolled up and removed when the floor was soused with buckets of water and brushed out with brooms, a major operation taking place once every month or so and engaging the combined efforts of Giles and Irene.

Irene, the third member of the household, was a nineteen-year-old London girl who had arrived three years before, equipped with a letter from her mother, and who had established herself in the servants' quarters. In a house so abundantly supplied with vacant rooms she had had a choice of more spacious accommodation, but the servants' quarters were the warmest rooms in the house, deriving benefit from the kitchen range below. Moreover, Irene was not accustomed to a lot of space. She liked walls that closed protectively about her, a low ceiling and a small window that didn't let in too much light.

By reason of the claims stated in her mother's letter, Irene occupied a strong position in the household, but refrained from exploiting it. She dusted, cleaned, cooked and attended Lady Evelyn, making her bed, washing her hair and looking after her clothes, some of which dated back to the years before her marriage, and were so numerous that the wardrobes in her bedroom and the two brass-bound trunks which had accompanied her to Egypt on her honeymoon in 1908, would not contain them. As Irene was of similar height and size to Lady Evelyn in 1908, a substantial proportion of Lady Evelyn's clothes had found their way to the servants' quarters above the kitchen.

Lady Evelyn enjoyed shopping and enjoyed driving her car. At least once a week she and Irene went to one of the nearby towns to buy groceries and to the market where Lady Evelyn always bought fish, choosing kippers and herrings with knowledge and care. She was always happy to stop at the antique shops or the second-hand bookshops where Irene sometimes found a book to add to her library.

Irene liked the crowded towns on market day and in the Mini with Lady Evelyn beside her felt no aversion to the countryside, but back at Thawle, once her duties were over, she spent most of her time in her rooms or in the kitchen –

one of the three kitchens of Thawle that was still in use — and rarely went out of doors. When she did, she kept close to the house.

The Spaniels

THE ONLY useless members of the household were the two spaniels, which on that Saturday evening, barking with sorrow and alarm, ran about the prostrate body of Lady Evelyn as she lay at the top of the steps, only pausing in their lamentations to dab their tongues on her mouth and eyes.

Guy and Giles, stumbling about amongst the hysterical spaniels, carried Lady Evelyn upstairs to her bedroom and lifted her to her bed.

'Weighs no more than a handful of hay,' said Giles.

Guy burst into tears.

'Now, Lord Guy, there's things that have to be done.'

But all they could think to do was to take off her shoes and cover her with an eiderdown. Giles rounded up the spaniels and went downstairs to ring up Dr Templeton.

Guy knelt by his mother's side, holding her cold hand. On the terrace she had smiled at him and clutched her buttercups. Now her eyes were closed. Guy stroked her hair and implored her to look at him. The spaniels had dashed back to whine and scratch at the door but it seemed to Guy that the sunlight entering the room through its majestic western windows and cast about by the moving branches of trees was causing as much agitation as the spaniels. Distracted by the reflections of chestnut flowers tossing back and forth in the mirror on the *bureau de bonheur* Guy raised his eyes from his mother's white, shrunken face to find that even the furniture in the room was losing solidity. The legs of the love-seat crumbled like kindling in fire. The ormolu clock melted to a golden liquid. Roses and carnations dropped from the brocade canopy framing his mother's bed, their drifting

27

petals flung against the walls or consumed by the swaying light. The spaniels began to howl.

Lady Evelyn opened her eyes.

'Guy, get me out of this dreadful place. That old woman in the next bed snores like a trumpet and those stupid nurses gossip away all night. Clattering that trolley around and all those teacups.'

Guy immediately understood that she was in the public ward of the Bath hospital where she had been taken in an ambulance after having been knocked down by a bicycle in Milsom Street.

'Darling, you're back in your own bed with your own pink pillow.'

'All that clatter,' said Lady Evelyn. 'Those noisy teacups.' She had closed her eyes. She opened them. 'Where's my teacup?'

Giles had returned to say that Dr Templeton would be there as soon as was humanly possible.

'Get her teacup,' said Guy. 'It's on the terrace with her bunch of buttercups.'

Clasping the teacup to her breast, Lady Evelyn said, 'Fetch me Irene.'

'But, Mummy, you're ill. I can't leave you to go chasing after Irene. Heaven knows where she is.'

'She will be up in her room or in the kitchen.' Lady Evelyn raised her hand and stroked his tears. Her smile revived her face to health and beauty. 'Now, Guy, you mustn't be jealous. Jealousy is the only flaw in your lovely nature. Fetch me Irene.'

The Family Portraits

WHILE HIS mother talked to Irene, Guy sat at the top of the stairs looking down on the hall and to fend off thought began counting the unicorns on the Sèvres tiles.

28

Twenty-five pairs of de Boissy eyes looked down from the walls. Abandoning the unicorns, Guy stared back at his ancestors, some of whom appeared to be regarding him, affectionately or cynically. Some, gazing across to the opposite wall, appeared to be regarding one another. Most of them were women, for generally painters prefer women to men unless they can put a man on a horse, and prior to Lord Charles, the male members of the de Boissy family had preferred the salons of Paris and the attentions of pretty women to equestrian pursuits.

One portrait that Guy particularly liked because it was so different had been painted by Alma-Tadema and depicted Lady Clarissa – third wife of Lord Peter and mother of Lord Edward. Lady Clarissa neither regarded Guy nor the portraits on the opposite wall, but from a reclining position on a Greek couch, turned her ardent gaze to a marble cupid, which, poised on one toe on a broken column, was engaged in aiming an arrow at her breast.

Closest to Guy on the south wall hung the portrait of his mother, which had been painted in her twenty-fifth year by MacEvoy who had insisted on her wearing a mauve dress and a green shawl. It was a hazy picture by an artist who excelled in haziness, but in spite of the blurred outlines of her face, he had caught the vitality of her expression and a suggestion of laughter on her lips. A fine portrait can impose on its subject an illusion of immortality. Captured in a felicitous moment, MacEvoy's Lady Evelyn seemed forever attached to life, forever faintly, tenderly and ironically smiling at her son.

Fears and sadness slipped from Guy's spirit, like demons returned to hell by the grace of God.

God, moreover, was advancing down the hall in the form of Dr John Templeton.

John Templeton

JOHN TEMPLETON's father, grandfather, great grandfather and great great grandfather had chosen medicine as their profession. This long family connexion with medical practice was reassuring to his patients who felt that not only knowledge, but devotion to duty, integrity and correct behaviour must surely have been instilled in the Templeton blood and passed on from generation to generation. He had inherited Lord Charles from his father and had attended Lady Evelyn for twenty-five years. Now, at the age of sixty-two, not only his experience and his family history, but his physical aspect, commanded respect and faith, so that as soon as he had entered Lady Evelyn's bedroom and closed the door behind him, Guy knew that his mother would be restored to good health.

But when Dr Templeton came out of Lady Evelyn's room and closed the door behind him, his movements lacked their customary precision. He approached Guy in a fluid way, as though his thoughts were wandering.

'Guy,' he said, 'let's go downstairs.'

Cadeaux de Remors

WHEN, some years before, Lady Evelyn's heart condition had first become evident, Dr Templeton had advised her to move into a downstairs room.

'Nothing on earth,' Lady Evelyn told him, 'let alone a silly murmur in my heart will drive me out of this room.'

'But, Lady Evelyn . . .'

Lady Evelyn put a hand on his and smiled. 'John, in this room my three children were conceived and it is filled with the delightful presents Charles gave me on the many occasions when he felt ashamed of himself: my lovely Fantin La Tour and the bureau in the corner which always makes me laugh, because no piece of furniture could more strikingly bring to mind that blousy girl with her short bow legs and bulging stomach. Even the ormolu reminds me of the jewellery she wore to such excess at ten o'clock in the morning. And my lovely Commedia dell'arte clock which arrived after an affair of such extravagant indiscretion that Charles, who usually enjoyed his confessions, couldn't bring himself to tell me about it. But of course there was no need. I only had to look at Harlequin, Pantaloon, Pierrot, Scaramouche and Punchinello dancing about playing guitars and banging tambourines to understand immediately what it had all been about.'

Somewhat embarrassed by these revelations, John Templeton said, 'Couldn't you move your bureau and your clock to one of the downstairs rooms?'

Lady Evelyn retorted, 'You, who devote yourself to the ills of ageing bodies such as mine, are curiously indifferent to the important trivia that keep your patients happy and alive. You look at us as we are at the particular moment when you happen to be looking, with such concentration you forget to pay account to what has made us. We may be crumbling away before your eyes, but within we are growing larger in experience and memories. Why try to preserve what is fallible and destructible at the expense of what, who knows, might be immortal?'

'Of course I know what you are saying, but I don't see what it has got to do with moving downstairs,' said John Templeton.

'I didn't think you would. Let me put it this way. What, of myself, shall I try to preserve for Guy? My withering frame, my faulty heart, or the splendid years of my life? I won't say that I am happier today than I was when I married Charles, but whatever you may have to say about my physical condition, within myself I am richer, stronger, harder, and more complete.'

But Dr Templeton throughout his life, and increasingly

as he grew older, had always found it difficult to give in or retreat. 'But, Lady Evelyn, the stairs. Why can't you be just as rich and complete downstairs?' His brows had closed in opposition to her argument and his lips had disappeared. Again, Lady Evelyn put her hand on his.

'Dear John, forgive me for refusing to listen to your advice, but exile was once considered to be a punishment worse than death. If I moved downstairs, my Fantin La Tour, my silly pot-bellied bureau, my lovely clock and all my *cadeaux de remors* would retreat into sulky retirement, withdrawing not only their power of evocation but their sense of humour. Rather than move downstairs I would much prefer the stables with Giles and Rolling Home. But I have no intention of moving anywhere. I am determined to stay in this room till the day I die unless you are cruel enough at some time to take advantage of my helplessness and carry me out on a stretcher to expire in misery in some hospital ward where I cannot watch the chestnut trees through my window and share the long nights of my old age with my two dogs, twitching away their dreams on my cold feet.'

Prescott

EVER SINCE that day Dr Templeton had smarted under Lady Evelyn's accusation of his failure to regard her as something more than a problem in flesh and bone.

'She will need constant attention,' he said. 'Day and night.'

'Couldn't we get old Prescott,' said Guy. 'She's a terrible boss but they're used to one another and Mummy wouldn't like some stranger washing her and all that. Irene will help. Awful as she is she's very good with Mummy.'

'I'll see if I can engage Prescott, and I don't see any reason why your mother can't stay here if that is what you want, but I'll have to call in Dr Gould tomorrow and get his opinion. You realize that this is going to cost you a lot of money and if she went into hospital, the National Health . . .'

'Mummy would have a fit. There isn't any money but couldn't I give Prescott a ring or a picture or something.'

'I imagine Prescott would be perfectly happy with a ring,' said Dr Templeton, who had not been thinking specifically of Prescott.

That night Guy sat by his mother's bed, attributing her unconsciousness to the sedatives that Dr Templeton had given her. So at ease were his thoughts that he dropped off into periods of untroubled sleep.

The following morning Dr Templeton returned, accompanied by Prescott who, equipped with the qualities of leadership she had acquired as a nursing sister during the war, rounded up Guy, Giles and Irene and was soon settled in Lady Evelyn's dressing-room. In the afternoon Dr Gould arrived and, half an hour later, swiftly departed.

In the evening Dr Templeton returned to disclose to Guy that in his opinion, supported by the opinion of Dr Gould, Lady Evelyn could not be expected to live for more than a few days. Three, five, seven at the outside.

Guy abandoned himself to grief.

Wilfred

THE MAJOR part of his forty-two years Guy had devoted to his mother. He was under the impression that he remembered his brother Wilfred, but as he was only two when Wilfred died, his memories of him were probably provided by stories recounted by his father and Lady Evelyn. He enjoyed looking through the photograph albums recording the early married life of his parents and was particularly drawn to a light brown picture of a small child, wearing a sailor suit and a large brimmed hat set on dangling curls, astride a donkey on the beach of Trouville. Lady Evelyn held the donkey's bridle with one hand and tilted a sunshade over her head with the other. Guy was not permitted to take the photograph out of the album, but a painting by Boudin of the Trouville beach on a windy day hung in his bedroom. The wind pulled at long skirts and puffed out capes. Dogs rushed about and one of the children could have been Wilfred.

Wilfred was born in 1907 and lived through an era that offered little opportunity for the expression of his adventurous nature. At the age of eleven, he escaped from school to enlist in the army and enjoy the last year of the war, but had been turned down by a kindly recruiting officer on account of his flat feet. At the age of nineteen he passed two years in moderately riotous living fashioned on the reputation of his father, only to fall out with his cheetah at the age of twenty-one.

Between the span of years – Wilfred twenty-one, Guy aged two – Lady Evelyn had conceived another son who had died two weeks after his birth. This event was not disclosed to Guy until he was too old for it to bother him.

Guy had indulged in a romantic affair or two when his father was alive and the horses at the top of their form. Lord Charles subscribed to the theory that fine horses and pretty women went together, enhanced one another and were of like kind. So Lady Evelyn, forever tolerant and amused, was called upon to entertain charming young couples, or older couples with charming young daughters, and Guy was permitted to pick up the leftovers, Lord Charles's enthusiasms being swiftly satisfied and swiftly abandoned for the one love of his life to whom he always contritely returned.

At the time of her father's death Guy had been engaged to a girl named Georgina Bray. If he had felt at leave to choose a bride for himself he would have preferred to Georgina the fifteen-year-old daughter of Dave Dawes who ran the pub at Thawle-on-Rustle, but he had always done as he was told and when his father placed Georgina's hand in his and inexplicitly instructed him to marry her, he accepted what appeared to be not a bad fate on the whole. For Georgina was pretty, lively, and a good horsewoman. But she was also passionate. Guy's kindly indifference bored her and after Lord Charles's death she broke off the engagement and rushed into more ardent arms just in time to be married and achieve a measure of respectability for Lord Charles's son.

Guy accepted these events without regret, for his mother's beauty, wit and loving nature had set a standard of feminine perfection that had blighted his sexual life, and when his father died dutiful grief was ousted by the satisfied sense that a rival had been removed. In the years that followed it occurred to Guy that instead of growing older he was growing younger. He was aware of a sense of silence and space in which he could freely move. A voice, possibly his father's, had ceased admonishing him and instructing him as to the direction of his maturity. Within the soft and tender nimbus that encompassed his mother, maturity was no longer demanded, or needed. He felt at peace and sank gratefully back into his childhood.

But now his wonderful mother whom he had always regarded as immortal was slipping from him into an unconsciousness from which no prayer or passionate exhortation could retrieve her. At first his grief was an unselfish response to her helpless condition, but soon his thoughts turned to his own predicament and he sorrowed for the years ahead when he would have to continue living without her. He pleaded for her counsel but from her calm face, its features becoming with every hour more wasted and spectral, came no instruction. Guy did not feel the weight of a hand on his shoulder, until he was severely shaken.

'Come downstairs,' said John Templeton.

Dr Templeton Asks for Wine

GUY CONDUCTED Dr Templeton into the Morning Room, so called because the morning sun struck across its windows, thereby over the years reducing to silvery shreds the rose silk linings of the Spanish curtains and fading the blue dress of a young woman, said to be the Comtesse de Bercy, who equipped with a greyhound and a large black hat, dominated the Gobelin tapestry on the southern side of the mantelpiece, and on the northern side, the sashes of cavaliers mounted on prancing horses.

This room, more than any other, Guy regarded as belonging to his mother, for it was here that in her splendid maturity she had served refreshments to the horse women and their attendant fathers, husbands and brothers, who, after they had partaken of tea or iced punch, would wander out of doors to stroke the silken noses offered to them over the stable doors.

On entering the room Guy was moved to a fresh attack of emotion by the sight of the chair that Lady Evelyn had preferred when performing her duties as hostess. Not a lady's chair, but a solid George II armchair of Virginia walnut, the cabriole legs carved with Indian masks, and upholstered in faded needlework depicting a delightful negro boy holding a tasselled sunshade over the head of a lady – all in a flowery landscape lively with dogs, deer and birds, chasing one another about in a frolicsome way.

So affected was Guy by the memory of his mother seated in her favourite chair and wearing a dress of some soft, clinging material with narrow sleeves breaking out at the wrist into frothy cuffs of Chantilly lace, that he burst out quite rudely, 'Would you mind sitting over there.'

Dr Templeton had chosen Lady Evelyn's chair in order to be able to look at one of his favourite pictures, a portrait by Perronneau of a stately, experienced child, a ribbon tied in a bow around her neck, and holding a kitten on the lap of her blue dress. He quickly removed himself to the solid wing chair that had been favoured by Lord Charles. Guy put his head in his hands and sobbed, quietly. Dr Templeton allowed him time to give way to his grief, but when his body stopped shaking and he raised his head, Dr Templeton said, 'Guy, your mother will have a peaceful death. It is selfish of you to question her good fortune, and remember that when they die those we love do not leave us.'

His words came to Guy in confirmation of a truth which was indisputably demonstrated when Lady Evelyn reappeared in her chair, tossing back her cuffs of Chantilly lace and tilting a silver teapot over cups painted from designs by Angelica Kauffman that had gone in the 1950 sale following the death of Lord Charles.

Said John Templeton, 'I think we ought to have a drink. Sometimes it's the best thing to do. As your mother can no longer act as hostess in this house, you are the host, and I think you ought to offer me a glass of port, or brandy or wine. It is the attention to small matters of formality such as this that hold us together. The etiquette of social life sometimes appals us by its irrelevance and triviality, but it has its uses. It has prevented many a man from breaking into dangerous emotional excesses.'

Guy hurried down to the cellar, grabbed a bottle, and from the kitchen a corkscrew and two glasses that had once contained peanut butter.

Appreciatively John Templeton sipped the Château Lafite-Rothschild, 1846, remarking, 'Your father broached this wine when Traveller won the Derby in '36 or was it '37. I never thought to drink such a wine and have always interested myself in its value. I would think, today, about six hundred pounds a bottle. Possibly more. A fitting toast to your mother.'

'Mummy never cared for wine,' said Guy. 'She preferred light ale or a glass of Guinness. She knew so much about painting and the jade and all the other things but when I said Mummy I really would like a bottle of wine, she'd say that the wine was part of the de Boissy collection and had to be looked after like all the other things.'

John Templeton sipped what he roughly calculated to be twenty pounds' worth of Lafite-Rothschild. 'Wine isn't like jade,' he said. 'If you keep it too long it goes off.'

'That's what I kept telling her.'

John Templeton sipped. Thought. Sipped.

'You're going to have to pay a lot of probate duty,' he finally pronounced. 'You might have to sell this house. You will certainly have to sell some of its contents. So if you don't particularly care about the wine it seems a pity that it should add to an inevitably heavy financial burden and that you should hand over to the Labour Government which your mother detests as don't we all – well – er – it seems a pity. As I was saying,' said John Templeton, his voice falling away as he stared into his empty glass.

Guy filled the glass.

A moment later John Templeton continued, in a confident, ringing voice. 'Your mother looked after this estate and preserved it, largely for you. I suggest that from this moment, instead of giving way to profitless grief, you take positive action to carry on the work she began.'

'She always tells me I must,' said Guy, 'but I don't know what to do.'

The Louis XIV ormolu clock seated on a spirited bronze bull struck nine. Guy had had nothing to eat for nine hours and the wine turning in his head had dulled his grief by casting some question on the cause of it, for once again his mother's personality richly pervaded the room. He felt she had just gone outside for a moment.

'I am not,' said John Templeton, 'urging you into malpractice. I am simply asking you to consider your situation, and the fact that you have a duty to your family equal to your duty to the nation.'

'But I haven't got a family,' said Guy. 'Wilfred's dead, Aunt Jane went to America to become a nun and Aunt Diana married that horrible man in Scotland. Mummy said she used to be nice but she's been converted by that Scottish lot who won't have anything to do with us. Except Uncle Robert and he's so old.'

'I know,' said Dr Templeton, 'that your family have been fractious and quarrelsome, but although one or another has always done something offensive to the conservative faction – that Scottish lot, as you call them – you have been, and I hope will continue to be, an unbroken family line. The fact that members of your family have departed from some social, and if I may be frank, moral rules, is beside the point. The rules remain and your family, generally speaking, maintains them. Curiously, and it is difficult for me to explain why, these rules are immured in your house and your possessions. If these things are dispersed the rules will go with them. Your mother understood this, which is why, in the years since your father's death, she has struggled to maintain your estate and I do not think you should be too scrupulous about salvaging what you can of your inheritance.'

John Templeton's impressive face wore a kindly but firm expression. The solemnity of his words and the silence that followed them affected Guy with a sense of having been cast, brutally and without reference to his wishes, against the most daunting challenge of his life. Wisdom and judgement would be needed for the making of large decisions; application and courage for putting these decisions into effect. But where could he find these qualities when all he was aware of was the pain within him and the duty that had fallen upon him to endure it with fortitude?

He said, 'But I don't know what to do.'

'There is obviously a lot you cannot do. You can't conceal the furniture and it would be unwise to dispose of the tapestries which have been illustrated in *Connoisseur* if I remember, *Country Life* and probably a number of other journals. Your mother once told me that the French have had their eyes on the Watteau for years. They'd keep track of it, and the Ingres and the Perronneau. You might, however, get away with some of the less celebrated paintings.' Dr Templeton paused to run his fingers through the abundant hair on his right temple. 'What I have in mind,' he continued, 'is the cellar. The probate duty will be enormous on that wine. A lot of it is past its prime and who is to say how much has been consumed over the years. I would suggest that you get rid of some of the wine, particularly the earlier vintages. If there were any gifts that your mother would have wanted to bestow on relatives – or – er – devoted friends who have known her and looked after her, now would be the time – er – ' Dr Templeton collected a small dry cough in the palm of his hand, 'before it is too late.'

When he left, Guy had repudiated pain and had taken up the task of making decisions. Acting on what he believed to be his own idea, he presented Dr Templeton with a Marks and Spencer's shopping-bag containing a bottle of 1811 Grande Armée Champagne Cognac, a vintage 1929 Château Mouton-Rothschild and two bottles of 1847 Château d'Yquem.

The Library

WITH A DEVOTION to straight lines inherit in his nature and put to use in the cultivation of his vegetable garden, Guy assembled eighteen bottles on the kitchen table, which was almost as old as Thawle, the surface having been worked into depressions and corrugations by the application of several centuries of scrubbing brushes, so that the sand-coloured wood now resembled an ocean beach after a storm.

He removed the corks of four bottles of Romanée-Conti and poured their contents down the sink. But when it came to the Rüdesheimer Apostelwein 1727, he recalled how much he had liked it when he had last tasted it, around fourteen years ago. He poured a glass. On the turn, but what could you expect?

With glass and bottle Guy approached the Library which

contained Lord Frederick's collection of French books.

This room struck admiration and surprise in the minds of those who entered it, but rarely the feelings of serenity and ease generally expected of a room that is filled with books. For here England and France confronted one another belligerently and with no intermediary to reconcile their differing temperament.

Towards the end of the eighteenth century, the ceiling had been decorated with plump flesh, garlands of pink roses and floating blue draperies by a minor French artist from the court of Louis XV, whose talents and sexual virtuosity had appealed to Lord Frederick, grandfather of Lord Edward, and who had remained at Thawle for two years to paint the ceiling and serve his patron, leaving behind him in Thawle-on-Rustle and other neighbouring villages a legacy of spirited children with dark eyes and dancing Gallic curls.

Beneath the ceiling, the room was austerely English. Fine, elegant English. But reserved and disapproving.

Lord Edward had shared his grandfather's love of rare French books. He wrote in his memoirs that he could not recall a time when he was not permitted to enter the Library and investigate any book, no matter how unsuitable in subject or illustration for the fresh, unfolding mind of a five-year-old child, by which age his command of French enabled him to read many of the books that caught his fancy. Acknowledging his debt, he looked after the books with care and extended the collection in later years. But though his books and paintings and his collection of Fabergé reflected a strong preference for the culture of France, there were inconsistencies in his taste and strong aversions that his family and friends found difficult to reconcile with his enthusiasms. He was fanatical in his insistence that English furniture was far superior to French which he declared to be vulgar, impractical and uncomfortable. In his memoirs he stated that 'no one would consider furnishing a casino or a brothel with Hepplewhite or Jacobean oak'.

He removed all the French furniture from the Library

and rehoused Lord Frederick's books in five Sheraton break-front bookcases of Honduras mahogany, which, situated beneath the exuberant ceiling, wore the appearance of prim, tight-lipped non-conformists, who, against their will, had somehow become involved in one of the more theatrical celebrations of the Catholic Church. Whereas the ceiling, rioting above five large, noble shapes, austerely grave and unadorned by frivolous ornament, looked vulgar and obscene.

Lord Edward realized his mistake and considered having the ceiling redecorated in the pale duck-egg blue or clotted cream of the Octagonal Room, but acknowledging himself to be only an episode in his family's history, had refrained from doing so. He had attempted to bring ceiling and walls together by installing a restrained Aubusson carpet which quarrelled with neither. But to no avail.

The Rocks of Valpré

THE LIBRARY, on that evening, was occupied by Irene, clad in one of Lady Evelyn's house gowns, dating from the early years of her marriage. Pink, with a thin silver stripe and lace at the throat.

Irene lay on the floor, her elbows pressed into the white Easter lilies on the Aubusson carpet and her hands interlaced to support her chin. As Guy entered the room she raised her eyes from the book opened before her.

Irene's remarkable eyes, set within deep, shadowy sockets in her otherwise unremarkable face, turned down at the corners, like huge tears about to drop from her cheeks. More so at the moment, for tears there were, falling in slow, glistening tracks. Guy had never before seen tears in Irene's eyes. He was moved and forgot that he hated her.

'If you're crying about Mummy, she's perfectly all right and you needn't bother.'

'It's this book,' said Irene. 'You see, there's this girl called Christine and she's very young and full of life and she meets this Frenchman in a cave. Then the tide comes in so they have to stay all night, but nothing happens because he loves and treasures her and wouldn't lay a finger on her. But the word gets around, so he fights a duel in defence of her honour. Then she goes to England and grows up, and there's this Englishman, Trevor Mordaunt, who wants to marry her and he's got hold of the Frenchman who was put in gaol for something he didn't do and was destitute on the streets playing the song he sang to Christine in the cave when the tide came in. Only the Frenchman doesn't know that his benefactor who takes him on as his secretary loves the girl he's going to marry and Christine doesn't know that her future husband has this Frenchman as his secretary, until they all find out and then it's too late, because she's married to Trevor Mordaunt whom she respects because he is kind and honourable, but she loves the Frenchman, and the Frenchman can't do anything about it because he owes a debt of gratitude to his benefactor. And then the man who fought the duel blackmails her so that she spends all her money and her brother forges a cheque and sells all the jewellery her husband gave her because she doesn't want him to find out about the night in the cave when the tide came in, because if he did he'd despise her for ever. Only he wouldn't. He's forgiven her straight away, but she doesn't know that. Then the Frenchman dies in a tender scene and it all comes out and the husband loves her still and she loves him. And they forgive one another.'

Irene put her cheek on *The Rocks of Valpré* and the tears bursting from her eyes soaked into its thick, fleshy pages.

'The muck you read,' said Guy. 'Will you please go. I have work to do and require the privacy of this room.'

'All right, my love.'

It infuriated Guy to be called 'my love' by Irene and he had told her again and again not to do it. But she still went on.

Irene closed *The Rocks of Valpré* and began collecting together the angularities of her body – the spiky elbows and skinny shoulders, so white they were almost silver, matching the silver stripes in Lady Evelyn's dress, and then the pointed hips and knees, bony and knobbly like the legs of Rolling Home in his prime. While she was assembling these legs and joints into a rising position Guy thought of the towers and cranes he had made from Meccano as a child and half-expected to hear the creaking and scratching of bolts and screws. But in one smooth, undulating movement, like a gush of water thrown up by a fountain, Irene was on her feet, and departed, lifting her hand as she sailed from the room, in order, with the sleeve of Lady Evelyn's dress, to wipe the tears from her eyes.

Irene

I MUSTN'T CRY, thought Irene, mounting the stairs to her suite of rooms over the kitchen. When she had reached her bedroom door and out of earshot of Lord Guy, aloud she said, 'I mustn't cry,' because there seemed more determination in saying something aloud as though you were swearing on the Bible or making a promise, and nobody of any value in this world ever broke a promise, which was why Ambrosine got into such a plight having given her word and committed herself to marrying Augustus Gurrage, that brute of a man, when, if she had only waited a week, she would have met her kinsman, Sir Anthony Thornhurst, at the ball and married him instead.

But, nevertheless, Ambrosine only shed tears when her grandmother died. Irene had not shared Ambrosine's grief on the death of her grandmother, for *crème de la crème* of the French aristocracy as she was, she ought not to have put Ambrosine's material comfort in the forefront of the picture and cast her into the arms of that brute Augustus Gurrage with his drink and women. But, after the death of her grand-mother and in spite of what she had to endure, never did Ambrosine cry. Neither did Katherine Bush. What moral fibre they had, those wonderful girls. As for Evangeline . . .

Entering her bedroom, Irene confronted her reflection in the pier-glass that had been brought down from the attic above so that she might keep track of any improvement in the manner in which she comported herself in Lady Evelyn's clothes. Evangeline would never have cried in spite of having nothing to see her through life but her red hair, her green eyes and marvellous skin. Irene's hair, though just as abundant as Evangeline's and dressed in like style, was not red, but *blond cendré*, like Ambrosine's, a much rarer and subtler colour. But Irene couldn't imagine that even Evangeline's milk-white skin could have been any more milk white than her own.

Of course, Christine in *The Rocks of Valpré* cried all the time, even over that ridiculous dog Cinders, but the Wyndhams were a worthless lot, getting themselves into debt and forging cheques. Marie Corelli's heroines sometimes cried too, but in Irene's opinion neither Marie Corelli nor Ethel M. Dell were in the same class as Elinor Glyn. In fact Ethel M. Dell had written whole books without mentioning a member of the aristocracy, all the heroes were misters and the heroines doting on dogs like Cinders, who was certainly mongrel. Any dog called Cinders couldn't possibly be well bred. In *The Gate Marked Private* the two men who were supposed to engage your interest were named Peter Garnett and Silas Hickory, the only member of the aristocracy being Lord Avencome, much on the side-lines. On the last page, when Silas puts his arms about Bobby and she goes into them 'like a bird into its nest', Irene couldn't help thinking that rather than the arms of Silas, she would have preferred a more aristocratic nest such as the arms of Sheik Ahmed Ben Hassan, who, even though you had to endure being raped by him every night, was not an Arab but son of the Earl of Glencaryll, a fact proved by Raoul Saint Hubert who was familiar with that famous Glencaryll scowl.

The books that Irene was recalling for consolation and advice had come into her possession by way of her grandmother who had been in service, but was a great reader. When her mistress, Mrs Oliver Fletcher, became widowed and moved into a smaller house, Mrs Fletcher had given these books to Irene's grandmother, whom she could no longer afford to employ, as a parting gift. On her grandmother's death they had gone to Irene, who with the assistance of Lady Evelyn had subsequently added to her collection from nearby second-hand bookshops.

Irene took off her dress and went into the bathroom adjoining her bedroom and the dressing-room where Lady Evelyn's dresses hung on a rail knocked up by Giles and protected by an Egyptian cotton curtain dating back to Lady Evelyn's honeymoon days. The bathroom had been decorated towards the beginning of the century with a wallpaper depicting roses, some in full flower and some in bud, that were climbing up trellises and attached to them with bows of blue ribbon. But now somewhat streaked by water that had been leaking for years from a gutter above, which in a hard winter filled with snow. The room contained an enamel bath raised from the floor on short, chubby legs, and little used because hot water had to be carried in buckets from the kitchen.

For eight months of the year the three rooms were very cold, Giles only being able to spare sufficient time from his attentions to Rolling Home, the saddles and racing trophies, to cut wood for the kitchen range and the fireplaces in Lady Evelyn's bedroom and the Morning Room. When she was troubled by the cold Irene consoled herself by consulting *The Reflections of Ambrosine*. On the first page of Elinor Glyn's masterpiece, Ambrosine Eustacie Marquise de Calincourt declares:

'I have wondered sometimes if there are not perhaps some disadvantages in having really blue blood in one's veins like

Grandmamma and me. For instance, if we were ordinary common people, our teeth would chatter naturally with cold when we have to go to bed without fires in our rooms in December, but we pretend we like sleeping in "well-aired rooms" – at least I have to. Grandmamma simply says we are obliged to make these small economies, and to grumble would be to lose a trick to fate.'

Irene was determined to lose no trick to fate which had played an impressive role in her life, and blood, blue or otherwise, confined in the veins, was not exposed to public scrutiny, so who could question her about it? But all the greater was the need to be constantly aware of the behaviour appropriate to blue blood. Irene's teeth never chattered, but she said her prayers in bed instead of kneeling beside it and when getting in and out of clothes, exposed her naked skin to the chilly air for as short a time as possible. The bath remained largely neglected, but the plumbing worked and twice a week she boiled a kettle on the kitchen range and in a large enamel basin washed her feet, her armpits and between her legs. And every day and night she washed her neck and face in cold water which closed the pores.

These tasks, on that night, concluded, Irene in a flannel nightgown lay on her bed, exerting all her will to stop crying. Turning for support to her bookshelves, she opened *The Sheik* at the page describing Ahmed Ben Hassan's first assault upon Lady Diana Mayo, and was astonished to discover that Lady Diana Mayo had not only cried but had grovelled in misery at Ahmed Ben Hassan's feet, pleading for mercy. In spite of having read the book twelve times, Irene had forgotten this passage, possibly because it offended her. Lady Diana should never have grovelled, even if she had pulled herself together later.

But putting the book down, she derived some solace from cold, proud Lady Diana's display of weakness, until at length she was released into the comfort of uncontrolled grief. Turning her head, she sobbed on her pillow. Never, not even when her mother died, had she felt so lonely.

'Please, Lady Evelyn,' wept Irene, 'please don't die. Not yet. Please, not yet. I'm very young and I'm all alone. Please, Lady Evelyn, please don't die.'

Percy

AFTER IRENE had departed, Guy approached his father's desk. Having extracted the inventory of the contents of the house which had been compiled after Lord Charles's death, Guy visited the kitchen for a box of matches and, leaving the inventory blazing in the Library fireplace, mounted the stairs to one of the attics at the top of the house. This room being deprived of light, Guy returned to the kitchen for a torch. The battery was flat but he found a packet of candles left over from the previous winter when the electricity had been cut off.

The flame of the candle disclosed boxes and trunks, a Victorian chaise-longue, a bed, several chairs wanting legs or backs, and brought to life the round black eyes of Percy, the rocking-horse which Lady Evelyn had bought at Hamleys on an occasion that Guy thought he remembered. He had been three years old, but a lively impression remained in his mind of his beautiful mother, her hands tucked into a fur muff and wearing a green velvet turban designed by Erté, with a trim of black aigrette feathers over her right ear, and shedding about her such an aura of charm and graciousness that everyone in the shop had melted at her feet in adoration.

Guy stroked Percy's nose and gave it a push. Percy's head retreated into the shadows behind him and advanced into the candlelight. Like Rolling Home asking for sugar, Percy pushed his nose into Guy's chest. His red nostrils snorted with anticipation and his pointed ears pricked for the slightest sound.

'Dear old Percy,' said Guy, clasping his arms around the dappled neck and burying his cheek in the silver mane. Guy wept, without knowing why, because it had been such a happy occasion that Christmas at Hamleys with his beautiful mother in her beautiful green hat.

The candle went out and whilst he was relighting it, Guy remembered the boxes. He selected four. Two small ones and two quite a lot larger.

The Elephants

SMOKE FROM the Library fireplace, where the inventory was still smouldering, obscured the little illumination provided by three twenty-five-watt bulbs so that all that could be seen of Lord Frederick's collection of French books was a faint glitter of gold embossed on dark red leather.

The smoke slowly and majestically drifted amongst the twenty-five elephants which, along with the other items of Lord Edward's Fabergé collection, Guy had removed from a William and Mary oyster-wood cabinet and arranged on the floor.

He had never cared much for the cigarette-cases and Easter eggs, but as a child had played with the birds and animals, and was now drawn back to a time when he had provided a jungle for the elephants, arranging stalks of parsley and spinach leaves amongst big boulders of beach pebbles in a baking dish which had survived from the nineteenth century and was sufficiently large for roasting saddles of lamb and sucking pigs. In the centre of the jungle, between shelving banks of sand, he had inserted a soup plate filled with water and fringed with fern where the elephants met for their evening bath.

The elephants all had names which he now tried to remember, but a bottle of Rüdesheimer Apostelwein 1727, though helpful in bringing the past vividly to life, had obscured details like names.

The most important elephant was Ranji, the automaton Indian elephant with a mahout on his back, the mahout and the gold rug being picked out in green and white enamels. When Guy turned the large rose diamond set between Ranji's eyes, Ranji came to life, walked about and swung his head in a stately way. But Guy preferred the smaller jungle elephants. The tiny nephrite one with the upturned trunk he thought was Lucy, but it might have been Anne. Two big ones in obsidian and aventurine quartz answered to Mark and Claudius and the darling creature in rose pink rhodonite, seated on his haunches and twitching an ear, was certainly Jimmy.

The jungle also sheltered a white chalcony spaniel twice the size of Claudius, an amazonite shorthorn bull, smaller than the spaniel but larger than Jimmy, a lapis-lazuli chimpanzee, a toad, two kingfishers, a white agate pelican with gold feet, an enormous snail and an opal puppy.

But Ranji with his mahout and his splendid rug was never taken to the forest pool for a bath. Ranji belonged to Lord Curzon's Durbar, religious festivals and public occasions.

Instructions from Lady Evelyn

'MY DEAREST GUY,' said Lady Evelyn, speaking from her bed on the evening of that day, several years before, when Dr Templeton made clear to her the condition of her heart and advised her to move downstairs, 'I have been rather ill as you know and in the course of making me better John has discovered that I have a weak heart. He tells me that if I don't move downstairs, which I have no intention of doing, I shall probably die.'

'Don't be silly, Mummy. I've never seen you looking so well.'

'I feel very well, and yet somewhat changed. I find myself thinking in a different way. I am not so interested in making plans any more. I am more concerned with tidying things up. The last days have made me realize that although I may not drop dead of a heart attack as John expects, nevertheless I am growing old and I shall some time within the next few years, if not immediately, die of something or other because everyone must. And I am worried about you. When I die there won't be very much money, so what will you do?'

Guy refused to believe that his mother would ever die, but he answered her dutifully. 'I shall stay here and grow my vegetables. I don't want a lot of money.'

'But this estate will have to be valued for probate. What will you do about that?'

'I suppose I would get in Sotheby's or someone.'

'That would be a mistake. Sotheby's are respectable and incorruptible and they would want to be paid. What you need is a valuer who is neither respectable nor incorruptible and who will not want to be paid because there won't be any money to pay him with. You must call Reggie Thring. Reggie is a terrible snob, which is to your advantage, and his wife Clare had an affair with your father which brings him into the family. I'm not saying that Reggie is a dishonest man, but there are points of weakness in his character and you must exploit them. It will be a give-and-take situation which Reggie will understand.'

'If by weakness you are talking about Clive, I don't see
...'

'I am talking about Reggie's passion for Fabergé. When I die you must call in Reggie to value for probate. He will not connive with you in a major fraud, but he will lean to your side which is all you can ask of him. You will make it clear to him that he will not be paid and you will give him the most valuable of the Fabergé Easter eggs, which is the one that opens out into eight sections with the views of

Moscow, the cigar-case that Tsar Nicholas presented to your great grandfather and the model of Tsarina Alexandra Feodorovna's coronation coach. And don't wait until I am dead because you don't want your gifts to Reggie to be included in the probate valuation.'

Rolling Home Asks for Sugar

HAVING RETURNED to the William and Mary oyster-wood cabinet the Easter egg that opened into eight sections, the nephrite cigar-case with a miniature of Tsar Nicholas II surrounded by a garland of rose diamonds, the model of Tsarina Alexandra Feodorovna's coronation coach, three bears, four dogs, a crystal hippopotamus and a jasper dormouse with platinum whiskers, Guy installed the remaining pieces of his great grandfather's Fabergé collection in the two smaller boxes he had brought from the attic.

Outside, the sky being clear and lit with stars, he had no need for a torch and candles. As he passed the stables, Rolling Home appeared at the door of his stall, dipping his nose and pricking his ears. Guy, suddenly afflicted by a feeling that life was making too many demands upon him, put down the two boxes and returned to the kitchen for sugar.

As Rolling Home politely took the sugar from the palm of his hand, Guy hardly knew whether he was stroking the soft, breathing muzzle of Rolling Home or the painted wooden nose of Percy.

Beyond the stables and within the high brick walls that enclosed the orchard and the vegetable garden, Guy buried his great grandfather's Fabergé collection under a walnut tree and returned to the cellar for another bottle of Rüdesheimer Apostelwein.

The Books

THE SMOKE in the Library had settled to a pleasant haze. Guy felt that most of it had got into his head. His thoughts seemed to have soft edges and blundered about in a foggy way without any consistent direction. On his knees on the floor, he attempted to scrutinize the collection of drawings, etchings and water colours compiled over the years by Lord Peter, Lord Edward and Lord Charles. Hardly aware of what he was doing, he put to one side a drypoint by Helleu of the Duchesse de Gramont because it had always reminded him of an early photograph of his mother. Returning to the other etchings and drawings, again, he was conscious of too many demands.

The reduction in the volume of smoke had unveiled the gold lettering on the backs of Lord Frederick's books which now glittered assertively, calling him to a recognition of their value and rarity. Abandoning the drawings, he wandered amongst the books, pulling out one here and there.

He had read few of the books but often opened them to look at the illustrations. Engraved portraits bored him but he loved maps showing cherubs with fat cheeks blowing out winds, whales spurting water and sailing ships tossing around the shores of inaccurately drawn continents that were lively with animals of every variety and savages brandishing weapons. He loved the feel of the thick pages, the deckled edges, the smell, and the coloured patterns inside the covers that looked like leaves, feathers, winding streams and paving stones set in gold cement.

He opened a book that had came from the library of Talleyrand and pressed it to his face. It smelt of snuff and three hundred years. On the title page two cherubs swung back and forth on garlands of roses. He turned the pages upon a girl who had pulled down her dress and was squirting milk from her breast into the open mouth of a faun. Guy tucked the book inside his jacket.

But what of the others? Hundreds of books – perhaps thousands. He had never counted them and now it wouldn't be easy to find out because the inventory had been reduced to scraps of burnt paper that were lifting from the grate and fluttering into the room like an invasion of moths.

Not realising how simple the disposal of Lord Frederick's books would eventually be, Guy felt oppressed by his responsibility in preserving them. He envisaged them being sold in public auction to fall into the hands of enthusiastic collectors who would respect them for a while, but whose children, the way things were going, would probably be illiterate and regard them as worthless rubbish; or worse still they might be scattered far and wide to languish in American university libraries. Guy thought of the books as a family which had been brought together from diverse sources and had settled down with mutual affection and shared affinities in the harmony that only the nature of a discriminating collector can bestow on the objects of his choice. He felt strongly that something had to be done about them. But they couldn't be buried like the Fabergé. Or the silver.

Postponing the difficult problem of the books, his mind turned to the dining-room and the silver. But on the point of leaving the Library to deal with the silver, he remembered the drawings, scattered about the floor. Pending a better solution for their disposal, he collected them together, took them to his bedroom and put them under the bed. Those that would not fit under the bed he installed in a large chest of drawers under a pile of old jackets and riding breeches. The sight of the bed had brought on an attack of weariness. He lay down and slept.

The Walnut Tree

NEXT MORNING Guy hurried outside to check up on the walnut tree. He had awoken from a dream in which, during a violent storm, the walnut tree had been struck by lightning and uprooted, causing the elephants to be scattered above ground. And although such tiny creatures would hardly have been noticed unless someone had been actually looking for them, in Guy's dream they got to their feet, shot up in size and blundered about amongst the wild strawberries and the raspberry canes. Anyone could have seen them from the stables which afforded a view of the orchard through an unrepaired gap in the wall, or by looking down on Thawle from a helicopter.

On waking, Guy struggled out of his dream and no longer believed in its total substance, but he could not help fearing that there might be some fragment of truth contained within it, deriving from concealed knowledge within himself, for how else had he come to dream it?

The orchard presented a peaceful appearance: the apple trees heavy with blossom and dew and the walnut tree firmly attached to the ground. Guy on his hands and knees diligently searched in the grass around the base of the tree for mislaid elephants that he might have dropped the night before. But finding nothing, he returned to the stables where Rolling Home waited outside his stall.

Giles was an early riser and Rolling Home had been grazing for an hour or so and had returned to his stall of his own accord and at the appropriate time to be saddled and await his master. When, by nine o'clock, Guy had failed to appear, he had lapsed into sleep and dreams, standing tipped to one side on three legs, the fourth leg bent in a resting position and his ears nodding about in a neglected way as if they were no longer needed for listening but as aids to contemplation. But as Guy approached he pulled himself together, assembled his ears and his resting leg and pushed out his nose for sugar.

Guy fetched sugar and whilst he was attending to Rolling Home, kissing the hard, flat forehead with its white splash between beautiful moist eyes and rubbing his cheek on the silky neck with its smell of horse, buttercups and clover, Giles appeared and wanted to know how Lady Evelyn was getting on.

Guy was overcome by a rush of anger. 'She's perfectly all right. And I won't be riding this morning.'

Returning to the house for the car keys but not stopping for breakfast, he set off in the Mini.

Prescott

PRESCOTT TOLD Dr Templeton when he arrived at midday that she thought it strange that Lord Guy should have left the house without putting his head in his mother's room to enquire if there were any change in her condition, but had dashed off, no one knew where, without even a shave to make him look respectable.

'Irene was with her,' said Prescott, 'while I went down to the kitchen for a cup of tea. I heard him starting up the car and ran out to speak to him. I'm sure he heard me, but he didn't stop.'

'Could there,' she enquired, after Dr Templeton had failed to make any comment, 'be any insanity in the family? Lord Charles did have a reputation for, what can I say, loose behaviour, and there's never smoke without a fire.' But even discussing medical matters with a medical man, she found herself unable to be more explicit.

'Lord Guy,' said Dr Templeton, 'has always been very sensitive. The previous child, as you know, was premature and did not survive. Lady Evelyn was forty-two when Guy was born. He was a delicate child. He did not go to school and had a private tutor because Lady Evelyn believed he ought not to be subjected to the rough and tumble of school life. However, he is now perfectly robust, in fact, remarkably strong, but extremely sensitive.'

'It is his insensitivity,' said Prescott, 'that troubles me. After that uncontrolled outburst of grief he doesn't seem to care that his mother is dying. So is there the possibility of something organically wrong or is he reverting to the habits of his father and dashing off with some girl from the village?'

'He is probably suffering from shock. What he needs is rest. Encourage him to take half a bottle of wine before he goes to bed. Perhaps it would be a good idea to bring a dozen bottles of wine from the cellar. Leave them in the Morning Room with glasses on a tray. It will put him in mind of having something to drink.'

'I don't feel,' said Prescott, Presbyterian and teetotal, 'that I ought to take wine from the cellar. It isn't my property.'

Said Dr Templeton severely, 'I am *prescribing* wine for Lord Guy. He is greatly in need of sleep and wine is much less harmful than sleeping pills.'

Clive St John

BRADFORD-ON-AVON being too close and gossipy, Guy headed for Bath where he was on friendly terms with a man running a hardware store down near the river. Around the corner another shop sold artists' materials and it was in this street that Guy parked the Mini.

But as he was hauling a carton of paints, brushes and turpentine into the back of the car, down the road, wearing a pink shirt and a yellow tie, came Reggie Thring's friend, Clive St John, preceded by his two abominable dogs with their hair pulled out of their eyes and tied between their ears with blue ribbons. The dogs were attached to Clive by scarlet leads and trotting ahead like short-legged scrubbing brushes, scooped up in their bewhiskered jowls a quantity of dust and pink confetti, for Clive was passing a church where there had been a wedding two days before. This being one of the more depressed streets in Bath – the fine Georgian houses selling for next to nothing because the Avon had flooded its banks for the past three winters and inundated the base-ments – the pavements were rarely, if ever, swept.

'Hullo, Guy, fancing seeing you,' said Clive. 'That looks far too heavy. Let me help.'

'You've got your hands full,' said Guy, struck with guilt.

'Not at all,' said Clive, lashing the scarlet leads about one of the beautiful lamp-posts that the Bath Preservation Society were defending against the onslaught of modern progress.

'I love painting,' said Clive, poking his spiky nose into Guy's carton. 'I did up the bathroom in March. Reggie wan-ted to call in that clever man who worked such wonders in the dining-room, but I said no Reggie please let me. And it's absolutely stunning. You should come and see.'

'It's the stables,' said Guy. 'The woodwork is in shocking condition. What are you doing here?' He asked resentfully, for this was not a street in which one would ever have ex-pected to encounter Clive.

'Reggie's at a house sale in the Crescent and I said I'd take the kiddies for a stroll.'

'But it's *miles* from the Crescent,' said Guy, showing anger.

'If you want me to,' said Clive, also showing anger, 'I *will* explain about how I bought some bread and some strawberry jam at that shop which is the only place where you get genuine pips, and then I had to pee behind the Abbey and now I'm off to that shop where you've just been to get some blood and bone for Reggie's hydrangeas. I could describe all that and more in detail, but it's really rather boring.'

'You don't have to,' said Guy, pulling himself together. 'And thank you, Clive.'

The kiddies had started to fight for the possession of one another's hair ribbons. 'Now, now.' Clive unwound the leads. 'Well, cheerio. How's your wonderful mother? I heard she wasn't very well.'

'She's wonderfully well,' said Guy, 'but she gets tired. She's having a rest for a day or two.'

Late that afternoon, on their way home to the village outside Bath where Clive and Reggie lived, 'Now why,' said Clive to Reggie, 'would Guy de Boissy buy a quantity of paint in a hardware store to do up the stables when I can't see him getting around to painting the stables, let alone painting them white, red, green and blue. And why would he buy a pound of potatoes when he's got potatoes of his own to flog in the markets, in order to divert my attention, which he did not, because I just slipped into a doorway with the kiddies and peeped out for a moment, and discovered that his real purpose was to nip into that shop selling artists' materials.'

'Why shouldn't he?' said Reggie, slowing down to take the bend at the top of the hill just out of Bath, where the main road to the south descended in long curves over fields flushed with the dying sun.

'Suspicious behaviour,' said Clive, 'always arouses my curiosity. And when Guy shot out of that shop like a bank robber with an easel and a carton of something, I strolled in and told the stupid girl behind the counter that I was a friend of her previous customer who had to dash off and that he wanted a copy of his invoice for the Taxation Department and could she give me one. Six tubes of titanium white, ten Indian red, eight cerulean blue and fourteen chrome yellow. Guy must be partial to yellow. That sounds to me like a lot of painting. And not stable painting. But strangely, to my way of thinking, he did not buy any canvas or bits of board, or whatever people paint on these days. Only paints and nothing to put them on. Now tell me, why do you think that Guy would behave in such a curious way?'

'I don't know,' said Reggie, and returned to the subject

he had been previously discussing, this being the house sale in the Crescent where he had bought, for the hideous prices that everything was bringing these days, a collection of vinaigrettes, two ribbon-back Chippendale arms, and a walnut break-front dresser with original handles and all the spice drawers intact, but in the meantime recording Guy's odd behaviour in that part of his mind which he reserved for the often useful findings of Clive's inquisitive nature.

Reggie lived in a Georgian house situated on sloping land overlooking a small village – its pub, store and cottages disposed about a stream that rippled swiftly over a shallow bed of pebbles and was contained within high banks dressed with kingcups and forget-me-nots. A bridge crossed the stream and on the other side of the bridge a wrought-iron gate introduced the drive leading to Reggie's house.

Reggie pulled up outside the gate, waiting for Clive to open it. But Clive had been angered by Reggie's inadequate reaction to the information supplied him concerning the eccentric behaviour of Guy de Boissy.

'Will you open the gate?' said Reggie, after they had sat in silence for some moments.

'I don't see why,' said Clive. 'At any moment Caliban will come plunging through the rhododendrons with beech leaves in his hair.'

When, after more moments, it had become clear to Reggie that Clive was not going to open the gate, he got out of the car to do so himself. His approach to the gate coincided with the arrival down the path through the rhododendrons of Frank Legg whom Reggie employed as a gardener. Both extended a hand for the latch of the gate. Reggie, aged fifty-two, tall, grey-haired and handsome in a well-bred Carthusian way, and Frank, aged twenty-five, stripped to the waist, and handsome in a fresh, lusty bucolic way, smiled at one another.

'Allow me,' said Frank.

'Allow me,' said Reggie, imbibing with delight and a sudden forgetfulness of all else, the pungent odour of Frank's sun-baked body.

Frank's hand had been first on the latch of the gate. Reggie closed his fingers upon it before returning to the car, where Clive sat, silent, his lips withdrawn in a thin smile.

The Attic

DIZZY WITH hunger, physical exertion and a sensation of desperate urgency, as though he and he alone had been given the task of pursuing a dangerous maniac driving a fast car round mountain bends and seizing the maniac before he could reach a spot where he would put his finger on a button and blow up the world, Guy gulped down a superbrunch-burger in the Wimpy Bar down the hill from Beau Nash's house, having left the Mini in the car park outside the public lavatories.

He arrived home at two and set to work. It took him some time to get everything up to the attic. A search for light bulbs disclosed the fact that there weren't any and in Thawle-on-Rustle it was early closing which Guy ought to have known but had forgotten, having lost track of hours, days, years, of all time in fact, concentrating as he was on the need for pursuing a dangerous maniac around mountain roads before it was too late. So he had to drive to Bradford-on-Avon for light bulbs and returned, having in the nick of time escaped an encounter with a tractor, a large van marked 'Inflammable', and a herd of cows.

By four he had got down to work. At seven he descended to the cellar for a dozen bottles of 1847 Château d'Yquem, poured ten down the sink and returned with the remaining two bottles to the attic.

At first he felt sorry for the Lancret lady in the shining pink dress whose graceful form, reclining on a grassy bank, was disappearing under a coat of Snowcem. The little dog at her foot which he had always loved because it seemed to be laughing, he preserved for the last stroke of his brush. But after having dealt with a wistful Roguelan lion and a portrait of a chevalier of the Order of Saint-Esprit which he liked because of the garters on the chevalier's elegant legs and the ruffles on his pantaloons, Guy came to terms with his distress, and told himself that he was only putting these delightful creatures – ladies in shining dresses, dogs, lions, horses and cavaliers – into retirement for a while. But the system he had adopted of preserving till the last moment those bits of the pictures he liked most was not helpful in arriving at harmonious compositions.

Concentrating on the need for achieving harmonious compositions, he began to enjoy his work and, becoming absorbed in problems of colour, space and form, forgot the dangerous maniac. By midnight, circles, oblongs, squares and diagonals were exploding in splendid arrangements in his mind. So delighted was he with a chrome yellow circle resting on the upper end of a cerulean blue diagonal, an Indian red egg on the lower end like a large, light-weight object riding a see-saw with a small heavy object pulling it down, that alongside his signature he dashed off the title 'Wig-wag'.

Around 12.30 Percy spoke up.

'It's no good, Guy. The frames aren't right. Nobody would think of putting that sort of picture into that sort of frame.'

'I think you're right,' said Guy.

'Abstract painting,' said Percy, 'ought to have plain frames. You're very good with your hands and you could easily knock up some frames. But you can't leave them in those antique carved wood frames all shining with gold leaf.'

'But what do I do with the frames? They're very valuable.'

'Put them in Seabird's stall,' said Percy. 'Cover them with hay and put a lot of apples on top and some saddles and other things in a careless way. Then take all those mezzo-tints from behind the sofa and hang them in the Morning Room because you've got to cover up the places where you took the pictures down.'

'You'd think,' said Prescott, 'that he'd take a turn watching by his mother's bed. Its four days and he hasn't put his head inside her door. He sleeps most of the day and every night I hear him tramping around up in the attic.'

'It's years,' said Giles, 'since he missed out on his morning ride. And what's he doing up in that attic every night with the lights turned on?'

'I don't know,' said Irene.

Sheik Ahmed Ben Hassan

GUY HAD FINISHED with the Morning Room and was working his way through the Octagonal Room, where the pictures, chosen to live in harmony with the Adam furniture, were, in his view, rather stodgy. Deciding that three quiet landscapes, bereft of dogs, horses, ladies, cavaliers and even birds, could be despatched into the outside world without regret, he returned them to the situations they had occupied for two hundred years and concentrated on an Oudry dog chasing pheasants. He had just applied the finishing touches when the attic door opened and Irene appeared, carrying a plate of steak-and-kidney pudding.

'What's that?' said Guy.

'It's your tea, love,' said Irene.

'You don't,' said Guy, sinking to snobbery that only Irene brought out in his nature, 'have tea at midnight.'

'It's food, love,' said Irene. 'You haven't had any food all day.'

Guy said, 'I don't want any favours from you.'

Irene, having arranged the plate of steak-and-kidney pudding with knife and fork on either side on the table that Guy was using for his paints and brushes, sat down on the sofa, placed her elbow on her knee and extended her hand in a horizontal position to support her chin.

'Hatred,' she said, 'is love in disguise. When Sheik Ahmed Ben Hassan . . .'

'I don't want to hear about your Sheik Ahmed Ben Hassan. As for saying that hatred is love in disguise, it's the most stupid idea anyone ever thought up. Love is love and hate is hate. They haven't got a thing in common.'

'Listen to you shouting,' said Irene, 'and getting all worked up. That's just what I mean. Sheik Ahmed Ben Hassan thinks he hates Lady Diana Mayo because he feels so strongly about her and she thinks she hates him because of what he's done to her until that day when she rides into the desert on Silver Star and he shoots down one of his best horses to get her back and when he carries her clasped against him and she feels the beat of his heart . . .'

'Enough of that rubbish,' said Guy, trying to keep calm, because it always infuriated him that Irene kept so calm when he lost his temper and it should, by all the rules of birth and upbringing, have been the other way round. 'I don't hate you. I am totally indifferent to you, apart from the fact that it irritates me beyond endurance to see you parading about in Mummy's clothes. I know I've got to put up with you because you are useful to Mummy and have wheedled your way into her affections, but this is a large house, you've got your rooms, so please keep out of my way and leave me alone.'

'Eat your pudding,' said Irene. 'It's a pity to let it get cold.'

'What do you want now?' asked Guy, when he had finished the steak-and-kidney pudding.

'I don't want anything,' said Irene. 'You always ask me, what do you want? It was the first thing you said to me.' Continuing, in the meantime, to regard Guy with that wanting expression which had so disconcerted him on the day, three years before, when he had first encountered her, standing in the hall by the front door, wearing a skimpy pink chiffon dress that hung from her emaciated form like the cobwebs draping the disused farm implements in the stables, and at her feet a small, bulging suitcase from which had escaped a loop of apple-green satin ribbon belonging to some garment within.

Guy and Irene

IT WAS HER face, rather than her unheralded presence, that commanded his attention. Her string-coloured hair, piled on the top of her head with an appearance of such weight and abundance as to impart an impression of exhaustion to the head supporting it, was insecurely fixed by long, undulating hairpins, which, he was to discover later, were forever falling out and interfering with the workings of the vacuum cleaner. Her eyes, like her hair, took up too much room. A vast white forehead introduced them, everything below being by comparison unexceptional; nose, mouth and chin too small and finely delineated to compete with the drama above. She regarded him as though he were someone she had specifically come to meet, not in any sentiment of welcome or friendliness, but more as some creature from outer space might gaze upon the earth, speculating upon the appropriate moment to move in and take over.

'I've come to see your mother,' she replied, in answer to his question.

'What about?' asked Guy.

Irene moved her body in a gesture which lifted her shoulders in two white bumps out of the top of her dress. 'It's a private and personal matter.'

Guy was by nature and upbringing hospitable and polite but he was annoyed by her casual shrug and the manner in which she now stared about her as though getting her bearings.

He said, a little sharply, 'When I know what you want I'll see what I can do for you.'

'I've told you. I've come to see your mother. This is where

she lives, isn't it? The door was open,' she added.

'What's that bag?' Guy pointed at the bulging suitcase. Irene also turned her head to regard it, dropping a hairpin with a clang on to the Sèvres tiles. A lock of hair descended and brushed her cheek. There was little difference between the colour of the cheek and the colour of the hair.

'Those are my things. You wouldn't want me to come without my things, would you? I couldn't manage the books on the bus. They're in the Bath railway station in the baggage room. Someone will have to collect them and the sooner the better because it costs two shillings a day.'

Before Guy could express his alarm and question the meaning of this statement, Irene had pointed to the Alma-Tadema portrait of Lady Clarissa.

'Why's she lying down? I suppose these are your ancestors and they're all sitting or standing up or riding horses.' (Lord Alexander, Lord Peter and the Lord Charles who had fought with Monmouth and along with his leader had sought refuge in the so-called Monmouth House in Shepton Mallet.) 'But that looks like Cupid with the bow and arrow and she's lying on a couch with hardly anything on. Was she one of the wives or just a friend?'

'That is my great great grandmother,' said Guy stiffly, 'and the way she is painted was the fashion of the period.'

Irene began to wander down the hall and Guy didn't know how to stop her without being unpleasantly rude.

'Is that your ma?' She had stopped before the MacEvoy which was hung rather high on the wall so that she had to lift her head to look at it. Guy felt that the weight of her hair might snap off her long thin neck. He had never seen a neck so white. It was obviously little if ever exposed to wind, rain or sunshine. In fact she looked as if she had lived indoors all her life, in a small dark room, Guy imagined, with very little fresh air and the curtains closed, which was one of the reasons why at that particular moment he felt he ought to treat her gently, though firmly. Because she looked so wan and frail.

'Yes, how did you know?'

'Because of the descriptions. And it's the latest,' said Irene before he could ask what she meant about the descriptions. 'And she looks quite young and you haven't got any sisters. I mean not any other sisters. So it must be her.'

A door closed. Irene's eyes turned from the MacEvoy and seemed to enlarge as they focused some distance behind him. Guy imagined he saw terror filling them up but a moment later the terror disappeared, leaving an emptiness of expression that was even more curious and forlorn.

Lady Evelyn came towards them, smiling and gracious as though welcoming an invited guest.

'And who is this? And what can we do for her, Guy?'

'I don't know,' said Guy.

'What is your name, my dear?'

'I'm Irene,' said Irene. 'The name's Blane. I just arrived.'

Remembering the scene later Guy recalled how his mother had stood in silence looking at Irene, not summing her up so much as taking her in, and that while Irene submitted to her scrutiny her nervous, angular body almost imperceptibly took on a look of grace and ease. But his mother always had that effect on people, so there was nothing remarkable about it.

'Come in here, my dear,' said Lady Evelyn, 'and let me hear all about what you have to say.' The Morning Room door closed behind them.

'She claims,' explained Lady Evelyn, after the books had been collected from the Bath station baggage room and Irene had been installed and Guy had demanded to know why, 'to be your half-sister. The love child of your dear father. You must admit that there is quite a remarkable likeness, so who are we, taking his warm, generous nature into account, to deny her claim?'

Lady Evelyn spoke from her bed, sipping the hot chocolate which Guy had brought before retiring for the night.

'Daddy,' said Guy, becoming very angry, 'was short and

broad-shouldered, like me. He had a square face, black hair before it went grey, the complexion of a sunburnt Greek and dark brown eyes. This creature is tall, stringy and blonde. Her eyes are a sort of indeterminate green and her skin looks like yogurt.'

'Why don't you say milk or cream? It sounds so much nicer.'

'Because I like milk and cream and I detest yogurt.'

'My darling Guy, a likeness is not necessarily the faithful repetition of height, bone structure, complexion or the colour of hair and eyes. It can show itself as a subtle reflection of the expression and movements of a face and body. I am confident that your father installed Irene's mother in some modest but comfortable establishment in London and during Irene's infancy and early childhood dandled his daughter on his knee. Children are worshippers and imitators and only by love and close observation could she have learned how to incline her head and move her hands in the de Boissy way.'

'Mummy, you astonish me. Her hands flap around as if they're going to fall off and her head sticks out on her scrawny neck like a spavined dandelion.'

'And you, Guy, astonish me by your lack of perception. Irene is the living image of your father and moreover she has brought with her a letter from her mother who is now dead and has left her destitute.'

'Destitute! Mummy, you are so naïve. Why doesn't she go back on the streets where she belongs.'

'Because she doesn't want to. We have had quite a few little talks and she has told me that although she was raped by her uncle when she was thirteen, no man has since laid a finger on her because she is keeping herself for the man of her choice. She believes in chastity, fidelity, one man for one woman, love at first sight and true romance for ever more.'

'No wonder, with all that muck she reads.'

'And she is only sixteen.'

'What,' asked Guy, 'did the letter say?'

'If you look in the top right-hand drawer of that ridiculous bureau you will find it.'

Guy read; 'My dear daughter, to spare you from the hardships of life, such as I have had to endure, I instruct you herewith to approach your stepmother, Lady Evelyn de Boissy, and inform her of the fact that you are the daughter of her late husband, Lord Charles de Boissy, and was conceived by him in the King's Arms on June 14th, 1946. Preserve this letter with your life. It's all you've got. Your devoted mother, Sally Blane.'

'Mummy!' cried Guy. 'She wrote that letter herself. It's a confidence trick. I absolutely refuse to believe that creature is my sister.'

Lady Evelyn, having finished her chocolate, put down the cup and patted his hand. 'That part of the story, accept or reject as you feel inclined. It is unimportant. But don't be difficult and make unnecessary trouble because I like her. You won't know what I mean and I'm not going to explain but she strikes a chord. She won't cost anything because she eats like a sparrow. She'll help in the house, and I really do need someone to fix my hair.'

Irene Goes

'WILL YOU PLEASE go,' said Guy. 'I'm very busy and I can't think with you sitting there staring at me.'

'Oh all right,' said Irene. 'But I think you ought to do something about those frames.'

Guy watched her departure to be sure that he was getting rid of her, but after the door had closed behind her, a sense of her presence still remained, for to what else could he attribute an immediate and vivid evocation of a painting in the Chinese Room.

The Chinese Room contained porcelain, jade and paintings, all awaiting his attention. The particular painting that had come to his mind in such a striking way was a scroll painting on silk, said to be Sung, but probably a Ming copy, depicting an egret standing on one leg amongst lotus flowers, quite still, leaving a ripple in the water, suggesting that it had just moved and was about to move again. Even its white plumes gave the appearance of having settled about its body at that very instant, after having ruffled up, and the lotus leaves had turned back in a wind that just at that moment had passed over them.

The egret was a leggy, scraggy bird, with nobbly knees and a long, extended neck; and yet so graceful and elegant.

Ozzie David

A WEEK AFTER Lady Evelyn bought the pink lustre cup and saucer from Magnolia Tree, and again it was a Saturday, Magnolia threw open the door of her shop to call out, 'Would you mind moving your car. You're blocking the entrance to my drive.'

The drive was a narrow lane, public, but Magnolia claimed it as her own as it petered out at the back of her cottage, where in a patch of kitchen garden she was raising fowls pending the time when she had amassed sufficient capital to extend the crowded premises of her Export Department. She had no use for her drive at the moment and the Ford Cortina parked at its entrance was causing her no inconvenience, but she believed in seizing every opportunity for putting those who came to her shop at a disadvantage before engaging in commercial transactions, particularly when they happened to be, not only London Trade, but that Portobello spiv, Ozzie David.

While Ozzie moved the Ford Cortina, his companion, a

Swedish dealer, who visited England three times a year to scour the country for broken famille rose plates, waited outside Magnolia's shop, looking thoughtful and aloof in the manner of a tourist, who after having admired the architectural splendours of the Abbey, decides to wander down the less celebrated but no less interesting lanes and byways of the town. He spoke no word to Magnolia, not only because he knew no English but also because, it was said, he was of royal blood and therefore held himself aloof from the riff-raff that peopled his profession. Not chosen, so much as forced upon him by a tyrannical socialist government, even worse, as far as Magnolia could ascertain, than the present Labour Government – Magnolia being a passionate conservative as was every member of the antique trade where private enterprise came into its finest flower.

'Nothing for your friend, I'm afraid,' said Magnolia. 'London Trade cleaned out all my Oriental last week. But I've got a very good Ugly Child for you.'

Ozzie regarded this work of art, executed in pastels and housed in an oval frame. The huge head, dressed with yellow curls confined in a blue ribbon, was set upon a fragile neck which was the only childlike thing about it, the face being that of a licentious roué, bags under the eyes and obscenely smirking.

'It isn't signed,' said Magnolia, 'but by the style of dress it's obviously eighteenth century. Ten bob to the Trade.'

'Beautiful,' said Ozzie, gazing upon it with an expression not unlike the expression on the face of the Ugly Child – pictures of Ugly Children, mechanical musical instruments and theatre programmes being his speciality.

Still maintaining the smile he had bestowed on the Ugly Child, he transferred it to Magnolia who thanked God that another of Ozzie's sources of income was the guide and transport service he supplied to foreign Trade like the Swede, doing the rounds of the West and Southern counties and picking up what he could at the same time at *their* expense. But always accompanied, he had no opportunity to slip into

71

her shop on his own and rape her on the spot as he would if he could. If she let him in on his own, which she never would.

'Is there anything,' said Magnolia, 'that you want from the window?' Into which Ozzie was extending thick fingers grafted with silver rings. 'Because if there is, I'd prefer to get it for you.'

'I'd like,' said Ozzie, 'to have another look at your "Pinkie" programme.' A request that Magnolia had anticipated, knowing full well that Ozzie hungered for this *pièce de résistance* of her theatre programme collection, but which he wasn't going to get hold of not over her dead body.

Holding it up, but not allowing him to touch it because on a previous occasion and probably on purpose he had soiled the corner with a print from his greasy thumb, Magnolia enjoyed the expression of tormented desire that Ozzie was unable to keep out of his face.

'You're still asking that ridiculous price?' Ozzie enquired.

Alarmed by a hint of weakness in his tone, Magnolia said, 'Five pounds ten. I put it up ten bob last week. It's appreciating.'

After a silence during which Magnolia viewed with satisfaction various shades of feeling moving across Ozzie's heavy features, Ozzie prophesied with a portentousness that would have done credit to Ezekiel or Isaiah, 'Those that do not cooperate with the Trade, live to regret it.'

After he had paid for the Ugly Child and departed in his ostentatious Ford Cortina, Magnolia rang up Alfie Middle.

Alfie Middle

ALFIE LIVED and operated his business on the northern side of the town from a warehouse which three hundred years before had served some purpose connected with the then thriving Somerset weaving industry. From humbler premises on the outskirts of Frome, he had started up in junk, rags and feathers and had prospered so swiftly his stock had soon overwhelmed the available accommodation and flowed on to the pavement outside. Neighbours had taken exception to the broken sofas disgorging their substance from slits in the upholstery and the heaps of mattresses, eiderdowns and pillows that obstructed their approach down the hill to the main streets of Frome. The situation might have erupted into dramatic incident had not Alfie had a stroke of luck up in Birmingham, which was the principal market for his rags and feathers. Here, in an abandoned warehouse, he came across 2,156 Victorian wine carafes made of thick, dimpled glass and 1,455 ice-cream dishes destined around 1890 for restaurants in that city but never delivered. Some poor optimistic fool having miscalculated the market and overstocked. A building contractor who had bought the property for demolition and deeming its contents to be of no value, allowed Alfie to clear the premises.

The frugal, cautious Somerset Middles who contributed to a portion of Alfie's nature warned him that neither the wine carafes nor the ice-cream dishes were of the least use to anyone in this day and age and would hang around his neck for ever more, but remote gypsy ancestors responsible for his sparkling black eyes, his sheepskin jacket, the gold rings in his ears and his devotion to the thin, plinky music of merry-go-rounds, pianolas and musical boxes, advised him to take into account the human disposition for a bargain.

Within three weeks Alfie had disposed of all but four carafes and three ice-cream dishes. Londoners were turning from beer to wine and nobody could resist a piece of thick, dimpled Victorian glass at three shillings a piece. Carafes and ice-cream dishes flowed through the nearby towns, up to London and even back to Birmingham. Local dealers bought in bulk and in Portobello the price went up to fifteen shillings. Alfie cleared £800, threw in another £400 from rags and feathers, and turning his back on the unappreciative natives of Frome, bought the warehouse facing the main road to Wells from which he now conducted a much up-graded business. Although still solidly based on junk, rags and feathers it encompassed paintings housed in an annexe entitled 'The Gallery' and antique furniture comprising brass bedsteads, walnut chiffoniers with marble tops – some of them rather far gone with wear and worm, but still worth while because of the marble tops, which when wedded to old sewing machines made practical outdoor tables for small London gardens – and pine chests sold at four quid to London Trade, who stripped them down and flogged them in Chelsea for thirty quid apiece. 'The Gallery', due to the quality of the paintings, brought small monetary return, but with nothing over ten bob it was a big attraction and filled his shop on Saturday afternoons, the word having got around that an Australian dealer had bought there for five bob a Conrad Martens which he had subsequently sold for £400 in Adelaide.

This same Australian dealer was on that day hopefully working his way through stags at bay, Highland cattle amongst the heather, dogs pursuing pheasants and the Pyramids at sunset, in search of a mislaid masterpiece.

'Make it brief, Magnolia,' said Alfie, 'I've got that Anti-polian in the Gallery.'

'I just rang to warn you,' said Magnolia. 'That Portobello Yid spiv, Ozzie David, is on his way to you with the Cracked Swede.'

'He's after my bird,' said Alfie.

Alfie's bird, the pride of all his possessions, was a sparsely feathered creature, said to be a nightingale, attached to a perch in a cage. After a coin had been inserted into a slot at the bottom of the cage, it shuddered, opened its beak, spread tremulous wings and burst into song. It was the *pièce de résistance* of Alfie's mechanical music collection and identical to another bird in a cage which had been illustrated years back in *The Connoisseur*, except that the bird in *The*

Connoisseur had more feathers. Alfie had been unable to read the article explaining about the bird but had it by heart after Magnolia had read it aloud to him, framed it and hung it on a nail alongside the bird on the inside front wall of his shop so that customers could not fail to miss it as they came and went.

'Did he get your "Pinkie"?' Alfie asked.

'Over my dead body,' said Magnolia. 'They make me sick that London lot. They think they can come down here and for next to nothing strip us naked, absolutely naked of all our best pieces. We do all the work, travelling hundreds of miles day and night and driving ourselves to the bone, when all they have to do is sail out from London in their Ford Cortinas, filling themselves up with beer at every pub on the way and say I'll have this, I'll have that. Beat you into the ground and when you've dropped your price just to get rid of them they cruise back to London stopping at every pub and mark up for fifteen quid something they've got out of you for ten bob.'

'I don't care,' said Alfie, 'so long as I make my profit. It's up to them what they sells for. But he's not getting my bird.'

'Well, I care,' said Magnolia. 'They despise us. They think we're illiterate natives like those illiterate natives down in Cornwall. I'm a direct descendant of Beerbohm Tree and I know more about theatre programmes than Ozzie David. My theatre library is the most extensive in the West Country and I'm not going to let Ozzie David treat my shop as an annexe to his dump in Portobello. I demand respect and cooperation. We're all in this together, Alfie. It's a fraternity, and I've got no time for that greedy London Trade with their Ford Cortinas who don't care a fig if we starve. Where would they be if we starved? Where would they go for their stuff? It all comes to us and I'm telling you that Portobello lot and Camden Passage's getting to be just as bad, and that lot in St Christopher's Place are just a gang of sharks that have brought the antique trade into disrepute. It's you and me, Alfie, and people like Reggie Thring who have maintained the dignity of the antique business.'

'Well said, Magnolia,' said Alfie. 'Well said.'

'What I rang to say,' said Magnolia, 'is that Ozzie says that Lady Evelyn de Boissy is ill and everyone thinks she's dying. Had you heard?'

'Not a word,' said Alfie, who did not move in the sort of company who would be likely to know that Lady Evelyn was dying.

'Ozzie says he met Clive St John up in Sotheby's and Clive told him because Clive heard it from Reggie who heard it from Dr Templeton who looks after Lady Evelyn and Dr Templeton told Reggie because Lady Evelyn told Reggie she wanted him to value the estate for probate when she dies.'

'I expect,' said Alfie, 'that those attics where they kept the maids will be full of beds and mattresses.'

'It was only a week ago,' said Magnolia, 'that she bought my pink lustre cup and saucer. Very tottery even then. Nearly knocked over my hat stand with all my beads.'

'I've got to go,' said Alfie. 'They're here.'

'Don't let them get your bird.'

'Over my dead body,' said Alfie.

The Empress Alexandra Feodorovna's Coronation Coach

'FABERGE,' said Reggie Thring, taking a turn at the end of the room and casting a glance into the Chippendale mirror which dressed the eastern wall, 'takes its name from Gustav Petrovitch Fabergé who established a firm in St Petersburg in Russia around the middle of the last century for the manufacture of jewellery and *objets d'art*, or *objets de vertu*, as I prefer to call them. When the firm was taken over by his son, Peter Carl, these *objets de vertu* were bought by the kings, queens, tsars, tsarinas, emperors and empresses of Europe and by anyone else who could afford them, one such being Lord Edward de Boissy who assembled a collection of Fabergé which although it could not compete in value and magnificence with the royal collections was outstanding for its quality and taste.'

Whilst talking, Reggie continued to stroll about and paused before another of the five mirrors which enhanced the room with an illusion of size and space and brought into it skies, clouds and trees, and which multiplied to an at times disconcerting effect the movements and attitudes of the people who happened to be within the room – on that Saturday afternoon Reggie himself, clad in a rose silk dressing-gown, and his gardener Frank Legg, lying stretched out in his underpants on Reggie's Queen Anne bed. The bed was too short for Frank and his large but shapely feet stuck out at the end. It was also too short for Reggie, but Reggie loved the bed and slept on his side with his knees tucked up. Clive St John had gone to London for the weekend.

'This lovely piece,' said Reggie, displaying it on the palm of his hand, 'is a model of the Empress Alexandra Feodorovna's coronation coach. This cigar-case carries a portrait of Tsar Nicholas II enclosed in a rose diamond frame, said to be a present to Lord Edward from the Tsar himself, and the blue enamel Easter egg opens out – let me show you – into eight sections depicting views of Moscow painted on mother of pearl by Krijitski and mounted in octagonal gold frames. When closed, as you see, it is contained within a fine gold net set with rose diamonds and pearls. The three pieces are worth something like sixty thousand pounds.'

'Wow,' said Frank, scratching the sole of his right foot with his left foot's big toenail. 'How did you get hold of that little lot?'

Reggie, having returned the three pieces of Fabergé to their positions on the mantelpiece, regarded himself in the mirror, combed back his abundant hair with his fingers and arranged amidst the silver grey that predominated, two interesting streaks of tobacco brown. This done, he tightened the cord of his dressing-gown and turned to regard the beautiful – brown to the waist and white below – body of his gardener.

'They are payment for a probate valuation that I have been asked to execute for Lady Evelyn de Boissy when she dies. Her son, Lord Guy, brought them here yesterday.'

'If his mother isn't dead yet,' said Frank, 'why does he pay you with things worth what you said for something you haven't done yet because she isn't dead. Why doesn't he wait till its happened and pay you then?'

'Because there isn't any money,' said Reggie.

Frank thought for a while before giving the whole thing up.

Reggie, immersed in memories, continued to pace the room. The southern window overlooked a sloping lawn which appeared to flow like a river from banks of rhododendrons in full flower and fell in a precipitous descent to the stream in the valley below, where the store, the pub and the dozen cottages of the village collected mist in the late-afternoon light. Woods, as yet undefiled by modern development, clothed the opposite hill, still bathed in sunshine, and although Reggie's side of the valley had witnessed a recent eruption of bungalows Reggie, from within the garden which enclosed his house, was able to suspend awareness of them.

'Even as a child,' he recounted, 'I was attracted to fine furniture. I remember a Regency rosewood table with a stretcher and claw feet. Regency hadn't arrived in my father's day, being too new to be old and too old to be fashionable. And rosewood was considered of little account. It was stuck out in the hall and everyone put their hats on it. I must have been quite small, still on the floor, because I don't remember the top, except for the hats. But I got to know the base so well I can see it today. I stroked the golden streaks in the dark wood and told myself they were streams winding through banks of bracken fern. I imagined myself paddling a boat along those streams. My father tried me out on half a dozen careers designed to bring fame and fortune to the family name which was not particularly illustrious and needed some fame and fortune to bolster it up – we owed all we had to my uncle who made a lot out of jute in Calcutta – but I always knew I wanted to do something with furniture.'

'You must have been a nice little chap,' said Frank, 'but I wish you'd get rid of a few of those mirrors. You're supposed to be talking to me. At least I suppose that's what you're doing, but instead of looking at me while you're talking to me you keep looking at yourself in all those mirrors. And I don't blame you because I'm doing the same thing. Instead of looking at you while you look at yourself and talk to me, I'm looking at myself and forgetting to listen.'

'I thought you weren't listening,' said Reggie.

'I've never seen myself before,' said Frank, 'in so many different positions and it catches my eye and makes my mind wander. I suppose it was his idea. Likes to keep an eye on what he's doing.'

'On the contrary,' said Reggie, with a guilty impulse of loyalty to Clive. 'They were my idea. They fill the room with flowers,' and he waved a hand at the profusion of rhododendrons cast into the mirrors from the garden outside.

'Flowers are for outside,' said Frank. 'It's unhealthy bringing them indoors. Get rid of those mirrors. They make me feel shy.'

'What I was about to say is that I learned a great deal of what I now know about fine furniture from Lord Charles de Boissy,' said Reggie. 'The house is my affair and the garden is yours. I hope you remember that I listened to you and conceded to your opinion when you objected to the marble nymph on the bottom lawn.'

'It didn't fit,' said Frank. 'You have to make up your mind what sort of garden you want and stick to it.'

'Lord Charles and I both went to Charterhouse,' said Reggie, 'which was a bond, and Clare who attended just about every race meeting in England was forever wanting to stroke horses. They asked us to their parties. I soaked, but literally soaked, it in. The Fabergé – a fantastic collection – the silver, and the furniture. The pictures. And they were so well informed, particularly Lady Evelyn. Most of it's gone, of course, including the horses.'

'What do you mean, the horses went?' asked Frank, showing interest at the mention of horses.

'In the 1950 sale after Lord Charles's death. Most of the land and all but one of the horses. The best of the paintings. A Rembrandt authenticated by three experts and rejected by two. But three to two substantiates a claim. A Poussin, undoubtedly right – lovely naked youths and girls dancing around with flower garlands, a delicious Boucher of Madame de Pompadour getting into her bath. That woman was always getting in and out of a bath. And a Gainsborough, very dubious in my opinion. Much too bright, but it sold to America where they like their Gainsboroughs bright. Lord Charles left what remained of the estate to Lady Evelyn who has defended it even in the face of starvation. I don't believe she has parted with a stick of furniture, a painting or a piece of Fabergé since the 1950 sale, because if she had wanted to do so she would have called me in.'

'But you've just told me,' said Frank, 'that you've got sixty thousand quid's worth in those three little knick-knacks up there.'

'They are a bribe,' said Reggie. 'They are a message from Lady Evelyn telling me that her estate is threatened with demolition and asking me to salvage everything I can for Lord Guy.'

'How can you do that?' asked Frank.

'By keeping my valuation as low as I can. And I don't mind admitting that I am torn. Very torn. Because I am dying to get my hands on some of that furniture. All the gaudy French went in the 1950 sale and now, thank God, there is no Boulle, no vile, but vile ormolu, and no Louis XIV chairs sitting around like old women with their legs apart looking as if they've piddled their pants.'

'I wish you wouldn't,' said Frank, 'talk like that. It's very unmanly. You get it from *him*. You don't say things like that to other people, so please don't say them to me. You embarrass me.'

Reggie turned his back to pace once more down the room. 'Nothing,' he continued, after a pause during which he digested Frank's rebuff, 'that remains in that house twinkles or sparkles. Everything gleams and glows. Walnut, satinwood, tulip wood, oyster wood, mahogany, coromandel. Delicious wood groomed to an unctuous splendour by the dedicated hands of centuries of little housemaids with their wax and cloths and feather dusters.'

'I suppose it all means something to someone,' said Frank.

'If you and I,' said Reggie, 'are to achieve a relationship, you will have to learn something about these matters, which is not beyond you as you have a good, if uncultivated, brain and considerable sensibility.'

'Talking of cultivation,' said Frank. 'What do you know about making compost and pruning roses?'

'Nothing,' said Reggie, 'and as you must have your area of precedence, I am willing to sit at your feet and learn.'

'If his lordship, Mr Clive St John, will allow it,' said Frank.

Suddenly Reggie was conscious that the happiness of that afternoon, following upon the delight of the previous day when Guy had turned up with the Fabergé, had darkened around him, threatening him with the punishment of problems and hard decisions.

Frank's eyes fixed his own in a gaze that was startlingly authoritative. 'He runs your life and you're afraid of him. Why don't you get rid of him?'

Reggie raised his voice. 'I don't want to hear you saying these things. His train arrives in half an hour and I've got to meet it, so you'd better go.'

'Calm down,' said Frank, rising from the bed. 'But I'm telling you that a decent down-to-earth fellow like me doesn't care for these underground meetings when Mr Clive St John decides he wants a day in London.' He pulled on his pants and tucked in his shirt. 'What's more, when he's gone I'm going to grab those yapping monsters by the scruff of their necks and cut off their heads with my pruning shears. Then we can get hold of a couple of labradors. Much more manly,' he added, throwing in Reggie's direction a dazzling smile, the teeth so white, the eyes so dark and sparkling with laughter.

Reggie smiled back, his spirit reimbued with happiness. But driving to Bath happiness claimed its price and left him to the consideration of its consequences. At least fifteen minutes late for the Paddington train, which was usually late, but today would be on time, so that Clive, his face tense with the irritation of waiting and knowing why he had been kept waiting, would be pacing up and down outside the station, or seated in the waiting-room on one of the benches, tapping his foot.

The Mongolian Ponies

DR TEMPLETON came every day to attend Lady Evelyn. No improvement showed in her condition, but also no deterioration. The day prophesied for her death passed, and Lady Evelyn lived on into the next week and yet the next, which gave Guy ample time to tackle the Chinese Room.

He painted the celadons, the tortoises and the Mongolian ponies in one of the greenhouses, but took the Chun bulb bowls up to the attic. It was hard work. The celadons, though sturdy, were in impeccable condition and had to be carefully wrapped. There had been quite a lot of rain and the path leading past the stables was soggy with mud which the ducks enjoyed, but Guy had to abandon the wheelbarrow. The celadons were heavy enough, but nothing compared to the tortoises and the Mongolian ponies. By eleven he had finished and, leaving them to dry, fetched a bottle from the cellar and went up to the attic to attend to the Chun bulb bowls. Not a long job except that the paint kept contracting from the glaze.

'Too much turps,' said Percy. 'They put in a lot of turps when they painted my dapples but when they got around to my hooves and wanted a thick, shiny black, they reduced the turps by half, I would say.'

Leaving the bulb bowls to dry, Guy returned to the uncompleted task of the paintings.

He had left his favourites, the Ingres and the Fragonard, till last, hoping that something might happen to prevent his having to subject them to the ignominy of shameful disguises.

Around midnight, he was coming out of the Peacock Room with the Fragonard when Prescott opened the door of his mother's bedroom and hurried along the passage at the top of the stairs. Guy hid under the staircase.

'Lord Guy,' he heard her calling. 'Where are you, Lord Guy?' Her voice, still calling his name, became fainter as she descended to the kitchen.

Guy mounted the stairs and on the landing by Lady Evelyn's door encountered his mother, looking at least forty years younger and clad, not in a nightdress and dressing-gown as he would have expected, but in a white satin evening gown of old-fashioned cut and waving an ostrich feather fan.

'Dearest Mummy, you're looking absolutely marvellous. The rest has done you good. I'm sorry I haven't spent much time with you, but you were always asleep and I've been awfully busy. What a lovely dress. I don't think I've ever seen it before.'

'I've always loved it,' said Lady Evelyn. 'Your father bought it for me for the opening night of "The Vikings", on April 15th, 1903. We weren't married and I was only eighteen. I hesitated accepting it but he said he wanted me to outshine everyone in the audience and on the stage, which, when you consider the wonderful triumph of Ellen Terry, was something of a compliment. Afterwards we went back-stage to her dressing-room and they all signed my pro-gramme. Oscar Ashe signed it and so did Holman Clarke. I think it is still in that trunk upstairs. Gordon Craig's sets were superb and it was performed in the Imperial Theatre in Tothill Street, which has since been pulled down. Alas! But of course it didn't run very long because most people don't want to spend a night with Ibsen even if he happens to be adorned by Ellen Terry. But, Guy, that is all in the past and you don't look well. You haven't shaved for at least two days and you're very flushed. I suspect you have been drinking too much wine.'

She waved her fan across his face but apart from a pleasant coolness, the feathers left no sensation on Guy's heated cheeks.

'Mummy, do you think you ought to be walking about like this? Shall I get you a shawl?'

'No thank you, because I want to talk to you and there's not much time. Prescott will be back and she's very bossy. You must return the Mongolian ponies to the Chinese Room. They simply do not look like a garden ornament.'

'I thought they did,' said Guy.

Lady Evelyn waved her fan. 'Those ponies are one of the most celebrated pieces of jade in this country. They have been described in the *Transactions of the Oriental Society* and have been exhibited at least six times in European exhi-bitions. They were presented by the Emperor Chien Lung to a Jesuit priest named Père Largillière who lived in China for years and attracted the affection of the Emperor.'

'I know,' said Guy. 'I always love that story.'

'I told it to you when you were a child,' said Lady Evelyn. 'I changed it a little because you were so sensitive, and it is a very terrible story, but you always wanted to hear it again. I think it was the suffering you liked most.'

'Tell it to me now,' said Guy, 'and don't change it.'

'When Père Largillière left China,' said Lady Evelyn, 'the ship which was taking him back to France was attacked by pirates who at that time ravaged the China seas. The pirates did not kill Père Largillière, preferring to enjoy slow and refined methods of torture. They took him on board their ship along with the Mongolian ponies which did not interest them, but they were not totally barbarian. No one is. They had heard of the excellence of French cooking, so after they had carved Chinese characters on his back – a poem, in fact, the pirate chief was quite a scholar – and had deprived him of his tongue, his ears, his toes and his testicles, which he didn't miss in view of his vocation, they left him with his eyes and his hands and put him to work in the galley. He was rescued after a skirmish off the coast of Java by a British ship which happened to be captained by one of your less notable ancestors, in fact this is all that is known about him and his only claim to fame. In gratitude, Père Largillière presented him with the Mongolian ponies and a document marked with the seal of the Emperor Chien Lung. Which explains why they are so famous.'

'Mummy, it is because of that dreadful story that I want to keep the ponies in the family.'

'But now we come to the happy part. When you were a child you used to sit goggle-eyed listening to the tortures, but this was the part that always made you cry. Père Largillière returned to his village, somewhere near Grenoble, and people came from far and wide to gaze at his peaceful face and receive his blessing. Even though he had no tongue and could not speak, he converted half those pirates to the Catholic faith, starting off with the cooks in the galley. I think he is now a saint and the people of his village have a special holiday when they get drunk and carry his effigy through the village lit with candles and covered with flowers.'

'It still makes me cry,' said Guy, crying.

'The trouble with you, Guy, is that you are too tenderhearted.'

'I get it from you, Mummy.'

'You get it from your grandfather, Lord Philip, who was so afraid of hurting somebody else he ended up by doing nothing at all, and I am pleased that you at least are doing something positive.'

'But, Mummy, when Father died, the greedy government grabbed the Rembrandt, the Poussin and heaven knows what and I don't see why they should have the Fragonard, the Ingres and the Mongolian ponies.'

'I think you might get away with the Mongolian ponies, though you will be taking a risk, but you must forget about the Ingres and the Fragonard. The Ingres should go back to France; nobody here would appreciate it – and I have left the Fragonard to the nation. Think how proud you will be when you take your little son to the National Gallery to show him the Fragonard.'

'But I haven't got a little son.'

'I know, my darling, and that's what you have to do.'

Guy was about to argue, but Lady Evelyn had gone away. Guy took the Fragonard back to the Peacock Room.

Irene's Hairpins

THROUGHOUT THAT evening, Irene, seated on her bed, had been sewing back the sequins which, on the last occasion she had worn it, had been torn off Lady Evelyn's 1913 Erté model from Poiret's salon. When taking it off, the thread attaching the sequins to the neck of the dress had caught in one of her hairpins, setting the sequins free to fall in a shower on the Shiraz rug that Lady Evelyn had lent her to warm up her linoleum. It was difficult finding the sequins on the rug because of all the colours, but Irene was satisfied that although she might have overlooked a sequin or two, she could close up the gaps so that the missing ones would not be noticed. When she had finished with the sequins she fetched a pink tassel from the top right-hand drawer of her chest of drawers where she kept the trimmings – lace, ruffles,

86

tassels, feathers, buttons and beads – that were waiting to be restored to Lady Evelyn's dresses.

Many of the dresses owed their elegance to severe lines accentuated by light-hearted accessories, which being fragile and in some cases perishable, had begun to fall away with the passage of time. The tassel had become detached from its parent garment prior to Irene's arrival at Thawle and because of the capricious nature of Erté's trimmings, she was not sure where it belonged, but after trying it out on a number of sleeves, bags and muffs, had decided to attach it to the 1913 dress. A pink chiffon frill fell from the waist of the dress, short in front and long at the back, over a severe skirt of sturdier material which narrowed to the hem and extended in a short train, sharply contracting to a pointed tip, like the hood of an arum lily. In order to walk comfortably, Irene had to take up the train and drape it over her wrist. She felt convinced that Erté would have realised that the weight of a tassel would keep the train from slipping off the wrist and provide a decorative enhancement. And even if, in an off moment, he had failed to supply a tassel, he would have approved of Irene's decision to sew one on. The tassel wasn't quite the right colour, but near enough.

Irene had chosen that night to repair the 1913 dress which she now put on, because since Lady Evelyn had taken to her bed she had felt sad and bewildered, a condition that her mother had described as 'feeling low'. The best way to deal with it, her mother had advised, was to put on your prettiest dress and sally forth as though you were going out on a special occasion. And although there might be no occasion in the offing, her mother had told her that when you sallied forth, looking your best, it was remarkable how often an occasion turned up.

Lifting the train of the dress, and draping the tassel over her wrist, Irene descended to the kitchen. After she had boiled milk, added cocoa and a teaspoon of sugar, she mounted the back stairs to the attic, carrying the cup of cocoa on a tray.

'I don't want your cocoa,' said Guy, 'or your steak-and-kidney pudding.'

Irene sat on the sofa. 'You don't look yourself.' Her expression was sympathetic and concerned. Guy felt ashamed. He drank the cocoa.

'Thank you,' he said.

Irene continued to sit on the sofa. She had draped the train of her dress over her arm. The pink tassel dangled below her meagre wrist. Guy's thoughts, moving haphazardly about her, blended with thoughts of his mother.

The sleeves of the dress were short to the elbow and fell in pleated pouches beneath her arms. But above, caught up in loops, falling off her shoulders and most of her breast, the pink chiffon, sparkling with a border of sequins, exposed a quantity of Irene's white skin. The sequins flashed, and catching the light, seemed to be moving about on the top of the dress. The skin looked as soft and calm as milk.

Guy was aware of a sense of urgency awakening in his body. 'Mummy thinks I ought to have a son.'

There was quite a long silence while they looked at one another and the urgency in Guy's body became more demanding.

'All right, love,' said Irene.

A number of Irene's hairpins had fallen down the side of the sofa, but much of her hair, though in disarray, remained attached to the top of her head. She took out the remaining hairpins and leaning over the side of the sofa put them underneath where they wouldn't be trodden on.

The hairpins were precious because they were irreplaceable. When she left London she had brought a good store with her which had belonged to her grandmother, but had been careless with them until she found that Woolworth's didn't have them, nor any of the haberdashery stores in Bath or Wells. Lady Evelyn had given her a few and had bought two tortoise-shell pins and a comb from Magnolia Tree's 3d. tray, but Irene didn't know where to go if she lost any more and kept a careful watch on the ones that were left.

Having put them under the sofa in a little pile she pulled down her hair and arranged it over Guy's shoulders and on the sofa cushion which was green and showed it off. The light of morning was coming through the window and made her hair look shining and lovely. She had washed it the day before and rinsed it in lemon, so that when Guy picked some of it off the sofa cushion and pressed it to his face, Irene knew it would smell clean and fragrant. She felt proud of it, not because it was hers, but because it was his. Like Lord Robert had said when he watched Evangeline brushing her hair, 'Isn't it wonderful and it's all mine.'

It was getting lighter all the time. The early mornings were nearly always fine and the sky clear. The rain came later. A blackbird was singing. Irene smiled, enraptured with happiness, and clasped closer to her diminutive breasts the head of the one and only man in the world whom she had loved since that fateful day when she was fourteen and her mother had taken her out for a three-course lunch, and who now was hers and hers alone for ever more.

Breakfast

NEXT MORNING in the kitchen, watching Irene pouring tea into her pink lustre cup and saucer, Guy wondered how he had ever thought she was anything but wonderfully beautiful.

'Would you like eggs and bacon, love?' asked Irene.

More than eggs and bacon, Guy wanted to put his arms around her, but he also liked the idea of postponing this expression of his feelings until a later moment, having in mind that when they had finished breakfast they would go back to bed.

Irene was frying bacon when Prescott appeared.

'Lord Guy, I looked for you everywhere last night. I couldn't find you. Then I thought that it would be cruel to disturb you. Sorrow is always harder to endure in the hours between midnight and dawn.'

Enthralled by the grace of Irene's hands as she turned the bacon, her fingers as white and flexible as the feathers of the egret ruffled in the wind, Guy paid no heed to the portent implicit in Prescott's words, and the need for fortitude that she was demanding of him by the solemnity of her expression and the sympathy in her eyes.

'We're just having breakfast,' he said. 'Would you like some eggs and bacon?'

'Lord Guy, your mother died last night, around midnight. And you mustn't feel sad because this is happy news. A happy release.'

'Don't be silly,' said Guy. 'I had a long talk with her on the stairs and she was looking absolutely marvellous.'

'She felt no pain,' said Prescott. 'She never regained consciousness. She just drifted off. It's the best way to go.'

'You must be out of your mind,' said Guy. 'Irene, I like my bacon crispy.'

'I know,' said Irene. But she had put down the fork with which she had been turning the bacon. And it was in her wet compassionate eyes that Guy realised his mother's death.

That night Guy painted another picture and when it was finished went to Irene's room. The sofa had been uncomfortable and moreover they had been squashing the drawings which wouldn't be good for them.

Waking around dawn he gazed into her sleeping face, brushed the hair from her cheeks and kissed her tenderly. Irene awoke.

Guy said, 'But you're my sister.'

'Why should you worry, love,' said Irene, 'after that affair you've had with your mother for all these years.'

The Woman with Blue Hair

THE FUNERAL in the Bath crematorium took place two days later. Dr Templeton saw to the arrangements but Guy also performed the duties required of him.

'I'm not,' he said to John Templeton, 'going to give that Scottish lot the opportunity of making up for their unkindness to Mummy by coming to her funeral. I'm going to put the notice in *The Times* on the day so they won't have time to get here because if they did I'd have to be polite to them and I couldn't bear it. But I'll send a cable to Aunt Jane, except that she seems to be so incarcerated I don't know whether they'd even let her read a cable from the outside world, and I'll ring up Uncle Robert. He was always sweet to Mummy and I wouldn't want to hurt his feelings. But I just want us and a few Somerset people because that's the way Mummy lived after my father died and I'm sure that's what she would want.'

Lord Robert sent a wreath, but no members of the de Boissy family attended the service. The mourners being Guy, Irene, Giles, John Templeton, Reggie Thring, twelve elderly men and women from Thawle-on-Rustle who had worked as maids and gardeners in Lord Charles's time, and a few yet more elderly couples and widows from neighbouring houses which had fallen into even more decrepitude than Thawle.

A few moments before the coffin was brought into the chapel, another person appeared and seated herself in a pew at the back: a woman of considerable age whom everyone present scrutinised but no one was able to identify. Her elaborately arranged blue hair was dressed with a small black hat, from the brim of which a veil hung down over richly decorated cheeks. She might once have been tall but her stooped back, missing all the discs in the spine, had reduced her height to around five feet. In every human being, however, there are always features that cling to youth. Her legs, long, straight, with muscular calves encased in violet stockings, and her narrow feet, displayed in purple shoes with very high heels, would have graced the front row of any chorus in the West End. Nobody knew who she was and after the funeral people forgot about her because so much happened to attract their attention. But later, talking it over between themselves, they remembered her again and wondered who she could be.

The Crematorium

IRENE DID not like the crematorium. It was modern and too stark. There was an altar with a cross, but the music wasn't real and there weren't enough flowers. She wished that Lady Evelyn's funeral could have taken place in an old church like the Abbey where the light was dim and the mystery hung like smoke. The high beautiful roof made you want to look up and think of God. And there would have been choir boys singing, their voices lifting to the beautiful roof.

In spite of the cross, the crematorium didn't look like a religious place. It might have been a hall or a council building where you paid your dog licence. But the Abbey wasn't a crematorium and Lady Evelyn had said she wanted to be cremated. Irene understood her preference. Better to get it all over instead of falling to pieces slowly over a period of twenty years, or perhaps fifty. Maybe a hundred. Who knows? Much better to be burnt with nothing but ashes left, and flames were beautiful, mounting up to the sky like the voices of the choir boys. It was easy to imagine a spirit liberated from the ashes, soaring above the flames and flying away into the arms of God. Irene was imagining the autumn bonfires at Thawle when Giles raked the leaves from the terrace and threw on top of them everything that needed to be got rid of. But of course a crematorium wasn't like that. Probably more like burning rubbish in an incinerator. But it didn't matter. What mattered was the ashes and the spirit flying to the arms of God. The thought was lovely and comforting, if only there had been more atmosphere to help it along. Even the clergyman reading the service didn't seem to be convinced about what he was saying. When he prayed Irene felt that he got through without mistakes because he had done it so often but had forgotten what it was all about. So she stopped listening and said her own prayer, making it up carefully and choosing every word. When she had finished she thought about Guy, kneeling beside her, very still, and wondered what he was feeling. But she didn't look. Even though he had behaved in such a calm, practical way, he must be feeling very sad and she wanted to hold his hand to comfort him. But it wouldn't have done.

Of course you had to feel sad. You couldn't help it. But for Irene the worst of the sadness was over. It had begun on the night when Lady Evelyn had given her the pink lustre cup and saucer. Later, when she closed her eyes, Irene had kissed her. It was the first time. They never showed their feelings. They understood, but they never said what they understood and she only kissed her then because she felt that Lady Evelyn had died at that moment. She never again opened her eyes. Irene kept on hoping because she had needed hope to keep up her courage. But when she took her turn by Lady Evelyn's bed so that Prescott could have a rest, she had known all over again that she was watching over someone who was already dead and that was the time when she did her grieving; sewing on tassels, sequins and lace, because you had to keep yourself occupied, but pricking her fingers with the needle because of not being able to see through the tears that always ran down and couldn't be stopped. But Lady Evelyn's public death, the one announced by Prescott in the kitchen, took place at a time of such happiness that Irene had got it mixed up with the happiness as though it were part of it. So she didn't feel grief any more, or just gentle grief that was almost smiling.

The clergyman had finished praying, and suddenly, for no reason that she could explain, Irene felt that the crematorium had become beautiful. There came a solemn moment. Absolute quiet and a feeling of everyone in the chapel forgetting themselves and joining together. The moment probably didn't go on for very long, Irene wasn't sure, but it seemed endless because it was so impressive. As though an angel had come into the chapel, put a finger to his lips and said, 'Hush.'

Without making any noise, part of the wall behind the cross went up to show an opening, just behind the coffin. Then the coffin began to move. At the same time Irene was conscious of a fractious sound disrupting the solemn quiet that filled the chapel. Turning, she saw that Guy was crouched huddled over his bended knees and that the sound she had heard was the chattering of his teeth.

She put a hand on his arm. Guy flung her hand away with such violence it struck her face and cut her lip against her teeth. She tasted blood in her mouth. Guy clasped his hands, tearing at his hair. Seizing at clumps of his hair he wrenched back his head as though to break it off his neck. His teeth clattered. His body shook. He began to gasp and groan.

Irene, blood on her mouth, grasped the arm of Dr Templeton and called to Giles behind her, so that when Guy surged to his feet and charged down the aisle to follow the coffin, Dr Templeton and Giles were ready to drag him back and hold his wildly threshing arms. But three others were needed to restrain his terrible strength.

From Guy's contorted face and clenched lips no sound came. He collapsed unconscious in their arms.

PART II
The Valuation

Empty Rooms

'I THINK it would be better,' said Irene, 'if you tied your dogs up somewhere or left them in your car. They are up-setting the spaniels.'

'Why don't you train them properly,' said Clive, 'and stop them rushing around and barking all over the place.'

'It's their job to bark,' said Irene. 'They're watch-dogs and they don't know who you are. You might be anyone. Besides, they live here and your dogs are only visiting.'

Having installed the kiddies in the car, 'What do you want her for?' whispered Clive, as they passed from the terrace into the front hall. 'Who does she think she is?'

'Harold Tippett,' whispered Reggie, 'has given her author-ity to look after things. I *told* you that.' But the tight, clicky little pulse beating at the corner of Clive's mouth, and the knowledge of all it might forebode, so daunted him that, making concessions to a comfortable life, he said to Irene, 'We don't really need you, Irene. We can find our way around.'

'I have the keys,' said Irene, 'and I am in charge.'

She had gone into mourning for Lady Evelyn and though it was a warm day wore a 1922 black velvet evening cloak, four severe white bands trimming the sleeves, which, ex-tending from shoulder to wrist, comprised the bulk of this garment. A white muffin-shaped ruff, trimmed with black, enclosed her neck.

She led the way, Reggie and Clive following at some distance to avoid treading on the hem of her cloak, which though looped close to her ankles, was too long for her and trailed behind, sweeping over the urns, flowers, archers and unicorns on the Sèvres tiles.

'She's wearing one of Lady Evelyn's gowns,' whispered

Clive, kicking off a spaniel which had taken a quick nip at his left ankle. 'She's probably salted a small fortune away up in the attics somewhere.'

'She's been wearing Lady Evelyn's dresses for the past three years,' Reggie whispered back, 'and for God's sake, Clive, we are not interested in Lady Evelyn's clothes.'

'They're probably worth a fortune. Portobello would go wild.'

'Shut up,' said Reggie.

'What has happened,' whispered Clive, 'to that Persian carpet?'

'I expect it was sold years ago to keep these poor people in bread and milk.'

'And the Ghiordes rugs?' said Clive, as they approached the end of the hall.

'I have been employed,' said Reggie, 'to make a valuation on the objects I see before my eyes and I do not see a Persian carpet.'

'Or two Ghiordes rugs,' said Clive.

'No,' said Reggie, but he was beginning to feel a greater unease than the only slightly disturbing unease he had experienced when Guy presented him with the Fabergé cigar-case, the Easter egg and the model of the Empress Alexandra Feodorovna's coronation coach.

'What's in there?' asked Clive.

'Nothing,' said Irene, confronting them with her back to a closed door and, influenced by a fleeting recollection of *The Garden of Allah*, extending her arms in a protective gesture which displayed to advantage the long, drooping sleeves of Lady Evelyn's evening cloak.

'Mr Thring,' said Clive, 'is a licensed valuer whose reputation for honesty and integrity . . .' He snapped shut on the word 'integrity', implying more than could have been decently said.

'How is Guy getting on?' Reggie desperately asked.

'Just the same,' said Irene, allowing her arms to droop and, to all appearances, caving in.

'I think,' said Reggie, gently, 'if you don't mind we ought to go through all the rooms.'

Irene fitted the key in the lock, opened the door, and, her body recharged with energy, flung it wide in a gesture as dramatic as her previous gesture employed in defending it from intrusion.

All three stood silently regarding the empty walls lined with faded silk – shredded, blotched with mould and stained by tracks of water that had seeped through a leaking roof – but splendid silk, rose and gold, patterned with the branches of flowering trees, providing perches for improbable birds. The vast, vacant floor extended to the eastern windows at that moment brushed by a spring shower, which worked on Reggie's imagination, as though it had taken place for some specific reason concerning their entry into the room. But now that they had arrived, the shower suddenly ceased, giving way to a rush of sunshine. The faded pink and gold on the walls sprang to life and a muted sparkle glimmered in the magnificent chandelier, its brilliance subdued by fifteen years of cobwebs and dust.

'Everything was sold when Lord Charles died,' said Irene.

'I know,' said Reggie.

'Then why did you want to see it?' asked Irene.

Reggie would have liked to have said, 'I didn't. Clive did.' Instead, he said, 'Everything here was French. It was a very beautiful room but a little overpowering.' The steady regard of Irene's eyes had brought him to the brink of panic. 'I never,' he rambled on, 'much cared for the French style, except in miniature. Jewellery, snuff-boxes, fans. And clocks. I like French clocks.'

'And Fabergé,' said Clive.

'Fabergé,' Reggie repeated. 'But not when it comes to ormolu rioting over cabinets and tables, and too much inlaid wood. All that bragging and boasting in the Wallace Collection. Have you ever been to the Wallace Collection?'

'No,' said Irene.

Calming down, Reggie declared in an easy way, 'My taste in furniture is essentially English. I do not like my consciousness of the beauty of form and the grain of wood to be overpowered by too much ornament.'

Irene said nothing as she locked the door.

'And that one,' said Clive.

'This room,' said Irene, stationed before the door, 'is also empty like the one you've just seen. Everything was sold.'

She stared at Clive who assaulted her with an outburst of charm. 'I just love to see these rooms with their lovely proportions, and remember them as they used to be. It brings back the past.'

'I thought,' said Irene, 'that you were supposed to be making a valuation of the things that are here and not wasting your time having a look at locked-up rooms. If you want to make it a social visit I'll invite you for tea and you can look around remembering the past.' But she unlocked the door.

Save for two empty packing cases and a bird's nest on the sixteenth-century Florentine marble mantelpiece, the room was empty. Shadows from trees outside tossed about on a ceiling embellished with pink-nippled breasts, blue draperies and galloping horses, now hazy with moisture and neglect. The broken pane in the window, through which the bird responsible for the nest on the mantelpiece had made an entrance, had been pasted over with cardboard fixed with Sellotape.

The next room was distinguishable from the others only in the quantity of soot that had fallen from the chimney and spilled across the floor.

'And this one?' asked Irene.

'Please,' said Clive.

The room was empty.

'And this one?'

'Never mind,' said Clive.

'Well then,' said Irene, with a smile which Clive said to

himself, for all its sweetness, might almost be called con-temptuous, if an upstart little Cockney tart could ever be capable of expressing contempt with her stupid little working-class face, 'we might as well go and look at the rooms where there is something to see.'

In the Library they settled their differences while Irene made tea and sandwiches.

'Why on earth,' said Reggie, 'did you have to make such a fuss about all those rooms?'

'I'm not a fool,' said Clive, 'or an ostrich with my head stuck in the sand. I want to know where we stand.'

When Irene returned with the sandwiches, Clive said, 'There were something like fifty pieces in Lord Edward's Fabergé collection. We can only find fifteen.'

'You got three,' said Irene.

'That leaves forty-seven,' said Clive.

'All sold.'

'When?'

'I wasn't there, so I don't know.'

Reggie, by the window, stared at Rolling Home, grazing on the lawn. He too had been shocked by the Fabergé. They ate sandwiches and drank tea in silence.

Conversation again broke loose in the Peacock Room, but languished in the dining-room where, although the Chip-pendale ribbon-back chairs were solidly in evidence, Clive opened cupboards and drawers to disclose objects of little consequence.

'Where is the silver?'

'They must have sold it,' said Irene. 'I wasn't here.'

'The Paul de Lamerie tea-and-coffee service and the James I beakers went in the 1950 sale,' said Reggie.

In the Octagonal Room Reggie knew he was talking too much and not very coherently, but Irene's calm silence and Clive's noisy silence so affected him that he simply couldn't stop talking.

The Octagonal Room served no useful function apart from that of adding prestige to the house and satisfying the whims of Lord Frederick who had a mania for reconstruction. It had been fashioned at great cost out of a passage leading from the main hall to a back stairway and was a room to be looked at; never to be used. Nobody ever sat down in it, or read a book. People walked into it, looked at it, and walked out again.

Whilst raving over the exquisite furniture, Reggie tried not to look at the square and oval shapes that stared at him from the walls. The walls and the domed ceiling were the colour of clotted cream, discreetly dressed with blue medallions and a gilded frieze. The clotted cream had darkened with age but the square and oval shapes appeared to have lagged behind in the ageing process and looked like patches of protected skin staring nakedly on an otherwise sunburnt body.

'Well, well,' said Clive.

'It's getting late,' said Reggie, feeling he needed time to reconsider his contract with Lady Evelyn. 'We'll be back tomorrow.'

'The implications,' began Clive, as they set off for home, 'that leap to mind concerning this situation . . .'

'I don't want to talk about it,' said Reggie. 'I'm tired. I shall go back tomorrow and as far as I'm concerned, you needn't come. You haven't been much help in any case.'

'Thanks, dear. You may live to swallow those words. You haven't been the only one making a list.'

'I introduced you to that house,' said Reggie. 'They took you in out of nowhere and never questioned who you were or where you came from.'

'So they did,' said Clive. 'Weren't they foolish?'

Frank opened the gate and closed it behind them.

'Why,' asked Clive, 'do we have to put up with that cave man with his grunts and muscles.'

'He's a very good gardener,' said Reggie.

'If you say so,' said Clive, adding gaily: 'Drive on, Lady Chatterley.' But after they had left the car in the garage and Reggie was looking for the keys to the back door, he said. not gaily at all, but in a dry cold voice, 'When I came back on Sunday night your bedroom stank of sweat.'

The Feather Collection

GUY'S BEDROOM distressed Reggie. He had never been in it before, and admitted to it now, felt he was reading a private diary.

He recorded on his list a Boudin of the beach at Trouville in a gusty wind, filling capes and pulling back the ears of running dogs. The only piece of furniture worthy of attention was a Jacobean court cupboard, which, when Clive opened its doors, proved to be filled with letters and photographs which Reggie felt were none of his business. Propped up on the court cupboard was an unframed etching showing four sketches of a woman's head which Reggie thought might be portraits of Lady Evelyn. But the subject turned out to be the Duchess de Gramont and the artist, Helleu was now out of fashion, he wrote the etching down at £2. Also on the court cupboard was a photograph of a young woman which had been presented to Guy in his twenty-sixth year and had never been removed, not because he had any sentimental attachment for it but because he had ceased to realise it was there. Reggie felt he knew the young woman in the photograph but couldn't put a name to her.

Pulling out the drawers of a specimen cabinet he came upon what seemed to be a collection of feathers. It was not what might be called a scientific collection – there were no finely printed cards attributing certain feathers to certain birds – but rather the sort of collection that might have been assembled in Victorian times by someone with a feeling for the decorative nature of feathers. The first two drawers displayed feathers arranged in circles with small feathers in the centre, medium-sized feathers in the middle and the largest feathers radiating from the circumference. In the third and fourth drawer the feathers were arranged in undulating bands of colour. Reggie was surprised how much colour there was. Like most people who do not look closely he was under the impression that English birds are largely some shade of brown. Although the collection must have been started in childhood, Reggie felt that it had been maintained. The feathers were in first-class condition and their arrangement impeccable, which surely indicated that over the years Guy had removed feathers which had succumbed to moth or old age and replaced them with new feathers. Once again Reggie felt he was invading the privacy of Guy's life, a sensation yet more manifest when the feathers brought him to the recognition of the photograph on the court cupboard.

Reggie's acquaintance with Georgina Bray had been restricted to half a dozen encounters at Thawle dinner parties. In later years she remained only vaguely installed in his consciousness as a girl who had been engaged to Guy, had broken the engagement off after Lord Charles's death, and who had rather quickly married someone in London. But one occasion involving himself and Georgina he had always vividly remembered.

During dinner Georgina, who had been seated on Lord Charles's left, had had rather too much to drink in Reggie's opinion, and had said something quite rude to Lady Evelyn. Reggie couldn't remember why, after dinner, he went into the Morning Room, but when he did it was to find Georgina, standing in the middle of the room, alone, looking flushed and sulky. Reggie felt an unaccountable embarrassment and after a moment, during which Georgina failed to acknowledge his presence, said something fatuous, like 'Is there anything I can get you?'

Georgina looked up and said, 'I want to show you the perfectly lovely present Guy has just given me.' She opened her bag and from its interior produced a blue feather. Holding the pin of the feather between finger and thumb, she twirled it back and forth, and gazed at it with a look of hazy concentration.

Reggie didn't know what to say and when Georgina again looked at him, her face was dressed with a big, bright smile. 'Did you know he collects feathers? I'm leaning over backwards to share his interests and I told him I'd go to the Zoo and ask the keepers to pull some out of the cockatoos but he said that he only collected feathers from the Thawle woods and that none had been plucked from living birds. He goes walking in the woods and looks for them. Some feather that some bird has dropped because it isn't any use to it any more and therefore can't possibly be up to scratch. He's been doing it since he was five years old and he says it takes a lot of time because birds, when they are in good condition, and the Thawle birds are in *very* good condition, don't drop a lot of feathers. But he says it will speed things up if I go with him because then there will be two of us looking for feathers.'

Georgina dropped the feather and both she and Reggie watched it fall, twirling, to the floor.

Reggie had good reason for remembering the events of that evening because next day he had learned that around two in the morning, after the guests had gone, Lady Evelyn had found Lord Charles lying dead on his dressing-room floor. And for Reggie an era, and a way of life that had centred around Thawle, had come to an end.

Clive had opened the top drawer of a large chest and was inspecting Guy's underwear.

Poor Guy, thought Reggie, stripped down and exposed to his feathers and his underwear. 'Come on, Clive,' he called sharply.

The Abstract Paintings

THEY ASCENDED stairways leading to rooms that had been occupied by servants, nannys and the de Boissy children in years gone by.

'What's in there?' said Clive.

'That's my room,' said Irene, 'and everything in there belongs to me. I brought my things with me from London and there isn't anything in there that doesn't belong to me.'

Reggie, feeling unable to face the revelations concerning Irene's private life that would certainly confront him in her room, hurried on down the passage. They climbed more stairs.

'What's in there?' asked Clive.

'It's a place where Lord Guy liked to work,' said Irene, 'because of the view.'

The room contained a Victorian chaise-longue, a rocking horse, an easel, and a Louis XIV satinwood table with a warped top, scratched and stained with ink. Much of the veneer was missing or peeling off, but retrievable, thought Reggie, writing it down at five pounds which was all it was worth in its present condition, and keeping it in mind. The table was littered with tubes of paint, tins of paint and jam jars containing brushes and liquid of various colours. A large number of unframed canvases painted with abstract designs were stacked along the wall.

'He took to painting,' said Irene, 'but they wouldn't be worth anything. They're not very good.'

Reggie turned one around to look at the back and quickly returned it to its place. 'No, they're not,' he said, and wrote something on his list.

'I wouldn't have thought they were even worth mention-ing,' said Irene. 'He bought all the paints himself and painted them and they're not very good.'

Reggie scratched out what he had written which for a reason which his conscious mind could not explain had been the word 'California'. Perhaps because he had always wanted to visit San Francisco, said to be a very pleasant city, all the year round. Or Constantinople, or Hong Kong. Anywhere far away from Thawle.

Downstairs in the Morning Room which they hadn't had time to get around to the day before, the furniture remained as Reggie remembered it, as though waiting for Lady Evelyn and Lord Charles to entertain them with refreshments and delightful conversation. He wrote down the quantity of mezzotints that crowded the walls at two pounds apiece because mezzotints, though going up, were still struggling to recover from the mezzotint slump that had set in around 1910. Tense with fear that Clive was going to say something about them, he kept his gaze unswervingly directed on his list to discover, when he finally felt able to look up, that Clive was no longer in the room.

Reggie waited for him on the front terrace. Armies of thoughts, all at loggerheads with one another, blundered about in his head. To keep them from getting entangled he attempted to engage Irene in conversation, but her expression was preoccupied and her answers reserved.

'You must miss Lady Evelyn very much.'

'Yes, I do.'

'It must be lonely here.'

'Giles keeps me company. And Rolling Home and the dogs. Animals are very affectionate. So are the ducks. I don't care much for the fowls,' said Irene.

'I wonder where Clive is,' said Reggie. 'Perhaps I should go and look for him.'

Irene shrugged her shoulders. Blue smudges under her queer eyes were the most noticeable spots of colour in her silvery face which looked pinched, and oppressed by its heavy load of string-coloured hair.

'Will it be high?' she asked.

'What?'

'The valuation.'

Reggie had never had to ask himself what he wanted to

do with his life. A sense of mission had fallen upon him when as a child he had rowed a boat in a golden stream winding its way through the base of a rosewood table. He was passionately obsessed by his vocation. But there was an expression in Irene's eyes at that moment which moved him to the point of making him forget that he was an antique dealer burning with desire to get his hands on almost everything Thawle contained.

He said, 'I don't know whether you know much about antiques.'

'I've picked up a bit,' said Irene.

'Then you must know that no antique has what you might call an actual value. It isn't worth anything until somebody wants to buy it, and it is only worth what that buyer wants to pay. Now you might argue that nobody would want to pay very much for the things in Thawle and that at auction, which is the criterion we set for a valuation, they would sell for very little, or you might say that because they are rare, old and beautiful and have been collected by the de Boissy family, they might sell for large sums of money. So they have a minimum and a maximum value, and I have to take a reasonable stand between the two. If I lean over too far in my search for a minimum value, which is obviously advantageous to the heirs of the estate, I can fall on my face. Quality and artistic merit have very little to do with the question. There are some exquisite mezzotints in the Morning Room which must have cost a great deal of money because years ago mezzotints were highly regarded. Today they are out of fashion and have very little value. But it would be unrealistic of me to pretend that the Gobelin tapestries and the furniture in the Peacock Room, the dining-room and the Octagonal Room were not worth a lot of money. Should I do so my valuation might be questioned and this would not be of any help to anyone.'

'I see what you mean,' said Irene.

Whilst he was talking about the valuation and justifying his position Reggie's mind had calmed down and settled into a peaceful melancholy. In the silence which Irene made no attempt to interrupt, he thought of Guy, overwhelmed by the death of his mother and the pillage of his house, about to be stripped of three hundred years' patronage of the finest artists and craftsmen in Europe and reduced to birds' nests, broken window panes and an old horse nodding his heavy head in a wilderness of buttercups that had once been a gracious lawn, printed with the bat-shaped shadows of sunshades and the brims of ridiculous hats. And this queer girl, folding around her, against the cold, the long sleeves of Lady Evelyn's evening cloak. But it wasn't cold. Reggie felt hot and would have liked to have taken off his coat. Irene, feeling his regard, raised her head to return it. A hairpin fell, striking a small, shrill note from the terrace stones. Reggie bent to pick it up.

'Thank you,' said Irene. Her eyes widened until they were so big that Reggie, looking into them, felt he was diving into another spirit and swimming about, lost and alarmed, in an element he had never before encountered. He didn't know where he was and couldn't find his way.

It was said that she came from London. It was said she was the love child of Lord Charles, half-sister to Guy. It was said that her mother was a prostitute and that she had been raped by her uncle when she was thirteen. Reggie knew nothing about such matters.

'They're hard to find,' said Irene, pushing the pin back into her hair.

Emerging precipitately from the front door, Clive was amongst them.

'Well, that's all,' said Reggie. 'I'll send the figures to the trustees.'

'What about the stables and greenhouses?' said Clive.

'What is in the stables and greenhouses?' Reggie asked Irene.

'Rolling Home is in the stables,' said Irene, 'but he's eighteen and he isn't worth his keep even. I don't expect he's got very long to live and he's gelded so he isn't useful for breeding, even if he could. There are some saddles and bridles and things and some photographs of the horses winning races, but they belong to Giles. Lord Charles left them in his Will. And some hay,' she added.

'And the greenhouse?' asked Clive.

'Spades, forks, two, no three ladders, flowers, flower pots, tomato plants, packets of things for killing snails . . .' Irene gave the impression of having embarked on a long, meticulously considered list of items which would diminish in importance as it progressed.

For reasons which Reggie did not immediately understand but which disturbed him, Clive did not insist on inspecting the stables and the greenhouses.

Objects Absent

DRIVING BACK home, neither Reggie nor Clive spoke until, mounting the hill out of Bradford-on-Avon and turning on the road to Bath, Reggie had to skid into a hedge to avoid an encounter with a Tate & Lyle sugar van.

'Shall I drive,' said Clive, 'while you let your thoughts wander?'

Stop bitching. I'm sick to death of your bitching, thought Reggie, but avoiding a quarrel as usual, he said nothing and pulled back on the road.

But Clive was disposed to talk. 'While you have been compiling your list,' he said, opening a pocket diary to show pages closely covered with his fine writing, 'I have been compiling mine.'

Reggie had noticed the absence of the caudle cups, the flat ware and the Jacobean tankards. Something akin to physical pain attacked him when Clive referred to Guy's abstract paintings in the attic which he had returned to inspect whilst Reggie was engaging Irene in conversation on the terrace. His memory had not recorded the love-seat, the *bureau de bonheur* and the dressing-table in Lady Evelyn's bedroom. On one occasion only, when she was convalescing from a virus infection she had picked up in Venice, had Reggie and Clive been admitted to her bedroom. Reggie had hardly spared a glance for the furniture about him, concentrating all his concern upon Lady Evelyn's wasted face. Clive, it was now revealed, had been more observant.

As his dry, thin voice continued to record objects absent, Reggie asked himself whether he had compiled equally detailed lists of the contents of other country houses in which he had been entertained. If so, for what purpose? And had his talent for observation extended beyond the furnishings to the wider area of human failings and indiscretions?

He listened numbly to the final items on Clive's list which were introduced in the form of a question requiring an answer.

'Weren't there some jade tortoises inscribed with poems by the Emperor Chien Lung, and some famous ponies?'

'There used to be,' said Reggie.

Slowing down to cross the bridge, he stopped the car by the gate. His beautiful garden mounted the slope before him. The rhododendrons were over; the roses in full bloom. The tall trees behind, hiding the new estate, had gathered together into their shadows.

He had bought the house eight years before, a year after Clare's death, and recalled with what pleasure he had reconstructed the kitchen and bathrooms, redecorated and installed his furniture. How had it come about that his beautiful house should now confront him like a prison cell fitted with instruments of torture?

When Frank opened the gate, smiling, his black curls hanging in clusters on his bronze brow, never before in Reggie's eyes had he looked so fresh and untainted by devious sophistication.

Reggie made for the whisky decanter, poured himself a stiff drink and handed one to Clive.

'What are you going to do?' he said.

Clive sipped his drink, not gulping it down like Reggie who was more urgently in need of it. 'Nothing,' he said.

Sorrow, anger, fear drained from Reggie's body, leaving him feeling empty and pure, but so weak he could hardly stand. He found his way to a chair and sat down.

'Then why go on like this?'

Clive sipped his drink. 'I haven't the least idea what you're talking about.' His narrowed gaze contemplated the top of the Chinese table before him on which, between two Ming blue and white dishes serving as ashtrays, he appeared to have arranged his thoughts for review. These thoughts impaled his attention. Meanwhile he took small resuscitating sips from his glass.

'Clive,' said Reggie, 'there is something in your nature that you must learn to control.' He hesitated on the word 'sadistic' and having failed in courage could only say, 'It's poisoning our life.'

His tone implored Clive, asking for the recall of that elegant, fair-haired young man to whom he had been immediately attracted when Clare, who had discovered him in a nearby pub, had brought him home to dinner. Falling amongst them out of the blue, equipped with gaiety, physical charm, a name he had probably acquired through Deed Poll, and a great deal of gossip, a touch malicious, but only a touch, about people he had, or, Reggie and Clare sometimes suspected, had not met. But after observing the dexterity with which he managed to ease his way into their circle of friends, they changed their minds and decided that Clive was capable of meeting anyone.

Having set foot in a wealthy, hospitable house, he maintained his position without feeling the need for offering any reciprocal hospitality. It was one of his achievements that though he had no money, he managed to live as if he had, without incurring the reputation of sponging on the rich.

For though lacking in material wealth, he was endowed with other resources. He worked hard, and employed his social talents with such purpose, it was generally agreed that he earned his keep.

During the years following his introduction to Reggie's friends there had been only one unpleasant incident when an irate old man, accusing him of unnatural sexual practices and the betrayal of a confidence, had ordered him out of the house and threatened to hound him out of the country. But this had been forgotten in the drama of Clare's death which took place two weeks later, after which Clive had moved in with Reggie. The irate old man went to the Bahamas for his health, and as Reggie was more generous with Clare's money than Clare had been, except when it came to betting on horses, there was no more talk of hounding Clive out of the country.

Clive's eyes turned from the contemplation of thoughts displayed on the Chinese table and flashed Reggie a glance. Hard and bright as a chip of ice. He sipped and sipped. 'I don't like being made a fool of. I like to know where I stand.'

'Clive, we were asked to go to Thawle to make a valuation for probate which God knows is going to be high enough. It is not our job to play Scotland Yard and investigate spaces and gaps. How is anyone to know *we* know about the contents of the house? We saw what we saw, and on what we saw we make our valuation.'

'I don't like being made a fool of. I don't like,' said Clive, quietly and slowly, 'being *deceived*.'

A feeling of nausea turned Reggie's stomach. 'Nobody is deceiving us. We were virtually told the situation we were going to find by Lady Evelyn herself when she presented us with three pieces of Fabergé.'

'*Your* Fabergé, worth I should say around £60,000. My miserable wine is probably worth about £5,000.' Clive sipped before adding, 'Would you feel inclined to make me a present of the Empress Alexandra Feodorovna's coronation coach? I have to think of my future which sometimes looks rather insecure. I am not indispensable. You can run your business without me and you don't need me in the garden. I haven't any horticultural qualifications. The Empress Alexandra Feodorovna's coronation coach might start me off in a new life if I ever have to make one.'

'And if not, what then?' asked Reggie, grasping to his bosom, out of love and admiration, years and years of longing and devotion, the Empress Alexandra Feodorovna's coronation coach. Whereas all Clive wanted it for was money.

'Nothing,' said Clive, smiling and throwing out a gush of charm, so potent and enlarged and yet so sinister, Reggie felt the need for another drink. Clive also refilled his glass.

He sipped and sipped. 'Why should I need anything while I'm with you?' he asked. 'And why on earth should I feel insecure?'

Reggie drank, crushed by the awareness of a deserved fate and the retribution falling upon him for past easy judgements and unconsidered folly.

How had it happened? How had he allowed Clive to get the upper hand? Because he had been unwatchful, never thinking that in the delightful balance of their relationship, either would want the upper hand?

And when had it begun to happen? Reggie wondered, working his way through his fourth whisky, Clive having departed to change into something more comfortable. Some time, not so long after Clare's death.

Reggie had been happy with Clare, and as generous as he could when the means for generosity had been in Clare's hands, and rather meagerly dispensed with at that. But he had been generous of himself. They had got on well together, and he had never raised the question of her indiscretions, only one of which had been Lord Charles. He couldn't blame her, for the generosity he was eager to spend had petered out in bed. But he had done his best and they had been happy, so why did he feel responsible for her death? Was it because they had not been suited to one another and when she died,

114

after a decent interval for adjustment, he had felt free, as though an impediment had been removed that had stood between him and the correct direction of his nature? And he had inherited her money.

Then Clive, soon installed, had unnoticeably at first, but later more demonstrably, behaved as though he possessed advantages. What advantages? Housed, fed, kept in comfort by Reggie. Reggie's mind kept returning to the same answer. The advantage of knowing that Reggie had not grieved for his wife and was secretly relieved to have seen the last of her? But he *had* grieved. Searching his heart, he honestly believed he had. It was only Clive who somehow contrived to make him feel that he had not.

It was not in Reggie's nature to regret or even remember the lapses into selfishness, spite and dishonesty that are scattered throughout the life of any man of his years. He had committed no major crime and had inflicted only minor injuries on those who were close to him. In natures of finer texture, episodes of pain, given or received, might have festered into haunting obsessions. But Reggie was sensible, worldly and tough.

When it came to his business affairs, his ambitions had been tempered by kindness and a meticulous honesty. He always gave a generous price and pointed out defects down to a quarter of an inch of restored veneer. 'I think that tree might have been retouched,' or 'That flag might have been added later because, you can see, it's blowing against the prevailing wind which is bending the tops of the trees,' were the sort of things he would say. But although he felt sympathy for the families whose furniture he sold in his shop, he accepted no responsibility for their decline. Neither did he suffer from the fashionable, international guilt for the murders, rapes, wars, famines and general distress in countries he cared nothing about and had never visited. So why did he feel guilty about Clare and in some way responsible for her death? Because he had gone to London and had not been present when it happened, and if he had been present might have prevented it? But how was he to know that when she went to that party with Clive, she would have an accident on the way home. Clive had stayed on at the party. Clare had driven back alone. Clive had never intimated that he felt any guilt at all for allowing Clare to drive home alone. And why should he? Clare wasn't a child. She was perfectly capable of driving home alone at night. Only Reggie felt guilt, for having been in London when it happened. Not there. Not watching. Far removed. Conveniently removed. Clive had been understanding and kind, moving in to fill the gap, comforting Reggie and helping him through his distress. Then settling down, charmingly, gracefully, but powerful with a conviction of privilege and the justice of his rights.

The Nursing Home

AFTER THEY had gone Irene took a mug of tea and a piece of cake to Giles who was doing his best in the vegetable garden, and went up to her room to change into the dress with the black flounces over the hips and the long sleeves lined with white satin. Lady Evelyn had worn it to Ascot in 1921, set off by a black cloche hat trimmed with osprey feathers, and had been photographed for *The Tatler*, but Irene, with all her hair, could not wear the Erté hats, designed for close-cropped heads, Irene's hair belonging to the era of wide brims, and chiffon scarves tied under the chin. She had, however, been instructed by Lady Evelyn that the 1921 dress would be incomplete without pale green gloves inset on the back of the hand with watches, which no longer worked, and these gloves she put on before setting out for the nursing home where Guy had been installed by Dr Templeton.

It was a practical house built around 1890 in a rural setting and in its spacious garden of lawns and trees the more robust inmates, seated on benches and chairs, were enjoying the afternoon sunshine. Some, finding the sun too powerful, had retired to the shade of a copper beech. Guy paced back and forth, looking so brown and healthy amongst so many frail trembling creatures he might have been mistaken for somebody's son making a visit to his elderly father.

The spaniels rushed up to him, to be fondled and embraced. They made affectionate whimpering noises of welcome and flapped their tongues on his hands. Guy smiled as he stroked their soft, steep heads, but scowled at Irene.

'You again.'

'I thought you'd like to see the dogs. They couldn't get here without me,' said Irene.

Guy dropped a spaniel. 'Why didn't you bring Mummy?'

'She can't come.'

Guy accepted her explanation and they began to stroll around the copper beech. The spaniels dashed off to snuffle their way to the wheelchair of an old woman who sat with a pale blue Shetland shawl draped over her knees, and whose gaunt head stretched out in right-angles from her arthritic back like the head of a saint on a cathedral door. She had made the acquaintance of the spaniels on one of Irene's previous visits when, apparently liking her smell, they had tracked her down, and since that day she always came to the garden equipped with a brown paper bag filled with biscuits which she broke into small pieces to make them last and slipped into the spaniels' slobbering mouths. When the biscuits were finished she stroked their heads and talked to them in a high, chirruping voice. The spaniels licked her hands and settled down on the fringe of the Shetland shawl.

'The vegetables are doing nicely,' said Irene. 'This weather is very good for the tomatoes. Yesterday we picked twelve. I made green tomato chutney with some of the little ones that looked as if they were going to drop off. Giles sends his love.'

'You never tell me anything about Mummy.'

Dr Templeton had given Irene instructions but she was never sure how she ought to interpret them. Dr Templeton had not taken into consideration the sort of things that Guy said to her or the pressure of truth that welled up in her when he asked her questions. Or the conviction she felt that she could deal with Guy's problems better than Dr Templeton.

'You remember,' she said, 'that before you came here she was very ill.'

'She got better. She looked marvellous that night on the stairs in her satin dress. She wore it to the first night of "The Vikings" and drank champagne with Ellen Terry.' He raised his voice. His hands began to tremble. Sweat showed on his brow. 'You're keeping her from me. You've always tried to alienate her affections. Send me Irene, she said, send me Irene. And you kept me out of her room!'

One of the nurses looked towards them.

Irene said as calmly as she was able, 'She needed a woman to look after her.'

'You call yourself a woman,' shouted Guy. 'How old are you? Sixteen? Eighteen? No woman becomes a woman until she's forty-two.'

'There were things I could do for her that she couldn't do for herself because she was old. Like her hair. You couldn't have done her hair.'

'Prescott would have done. She's a woman. She's about sixty.'

'Prescott is too practical and too severe. She liked me. I made her laugh. Didn't you want her to be happy?'

Guy shouted, 'She had four hair-brushes with tortoise-shell backs and silver shields engraved with her name. I used to brush her hair for hours on end. Now don't be silly, Guy, she used to say and then she'd laugh and snuggle me into her hair and I put my head on her shoulder. There was nothing so soft and white. She pulled her hair around me to keep me warm and I went to sleep.'

The nurse hurried towards them.

'Lord Guy,' said the nurse, 'it's time for tea.'

'I'm going home,' said Guy. 'I've got to see Mummy.'

'Please, you must be calm. You can go home as soon as Dr Templeton says so.'

Guy, who had always done as he was told, quietly repeated, 'I will go home as soon as Dr Templeton says so. Give her this,' he said to Irene, producing from the inside pocket of his coat a letter addressed to 'Lady Evelyn de Boissy, Thawle, Somerset'.

'I've brought his washing,' said Irene as the nurse accompanied her across the lawn. 'And an apple-pie.' The spaniels followed.

The nurse patted her hand. 'Don't be upset. You just have to realise.'

'I do,' said Irene, restoring clarity to her vision with the sleeve of Lady Evelyn's dress. 'He's worse today. Yesterday he was quite nice.'

'He has his ups and downs. You just have to be patient.'

'He was always a bit jealous,' said Irene. 'You see, for years he had her all to himself.'

'I know,' said the nurse, but her attention had been attracted by the gaping mouth of an old man who appeared to be dying. 'Just remember how lucky you are.'

Irene had no idea what she was talking about. Neither had the nurse.

Back in her room Irene took off her dress, and put on a pair of jeans and one of Guy's shirts. She wondered what she ought to do about the letter that Guy had written to his mother and felt herself weighed down by responsibilities. She asked herself whether she ought to face them or pass them on to Dr Templeton. Postponing her decision, she put the letter with the others piling up on the mantelpiece.

Outside the spaniels dashed about barking at blackbirds. Rolling Home dozed knee deep in swinging grass, and Giles bound the tomatoes to the hazel twigs he had cut from hedges at the bottom of the valley.

Irene was not deprived of human and animal companionship, but she felt very lonely. Evangeline, Ambrosine, Lady Diana Mayo and Katherine Bush, instead of being more real than real people, had become a little less. Yet hadn't they been through worse times than this? Hadn't they braced their shoulders and raised their indomitable heads in defiance of misfortune? For the first time in her life Irene asked herself whether courage or defiance of misfortune had ever been asked of them, for hadn't they, from Chapter One, been assured of a final triumph over their various predicaments, and in the end, happiness for ever after? Nothing looked very reassuring to Irene and the future towards which in blind faith she had made her unfaltering way seemed no longer preordained. A multitude of diverse paths meandered off into ominous obscurity and Fate, which until now had directed her course, had retired, leaving her to her own resources. Irene felt that orphaned, penniless, and battling to hold her own in an equivocal situation, she had few resources.

Taking down her hair, she braided it into a plait and descended to the kitchen to cook dinner for Giles, in the meantime occupying herself, grammar-book and exercise-book open on the table, with the daunting challenge of French verbs.

Clematis and Rhododendrons

'IF YOU don't want it,' said Clive, 'I'd rather like to have the car.'

Since the valuation Reggie had spent the days in his shop, resisted the temptation of enjoying the twilight hours in the garden, and had worked late at night preparing his statement for Davidson, Tippett & Cushing. To his relief Clive had refrained from interfering in this delicate operation. They had spoken little to one another and when they did their conversation had been brief and polite. But Reggie wondered uneasily whether the cessation of venomous verbal conflict, to say nothing of the withdrawal of physical intimacy, was not even more disturbing than venomous verbal conflict and physical intimacy might have been.

Talking or not talking, venomous or polite, Clive was *there*, but reticent and mysterious, so that when on Sunday morning he said, 'If you don't want it, I'd rather like to have the car,' Reggie immediately replied, 'Of course,' but wondered why Clive wanted the car, and why he had not volunteered an explanation as to why he wanted it, what project the use of the car involved, and if it involved a project, why he had not invited Reggie to collaborate in that project. But all these unanswered questions, problems and vague fears were nothing compared to the relief he felt at the thought of a whole day without Clive.

When the car moved slowly over the narrow bridge outside his gate, turned the sharp bend at the top of the hill and disappeared under the branches of the beech trees bordering the lane to the main road, Reggie wondered whether Clive, instead of going away for the whole day, might not have parked the car somewhere out of sight with the idea of sneaking back to catch Reggie in the act of what Reggie might be doing. With this thought in mind he decided to pass the day enjoying minimum pleasures. Putting his valuation away he strolled in the garden.

By ten o'clock he and Frank were discussing the possibility of growing clematis on the back wall of the house where the outlook needed improving.

'I like the little pink one,' said Reggie. 'Not that big purple thing. It reminds me of funerals.'

'You cannot,' said Frank, 'grow clematis on a northern wall. Clematis prefer a southern aspect.'

'Why?' asked Reggie.

'Because that's what they prefer like Eskimos prefer snow and Arabs prefer deserts.'

'Do you actually mean to say,' said Reggie, 'that when these creepers were growing wild in the woods which is where they came from they all had southern aspects?'

'No,' said Frank, 'but if they did, they grew better.'

Reggie said, 'It's all been thought up by gardeners and nurserymen to make the ignorant public believe that plants are complicated and difficult. Put a plant in the ground, give it water and it will grow. Plants, like people, prefer life to death.'

'Plants are very like people,' said Frank. 'You can't just order them around and say do this do that. Plants, like people, are prepared to die for their beliefs.'

They set off for the vegetable garden where the artichokes, also like prima donnas, required a particular situation, facing a particular direction and a particular sort of soil.

'What it all means,' said Reggie, after an hour's instruction which had opened out to him a world as complex and as prone to error as the world of antique furniture, 'is that you are driving yourself into a nervous breakdown juggling around a lot of opinionated and ungrateful plants all wanting what they haven't got. Lime, if they haven't got it, and no lime if they've got too much. Wanting sun or shade, whichever they haven't got, and thriving as the spirit takes them on affluence or poverty.'

'You've got the idea,' said Frank.

'It's like running a country,' said Reggie. 'It's like reconciling the demands of Ireland, Scotland and Wales, the miners, the bankers, the trade unions, West Indians, Indians and Pakistanis.'

'You would be surprised,' said Frank, 'how many plants in this garden are foreign migrants. But they've settled down. They're doing very well.'

'You mean,' said Reggie, thinking of the large importation of French furniture into Thawle in the eighteenth century, 'they haven't always been here?'

'There were no rhododendrons in England,' said Frank, 'until they were brought from the Himalayas. Hyacinths and cyclamen came from the Middle East. Peaches from Persia and the two cedars came from Lebanon.'

'I know that,' said Reggie. 'That's why they're called Lebanese cedars.'

'It amazes me,' said Frank with his beautiful smile, 'that you know anything. Never have I encountered such ignorance.'

Clive and Irene

NOW AT MIDSUMMER, cornflowers and poppies brushed the knees of Rolling Home who, sighting Clive at the front door, gathered himself together, hoping for sugar. His head came out of the poppies and he slowly advanced his right foreleg, followed by the hind leg on the other side, but pricked his ears in a youthful way.

There being no response to his vigorous knocking, Clive kicked off the spaniels and made his way to the kitchens where he found Irene making a fruit pie.

'I'm sorry to disturb you on a Sunday.'

'Every day is the same to me,' said Irene.

Clive waved a paper. 'We've just received this letter from Davidson, Tippett & Cushing about the valuation. Reggie's lists are almost complete and this is just a formal document, but it has to be witnessed by a Justice of the Peace, confirming that we have inspected every room in the house, which as you know we have, and the outhouses, which we have not.'

His tone was pleasant but, raising her eyes, Irene surprised in his features knowledge and intentions that were ill-concealed.

Clive fanned his face with the document in his hand, waving it back and forth with a rapidity which blurred the print. Irene suspected that it might be something he had come across in the letter-box advertising bargains at the local supermarket, but instructions from the treasury of wisdom contained on her bedroom walls advised her not to expose their conflicting interests to the light of day.

Irene's life had conditioned her to self-control. It was not difficult for her to refrain from saying, 'What do you mean? Why are you here? What do you want?' Silence gave nothing away and necessitated no retreat from an entrenched position. Returning her gaze to the pie, she pinched into small pleats the pastry on the rim of the dish.

'And so you see,' said Clive, 'before we sign this document I do have to take a quick look at the outhouses and the stables. It's only a formality but we do have to sign it and our signatures do have to be witnessed by a Justice of the Peace. It will only take a minute and I really am *so* sorry to trouble you.'

Irene washed her hands under the tap in the sink, rubbing off the greasy dough and drying her hands on a towel. As she approached the door leading from the kitchen, Clive called her back.

'Where are you going?'

'I'm going to call Mr Thring, just to make sure.'

She had turned to look at him, and now Clive confronted silence with silence. Irene believed the silence could go on for ever.

Clive put his hands inside his jacket, extracted a cigarette-lighter and put a flame to the paper in his hand. He held it until it was burned to a white triangular corner which he dropped to the floor.

'Now shall we look,' he said.

Irene nodded, knowing that if you had to give in, it is much wiser to do so too soon than too late.

Irene Drops a Stitch

THE SUNSHINE of that phenomenal summer had burnt the grass to shining gold. Still in mourning for Lady Evelyn, Irene had put on a white dress, which she had learned from a book in the Library was the colour for mourning in China. To afford protection for her silvery skin, she carried a sunshade and made her way across the lawn to the copper beech.

'What are you knitting?' asked Guy.

'A jacket,' said Irene.

'It's very small.'

'It's for a very small person,' said Irene.

'I thought so,' said Guy. 'You're pregnant, aren't you?' And when Irene made no reply, 'Have you been tumbling around in the hay with old Giles?'

'Don't be silly. He's much too old.'

'I always told Mummy you were a tart. No one would be too old for a tart like you.'

'No one's too young or too old,' said Irene. 'Think of your pa and what he did to fifteen-year-old girls and that blousy old barmaid at The Three Bells.'

'Don't you talk about my father like that. That's local gossip without any foundation. Don't you *compare* my father to some peasant who's pulled you into the bushes. And where's Mummy? Why haven't you brought Mummy to see me?'

'She can't come.'

'That's all you ever say. You've locked her up. You want her all to yourself like you always have.'

'You don't have to take it from me,' said Irene. 'Dr Templeton has told you, the nurse has told you, everyone has told you she can't come.'

'You're all in it together,' shouted Guy. Then, suddenly, as more often these days, the trembling stopped and he became a different man. 'Is he going to marry you?' he asked, with a look in his eyes of affectionate concern.

'I don't know,' said Irene.

'Will he look after you?'

'I don't know,' said Irene.

'Well, will he look after the baby? He ought to look after the baby and provide for it.'

'If he doesn't, then I will,' said Irene.

'The way you say that sounds as if you want it. Do you really want a child that some fellow or other has given you and doesn't care a fig?'

'Yes,' said Irene.

'You mean you love him when he doesn't care a fig for you?'

'That's beside the point,' said Irene.

'Well,' said Guy, 'I suppose it will give you an interest in life.'

Irene continued knitting.

'We'll look after you,' said Guy, a moment later. 'You've always got Mummy and me and Giles. We'll see you're all right.'

Irene, bending her head over her knitting, raised her hand and brushed the tip of her forefinger under her eyes. 'Thank you,' she said.

On her next visit Irene, after first having consulted Dr Templeton, arrived at the nursing home prepared to tell Guy what was going to happen. But she didn't know how to go about it, Guy being so unpredictable. There were days when she could tell him almost anything. On other days he shouted back if she said anything at all. Usually she started off on the vegetables to get the feeling of the mood he was in and because the vegetables had a calming effect. But on that day he didn't seem to be listening. He seemed to be turned in on his own thoughts. And eventually she felt she had to broach the subject.

'There's something I have to tell you,' she said, hoping that from Guy's reply she would be able to find out the best way of going on.

Guy showed no interest. He might not have heard.

'What's that you're knitting now?' he asked.

'Another jacket for when the baby gets bigger. It won't always be small. And winter will be coming on.'

'How are the vegetables going?' asked Guy. 'With all this sun the tomatoes ought to be very good.'

Irene had already told him about the vegetables, but he hadn't heard. 'The tomatoes are the best we've ever had. And you should see the marrows. You wouldn't believe it. Don't you want to know what I have to tell you?'

Guy began to tremble. 'No,' he said.

'But I have to, and it isn't anything to get upset about. It's just that there are financial difficulties and Mr Tippett says you have to sell some things.'

'I wanted crispy bacon,' said Guy, 'and she came into the kitchen with news. It was happy news, that's what she said. I don't want to hear any more news.' He raised his head to look at Irene. 'Have you consulted Mummy?'

'It hasn't got anything to do with your mother. Davidson, Tippett & Cushing are your trustees and they say there is only £17 in the bank and the rates to pay and there has to be a sale.'

'What do you mean a sale? That's not the same as selling things.'

'A public auction,' said Irene.

'What does Uncle Robert say?'

'He's very old, and he's up in Scotland. He leaves it to Mr Tippett and signs the papers. Mr Thring has been a great help. He's a very nice man and has been advising Mr Tippett about what ought to be sold. I have been advising them too.'

'What on earth can you advise?' shouted Guy. 'What on earth do you know, you pregnant slut?'

Irene stopped knitting because her hands weren't very steady and although knitting did not require much concentration if you did a lot of it, it did require steady hands.

'I know what you like. Mr Thring said we ought to sell a lot of the furniture above stairs because it isn't any use to you and it might bring quite a lot of money. There are prints and samplers and even some nice old Georgian chairs that are a bit knocked about and some very good Victorian furniture. And old dolls we found in a cupboard. He said Percy might bring quite a lot of money, but I told him you wouldn't want to sell Percy.'

'Or the elephants.'

'They haven't even seen the elephants.'

'That's right,' said Guy. 'I buried them under the walnut tree.'

Irene's hands, steadied by hope, recommenced knitting in an independent way, but realising the fragility of that beautiful moment of lucidity, she decided not to intrude upon it unless she should damage it.

'Don't you want to know about details?'

'Yes, I want to know.'

'The dining-room. It's so big and the furniture is very valuable, but after your pa died nobody went into it and there was a lot of dusting. And you and Lady Evelyn hardly ever went into the Peacock Room. It was very cold, and you've saved most of the paintings. I think Mr Thring knows about the paintings but he's not letting on. They're doing it,' she said, for Guy had not spoken, 'so you can keep the house. I hope you don't mind but I advised selling one of the bookcases in the Library. Mr Thring loved it so much and I thought we had to do something to thank him for saving the books. He measured them up by the yard and they're much more important than the bookcases. Mr St John raised objections but Mr Thring said that people today only want leather-bound books to show off their bookcases and that *he* bought leather-bound books for thirty shillings a yard to show off *his* bookcases and it didn't matter what was inside the books so that was all they were worth. Only of course he knew because he looked inside one or two and went very quiet. All last week I've been moving the books and they won't be sold. Is there anything you would especially like to keep apart from Percy ?'

'There's a picture in the Chinese Room,' said Guy, 'of a bird standing on one leg in some water with lotus flowers. I would like to keep that.'

'All right,' said Irene.

Guy asked no further questions. His shoulders drooped in an attitude of lethargy and submissiveness. He appeared to be waiting, without protest, for Dr Templeton, the sister and the nurses to order him back into his life. Irene felt that if only she could have taken him home and put her arms around him to comfort him everything would be all right. But Dr Templeton had instructed her, and that other doctor – one of the best psychiatrists in England, Dr Templeton had told her – whom she had only met once, had also instructed her. She was not allowed. She knitted, because it was better to keep yourself occupied.

Guy raised his head. His face, aged forty-two, but protected and unmarked by troubles, pleated into lines of suffering that Irene had never seen before. But there must have been some preparation for them, she thought. They must have been biding their time, for they fell into such exact and ready-made places, turning his smooth boy's face into the face of an old man with cares and sorrows.

'Even if they have to sell Mummy's bedroom,' he said, 'I would rather they did that and kept the Morning Room. Now that she's dead I would rather keep the Morning Room where I can remember her when she was younger and so beautiful, and not the bedroom where she lay for all those days not saying a word and slowly dying.'

Irene dropped a stitch.

The spaniels, which had settled down on the blue shawl of the old lady with biscuits in the wheelchair, dashed over the lawn, investigating bushes, chairs and legs, but finding their way at length to the feet of Guy and Irene. Guy took them up in his arms, kissed their black rubbery lips and stroked their floating ears.

While he played with the spaniels, Irene talked with the sister. 'He remembers,' she said, after having told the sister what Guy had said. 'Why can't he come home?'

'I'll tell Dr Templeton,' the sister said. 'He'll let you know.'

'I brought a fruit pie,' said Irene, 'and tomatoes and lettuces. I'm sure the food here is very good, but I think he likes to know he's eating things from his own vegetable garden.'

'Thank you, Irene,' said Guy, having been shown the fruit pie, the tomatoes and lettuces. 'Would you give this letter to Mummy?' He took it from his shirt pocket and handed it to her.

Irene put the letter, along with her knitting, into the 1918 concertina bag fashioned like a Japanese lantern. Tassels interspersed with beads dangled from the base, and it hung from her wrist on long ropes of plaited silk. Having collected the spaniels and installed them in the back of the car, Irene set off for home.

PART III
The Sale

The Auctioneers

THE AUCTION took place in October, the auctioneers, Boothby & Wigg, being of long standing in the West Country and under the capable control of Edward King who, now aged forty-three, had started his career with the firm at the age of twelve, after school and on Saturdays, as an odd-job boy.

During these years of apprenticeship Edward had been employed moving about lighter pieces of furniture and re-sorting the lots of bric-à-brac that the dealers rearranged to their advantage. He had worked till 8 p.m. on the night prior to the Boothby & Wigg Wednesday auctions, bringing to light such items as Sheffield candlesticks covered with a grubby mat under a trestle table and Staffordshire figures installed in saucepans or broken soup-tureens. He had checked stacks of kitchen plates and, unearthing a piece of early Derby, had restored it to its rightful position in the cabinet reserved for finer pieces of porcelain and jewellery. He learned to respect items that had lost their lot numbers and picked up knowledge that was to stand him in good stead when the time came for him to compile his own catalogues.

At the age of fifteen he had been promoted to the status of porter and supplied with a white coat. At twenty, as clerk to Thomas Webb, the then reigning auctioneer, he had sat beside the rostrum recording the bids, and when, five years later, Thomas dropped dead in the Bull around the corner, the hammer had been placed in his hand. Meta-phorically speaking, for Thomas had knocked down his lots with the blunt end of a pencil. Edward bought a hammer and charged it to the firm.

Thomas had been a true West Countryman and only found

it necessary to visit London once in ten years. His auction-eering technique was out of date. He made no attempt to stem the flow of chatter that rendered the bids inaudible, and he allowed the Trade to bully him. On several occasions when a dealer notorious for bidding up his own lots lowered his hand on the stroke of the hammer, Thomas, instead of knocking the lot down to him as he deserved, fell meekly back on the under bidder. Edward, recording the bids by his side, made a mental note that when he held the hammer in his hand he would not put up with that sort of thing.

He made a number of trips to London and attended sales at the larger and smaller auction rooms. He sorted out what he considered to be the most valuable lessons to be learned from these experiences and when he finally mounted the rostrum he knew exactly the effect he wanted to achieve. He was captain on the bridge of a ship, beneath him a deck peopled by undisciplined crew and ignorant passengers. It was his job to keep the crew in hand and instruct the passengers in the way they ought to behave. The slightest hint of mutiny, independence, levity, even a vaguely wandering thought, he crushed with an iron fist. On the occasion of his first auction his youth and inexperience provided a challenge to trouble-makers amongst a frivolous public and tough, cynical Trade. After the fifth lot, Edward put down his hammer, declaring that when everyone had stopped talking he would continue with the sale. Most of the public, who had luncheon engagements, dinners to cook and gardens to attend, stopped talking. Trade knew that Edward was interfering with the *laissez-faire* traditions of Boothby & Wigg and establishing a precedent for future dictatorial behaviour, but they also had calls to make and business to attend to. When silence reigned, Edward picked up a pin, which by a stroke of luck was waiting on the top of the rostrum for this fateful opportunity to express the *raison d'être* of its existence, and dropped it to the floor. On the hundred-and-tenth lot he again laid down his hammer to inform the public that the auction room was not a public restaurant and that there was a very good fish restaurant two streets to the right and, turn left, a sandwich bar around the corner, or if they wanted a licensed restaurant there were two – one French and one Italian – at the top of the hill, a recommendation based on the signs above their doors rather than on the food provided within.

But although he succeeded in whipping the public and the Trade into shape, Edward lost sight of the fact that an auction, with an audience and action on stage, is a dramatic event and he never learned the secret of keeping his auctions alive. He was a seller's auctioneer, not a buyer's. He squeezed the last two shillings off a twelve-shilling lot. His bids went up by one shilling to the first five pounds, by five shillings to the first twenty pounds, and if by chance the bids exceeded £1,000, they went up in tens instead of fifties. People went to sleep and missed their bids. He was lucky if he got through sixty lots an hour, whereas one of the more dynamic London auctioneers got better results charging his way through one hundred and fifty lots an hour, the panic-stricken public, like late arrivals dashing after a departing train, finding themselves in possession of lots for which they would not have paid half the price had there been time to consider.

The Viewing

TWO DAYS were allowed for the viewing, one fine, the other moist, but both displaying to advantage the Thawle woods, gathering mists from the valley and turning to russet and gold.

Amongst the inhabitants of neighbouring villages there still remained a few who could recount stories of splendid entertainments and wandering ghosts. One ninety-year-old claimed to have polished Lord Edward's riding-boots and two elderly widows contended for the privilege of having unhooked Lady Evelyn's dress when she returned from her honeymoon in Egypt. The de Boissy family, often abroad and engaged in the pursuit of their own pleasures, had earned only the smallest legacy of criticism and reproach. The charm of the house had spilled over the surrounding country-side like a perfume, pungent and intense at its source, though diminishing over extending distances. The younger generation, uninformed in history and scornful of the Thawle style, had little interest in the sale, but the older people turned up in force, hoping for some inexpensive souvenir. A number owed their dark eyes and good looks to the French artist imported by Lord Frederick from the Court of Louis XV, and now that illegitimacy had become respectable, brought their children with them to show off the Library ceiling.

The people who attended the viewing represented, however, only a small proportion of the interests involved. The Northern Ring, consisting of some forty dealers, sent only five representatives, variously instructed to keep an eye on one another, and the subsequent knock-down took place the day after the sale in a pub twenty miles north of Birmingham. The Southern Ring could spare only two delegates as there was another house sale running concurrently in Dorset. But the local Ring turned up in full strength and re-auctioned their lots on the spot, behind the stables. The London Ring, a rather loose organisation which, now that antiques were drying up, displayed a tendency to fragment in favour of private interests, was even more amply represented, its members having agreed on a free for all with no intimidation, repercussions or vendettas, but allowing for personal arrangements and gentlemen's agreements.

Members of the de Boissy family in Scotland had been advised of the sale and supplied with catalogues. Some, feeling that the furniture and pictures ought to be kept in the family, sent postal bids. Others engaged the services of Ian Matheson, an Edinburgh dealer who attended the sale and bid on their behalf. He informed them that their notions about the value of furniture were some fifty years behind the times, but they neither believed him nor listened to his advice. Taxes and the upkeep of their estates had drained them of money and over the past years few of them had bought anything but food and clothes. Only two lots found their way back to the Scottish de Boissys. A copper warming-pan which Lord Robert, getting the lot numbers wrong, had confused with a chair, and a sampler which Diana McFarlane, sister to Lord Charles, told Ian Matheson she wanted at any cost. It had hung in her nursery and had awed her and won her affection between the age of six and eight when she was going through a religious phase. The child responsible for the embroidery had stitched the date of its execution and her name, Margaret Anne, at the bottom of the sampler. She was the second daughter of Robert de Boissy, younger brother of Lord George, and had died of melancholia at the age of fourteen.

On the first day of the viewing, the auction staff, wearing white coats to distinguish them from the public, were at their stations by nine. The cars turning into the long drive that led to the front terrace of Thawle were directed by a bossy man wearing a red badge to a level stretch of land north of the woods, a portion of which in Lord Edward's day had been a croquet lawn, maintained by Lord Charles as an amusing relic of the past, but which had since been allowed to run wild and provided pasture for Rolling Home. The man with the red badge beckoned the cars into orderly rows. Two ice-cream vans were stationed on the front terrace and a stall pushing out steam from beneath a striped awning provided tea, hot dogs and sandwiches. Although most people had only recently finished breakfast, many started eating. In the front hall, in spite of notices prohibiting smoking and eating, the Sèvres tiles were soon smudged by the crushed ends of cigarettes and slippery with ice-cream. By noon the terrace was littered with minty papers, greasy brown paper bags, empty cartons and the sticks of toffee apples.

The Trunk

MAGNOLIA ARRIVED at nine-thirty and parked her van alongside Ozzie David's Cortina, Ozzie having arrived at nine-fifteen. Magnolia, carrying a bag of buns, for there had been no time for breakfast, made a tour of the hall and the ground-floor rooms. Her income prohibiting her from the likelihood of acquiring anything here, she took a quick look at the kitchens and mounted the stairs to the attics and servants' quarters where the less ostentatious pieces of furniture, prints, samplers and general junk were being examined by the Southern Ring and natives trailing hoards of querulous kids.

She marked her catalogue for the Stevengraphs, which Lord Charles had fancied because of Stevens' skill in depicting the low, extenuated gallop of racing horses, but with little hope of getting them because of the current inflated price of Stevengraphs. The Alkens would undoubtedly go to the West Country shippers, notoriously fanatical about Alken prints, and Magnolia left them alone.

She approached a trunk with a domed lid, reinforced with brass bands and secured by a large brass lock. She opened the lid to reveal a quantity of printed material all pell-mell inside. Magnolia picked out at random a slender publication with a pictorial cover, which looked to have been designed around the beginning of the century, announcing the performance at the Théâtre National de l'Opéra of 'Ariane opéra en 5 actes de Catulle Mendès musique de J. Massenet'. Beneath this text, which was displayed in various artistic styles ranging from an erotic, abandoned 'Ariane', a minute 'musique de' and an austere but commanding 'J. Massenet', a Greek ship sailed out to sea, leaving behind seated on a rock a woman of substantial size, clad in a white sheet that was slipping off, and holding her head in her hand. Magnolia returned it to the trunk and fished for more. The Haymarket, 1887, 'The Red Lamp'. The Avenue Theatre, 1893, 'The Black

Cat' and 'The Land of Heart's Desire'. Magnolia restored both programmes to the trunk with a violence which, disturbing its contents, disclosed the words 'Trilby', 'Yeats' and 'Colette Willy'. Faces appeared, decorating the margins of a menu from the Café Royal. The faces, though roughly sketched, looked familiar to Magnolia who felt she had encountered them before in reproductions of more finished drawings. She stuffed the menu deep into the trunk beneath newspapers displaying young women with pinched waists and bulging hips, attired in the latest 1900 foundation garments, closed the lid of the trunk, sat on it and ate, gulping down, hardly chewing at all, a bun. She hoped that a casual observer might attribute the bright rash that had broken out over her neck as it always did, giving her away, to a surfeit of calories and not to the intense, throbbing excitement that sends up the blood pressure of every collector when coming upon unexpected treasure.

But Ozzie David was not a casual observer. He had long ago learned that on a view day, viewing the viewers could be as rewarding as viewing the objects on view.

'Why are you sitting on that trunk, Magnolia Tree?'

'Because I'm eating a bun. I haven't had time for breakfast,' Magnolia confided. 'The Staff was supposed to turn up at eight to collect my latest American shipment which has to go off before five this evening, that's the deadline, but he didn't turn up till eight-thirty. You can't rely on anyone.'

The precipitous slope of the domed lid rendered the trunk inappropriate as a place to sit upon. Magnolia, beginning to slide, took her weight on her knees and, thrusting back, placed her buttocks on the top of the trunk. Ozzie observed this operation and was visited by a fleeting recollection of an amateur production of 'Arsenic and Old Lace', when an all but demented nephew stations himself on the lid of a trunk containing a body recently disposed of by his two homicidal aunts.

'If the lid of that trunk was flat,' he observed, 'it would

provide a comfortable spot for you to sit upon and eat your bun. But the discomfort you are enduring, sliding about perched up there, leads me to believe you have other reasons for sitting on that trunk.'

Heaving himself up, Ozzie sat beside her and turned to look intently into her face with a smile on his rubbery pink lips that Magnolia did not care for.

'Would you like a bun?' she said.

'No,' said Ozzie. 'I want to look inside this trunk.'

'You might wait,' said Magnolia, 'until I've finished my bun.'

'Those that eats a surfeit of buns,' said Ozzie, 'ends up with buns in the oven.'

'That is the kind of remark I do not appreciate.'

'I am surprised,' said Ozzie, 'that you understand it. Chaste as you are. And in case you don't, I will explain to you that buns put on flesh and man is heir to the sins of the flesh.'

'I don't go for that Old Testament stuff,' said Magnolia. 'My parents were missionaries and the New Testament is good enough for me.'

'It's a free country,' said Ozzie, 'so now perhaps you would be kind enough to dispose of your bun in order that I might take a look in this trunk.'

Magnolia's reply was drowned by the noise attending the arrival of Bill Thompson, Morry Fleet, Eddie Farrell and Harry Scale from the local Ring who surged up the narrow stairs and dispersed about the room, quickly filling it with checky sports jackets, bluster and smoke in spite of the 'No Smoking' signs. They turned chairs upside-down looking for worm and why should they when worm never bothered them and was never mentioned if you were silly enough to buy anything from them. Which, years ago, young and inexperienced, Magnolia had once done, but once only. They opened and shut the flaps of two country Georgian tables, searching for warp, which also never bothered them. Having pulled off one flap, attached by insecure hinges, and left it lying on the floor for everyone to trip over, they crowded around the Stevengraphs, the Alkens and a pretty sampler dated 1809 and signed in cross-stitch by a seven-year-old child whose poem, also in cross-stitch and surrounded by a floral border in some other sort of stitch, extolled the virtues of patience, obedience, the love of God and the pitfalls awaiting rebellious spirits and idle hands.

'Have you,' asked Magnolia, 'had a look at those Alkens over there?'

'Reproductions cut out of *Country Life.*'

'And putting them in walnut frames to tart them up. I've always said the aristocracy have no taste, no respect for antiques and practically no knowledge whatever.'

'Lady Evelyn,' said Ozzie, 'was no aristocrat.'

Surprised to the point of forgetting the urgent need of protecting her position as defender of the trunk, Magnolia said, 'What do you mean?'

'When it comes to a big house sale,' said Ozzie, 'I always do my researches. Otherwise you don't know where to look or what you're looking for.'

He drew from the inside pocket of his coat a small book with a blue cover, opened it and began to read. ' "Lady Evelyn was born in the East End in 1887. Her mother took to the gay life and her father died of drink. Lady Evelyn was brought up by an uncle and aunt who noticed that Lady Evelyn when she was around fourteen was turning out to be very beautiful, so, hoping for some reward for all the labour and care they had spent upon their little orphaned niece, they sent her around in search of employment. With the result that by the age of fifteen, in the year 1902, she found herself in the third row of the Gaiety Theatre. From the front row of the Gaiety, a year later, she caught the eye of Gordon Craig who gave her two lines in one of his flops which ran for two weeks in 1904. When she was eighteen she married Lord Charles de Boissy who was a great devotee of the theatre and all its charms," and, in my opinion, Magnolia, Gordon Craig was a fool to let her go because even though she may have muffed two lines in a bad play, for the rest of her life she played a part to such perfection anyone with a little foresight would have spotted her as the greatest actress of her day. No one born to the role could have done it better and Lady Evelyn never made a bad entrance or muffed her lines. Look at those treasures downstairs that Reggie Thring is wetting his pants to get his hands on.'

'Enough, Ozzie,' said Magnolia.

'The point I'm making is that Lady Evelyn was a true lady. She was beautiful and very refined. She knew quality when she saw it and what she didn't know by instinct she quickly learned. She wasn't going to part with those family treasures like most would have done even if she had to eat sausage and mash instead of pheasants and sucking pigs like she used to do in her day when she was a beautiful bride. She had been cast in the role of Lady Evelyn de Boissy and she played it to the last ditch.

'Nevertheless,' Ozzie returned to his book, 'the Scottish branch of the family would have nothing to do with Lord Charles or Lady Evelyn after their marriage. Graciously accepted as they were by other aristocratic families, the Scottish lot wouldn't budge an inch.'

'Typical,' declared Magnolia, who was warming to Lady Evelyn and regretted not having studied her more closely when the opportunity had offered on Trade Only Saturday afternoons. 'Never could abide the Scots. Stubborn mean lot. I'll give you fifteen bob, I said, for that plate, marked up at seventeen and six, but would they give me trade discount? We're entitled to trade discount, Ozzie.'

'Stubborn, Magnolia, as you say. And not only the Scots. Because as you yourself know, once you've taken a stand against someone, if you are a stubborn person you never back down.'

'What do you mean as I know?'

'I was referring,' said Ozzie, 'to your "Pinkie" programme and your obstinate refusal to part with it at a fair price.'

Magnolia tried for the more comfortable accommodation of her buttocks on top of the trunk.

'What's the matter?' asked Ozzie. 'Are you troubled with crumbs from your bun?'

Fixing Magnolia with his odious smile, he allowed the silence to spin out a while before saying, 'Let me return to my chronicle.'

Ozzie turned pages of the blue book. 'Married at the age of eighteen in 1905. Her first son Wilfred was born in 1907, chewed to shreds by a cheetah in 1928. Her second son was torn from her womb in 1910 and quickly passed away, and it's no good looking like that, Magnolia, because that is perfectly legitimate medical language as you would read in any respectable book. After a gap it looked as if Lady Evelyn would bear no more children, but she obviously tried because the present lord and heir to this estate was born in 1925 when Lady Evelyn was forty-two. And now I would like to look inside this trunk or do I have to fetch Eddie King and inform him that you are obstructing the viewing?'

'That crook,' said Magnolia, 'staring at that Dutch cupboard at the back of the room that he keeps for running up bids. Ran me up from seven and sixpence to fifteen bob for a carton of junk sheer junk, which I only went for to keep it out of the hands of that old bitch stinking of gin in that slum up by the Crescent who's been spreading malicious rumours about me. And all because I beat her to a jug and basin. My God, the envy in this profession, Ozzie, and the jealousy and tittle-tattle. I'm off to the States next month for a breath of fresh air. At least when they cut your throat they give you a good feed first. And when he knocked it down to me for seventeen and six I turned round and was she there? Down with 'flu I heard and I hope she never gets over it. You're taking your bids off that worm-riddled cupboard again, I said. I don't know what you mean, he said, and I'm going to lunch. You ran me up, I said, and I know because that's why I always sit at the back and there wasn't anyone behind me only that Dutch cupboard and I'm going to report you to the Auctioneers Association for malpractice. Whereupon he turned as white as a sheet and when you've got a skin as thick as his it's quite something if you can change colour at all.'

'And did you,' asked Ozzie, 'report him to the Auctioneers Association?'

'It's my trump card,' said Magnolia, 'and I'm keeping it for when it's needed which could be now, so I don't think you'll get any support from Eddie King in getting me off this trunk.'

Following a pause for thought, Ozzie said, 'Bill Thompson, Morry Fleet and Harry Scale have just slashed all four of Sydney Meyer's tyres because he failed to cooperate.'

'You've always said,' said Magnolia, 'that you were an independent trader who won't have any truck with the Ring.'

'Correct, correct. I am an independent man. But there is a difference between joining the Ring and playing balls with them as you might say.'

'Ball,' said Magnolia.

'What I would like to say to you, Magnolia,' said Ozzie, philosophising as it were, 'is that however you may prosper in this world and however far you may go, the important and honest bit of your life is where you begin. You could go on to being Prime Minister of England or President of the United States or the wife of a maharajah, but you'll always come back to where you begin. I'll bet my sweet life that amongst the effects of the deceased Adolf Hitler somewhere tucked away you'd come across a paint-brush for which he had a sentimental fondness because it strikes a chord. And I'll bet my sweet life that in this trunk there will be costumes from the Gaiety Theatre, satin slippers that have been filled with champagne, ostrich feather fans and letters from admiring gentlemen of noble birth. Because they never get it out of their blood. Grease-paint and all the lights and applause.'

'Ozzie,' said Magnolia, 'will you accept my word if I swear on the Bible, and my parents were missionaries who died at the hands of the Mau-Mau in Kenya, that there are no costumes from the Gaiety Theatre, no satin slippers and no ostrich-feather fans in this trunk.'

'I believe you,' said Ozzie. 'I believe that inside this trunk there will be theatre programmes, which, because Lord Charles was not only a devotee of the theatre but also a man of substance, will be inscribed with little affectionate notes and signed with such illustrious names as Ellen, Sarah, Max, Will, Oscar, Constance, Henry and Graham. Now let's have a look.'

'Fifty-fifty,' said Magnolia.

'I can't agree to your proposition,' said Ozzie, 'until I see for myself.'

'The Ring is still hanging around breathing beer at ten-thirty in the morning and it would be foolish to attract their attention. Fifty-fifty and I get first pick because I was here first,' said Magnolia, whose mind still clung to the image of that menu from the Café Royal decorated with famous faces that could only have originated from the pen of Max Beerbohm and each with its individual signature.

They shook hands.

'But I bid,' said Ozzie.

'No,' said Magnolia, 'I got here first.'

'Magnolia, that lot over there will get around to looking in this trunk no matter how long you sit on it with your bun. If I play balls with them they won't bid me up and I'll get it cheap, but they'll bid you up sky high because you hold out for independence. If I bid they'll let me have it because they know it's my line and when we knock it down after the sale they'll let me have it after they've made their bit of profit.'

'I thought you weren't in the Ring.'

'Well, I'm sort of in and out,' said Ozzie. 'You've got to be sensible, Magnolia. Being stubborn is the only flaw in your lovely nature. What's the point of you and me and the Ring bidding against one another. I'll get it at the knock-down and fifty-fifty on the knock-down price, turn by turn, and you get first pick because you was here first.'

Again they shook hands. Magnolia wiped her hands on her skirt. 'There's just a possibility,' she said, 'that they might be interested. So sit here and don't move while I look around.'

'I'll sit,' said Ozzie who, as soon as Magnolia had shoved her way downstairs, opened the lid of the trunk to inspect fifty years of Lord Charles's and Lady Evelyn's theatrical experiences.

Magnolia pushed her way past local peasants dragging their brats whose complaints of boredom had been staunched with ice-creams and hot-dogs, realising that for the first time in her life she had compromised with the Ring. Magnolia felt unclean and unhappy.

The Red Carnation

'HULLO, REGGIE,' said Magnolia, shoving her way through London Trade on her way to the kitchens. 'There must be quite a bit here to interest you but cut-throat competition by the look of it.'

'Some lovely things,' said Reggie. Ever since the valuation, strong feelings – memories, regrets, desires – had been building up within him and he found himself saying to the least appreciative audience, 'It saddens me.'

'It saddens me too,' said Magnolia. 'All that London lot invading our territory. Why can't they stay where they belong? Now that things are drying up in their neck of the woods they're spreading their tentacles far and wide squeezing us out.'

'What saddens me,' said Reggie, 'is the decline of a great family and the end of a way of life. The 1950 sale reduced the fifty rooms of this house to something like fourteen. This sale will reduce it to something like four.'

'They've worn themselves out,' said Magnolia. 'Lord Guy,

soft in the head and there'll never be another one. They can't even breed any more. Did I have to be sent into a loony bin when my father and mother were carved up by the Mau-Mau?'

Reggie's eyes turned from Magnolia to observe Clive who was engaged in conversation with a Mayfair picture dealer wearing a black and white check hacking jacket over black trousers, a white silk cravat and a red carnation, and who from the top of a pair of library steps was inspecting a painting by Pierre Rosseau of the Forest of Fontainebleau.

Reggie, controlling a surge of jealousy, wrenched his gaze from Clive. 'You've worked hard and built up a good business,' he said. 'You've built up a reputation in the West Country for integrity and honesty [and forthright rudeness – but he didn't add that]. But these people were different. They had money.'

'Exploiting the poor.'

'It was the way of things in those days. There is not an ungraceful or ugly object in this house.'

Magnolia snorted. 'What about all that Vicky rubbish upstairs. And those Alken prints cut out of *Country Life*.'

'The Vicky rubbish was provided to sit in and lie on. And it's very comfortable.'

'For the maids.'

Reggie tried hard to focus his attention on Magnolia, but his glance kept wandering off to Clive who was now holding the legs of the Mayfair picture dealer to support his balance on the library steps. Reggie, who had seen the creature at many London auctions and even spoken to him, was perfectly familiar with his name but his mind refused to recall it. The creature had now replaced his magnifying glass in his top pocket and had turned his eyes from the Forest of Fontainebleau to gaze into Clive's upturned face.

'I think you can be perfectly sure,' said Reggie, clinging to some continuity of thought, 'that when the fortunes of this family began to decline the maids and cooks were as well if not better off than the de Boissy family because they lived in the kitchens which were warm, and were in a better position to help themselves to the best cuts of meat.'

'Good for them,' said Magnolia. 'So would I. It wasn't for nothing they ended up on the guillotine.'

'Magnolia, the guillotine was an instrument that cut off your head, not something from which you were suspended, and do you feel responsible for some folly your great great grandfather committed one hundred years before you were born?'

Magnolia, deciding that Reggie's class prejudices provided an impenetrable barrier that would forever impede a civilised exchange of ideas, fired a parting shot. 'I still say they deserve what they've got.'

'Are you a socialist?'

'Good God no,' said Magnolia, appalled. 'And I've got to go now, Reggie. Your day's probably finished but I've got a lot of viewing to do. I haven't seen the kitchens yet or the greenhouses.'

When Magnolia had departed, Reggie stood alone in the crowded room. Though jostled by eager people and distressing thoughts, a sense of separation closed about him, disturbing, because it was alien to his nature. The people thronging the room had become removed and unreal as though they belonged to another time. More vividly presented and more sharply defined, Lady Evelyn, Lord Charles and Clare passed across his mental vision. And the many people he had met in this room, some of whom had disappeared to London, Paris or America, and others whom he rarely saw, their social lives contracted by age or poverty.

Leaving only Clive, the one substantial relationship that had survived out of that time.

Clive had taken the hand of the creature with the red carnation to assist his descent from the library steps and Reggie hated him for having drifted, after all those years, towards such an odious alternative. A mean-lipped man with a soft corrupt skin and foxy eyes.

Beside him a woman in a black hat extended her hand

to a pair of Sèvres vases, extolling their quality in French to a youthful male companion. Reggie saw Clare standing before a blazing fire, her figure flanked by these two same vases on the mantelpiece above. Saw her offer her hand to Lord Charles: saw Lord Charles raise her hand to his lips.

They had just returned from riding in the woods and Clare wore her riding clothes which became her because there had always been something severe and boyish in her looks, which was probably why he had married her. Reggie had noticed a smudge of green on the sleeve of her blouse and a twig in her hair. He had quickly turned to Lady Evelyn who was seated by his side and in her eyes had encountered an expression of satirical amusement. Hadn't she even so slightly shaken her head as though to say, Reggie, it doesn't matter? And after he had got over the shock, it hadn't mattered. It had mattered so little he hadn't cared when Clare died. Driving home, alone, after a party; leaving Clive behind, to follow later.

Why cling to those you no longer love? thought Reggie. And I want to be free. I'm glad to be free.

But the day was full of memories, confusion and distress. Suddenly Reggie felt suffocated in that room, busy with people, squatting on the floor, flipping back the corners of rugs, tipping up chairs to look for worm and climbing library steps to inspect, through a magnifying glass, the Forest of Fontainebleau. In spite of the number of people, there was no life in the room, nor any suggestion of gaiety. Few spoke to one another, though many must have been acquainted – dealers from London, Germany, Sweden, France. Their faces, withholding any hint of interest or delight and their grim closed expressions, appeared to affect the objects in the room, divesting them of their beauty and attachment to history. Nobody laughed in a room that had been once filled with laughter.

Reggie made his way outdoors and on the terrace, dogs, children, ice-creams vans and the flapping red and white awning of the hot-dog stall melted in a watery haze and sparkled with pins of brightness struck by the sun from the tears in his eyes.

After the Viewing

BY FIVE O'CLOCK most of the viewers had departed and the employees of Boothby & Wigg were engaged in moving the furniture from the downstairs rooms into the hall.

Magnolia, returning from the greenhouses to the car park, halted to regard Sydney Meyer standing a short distance from his van – one of the seven vehicles that remained. The disposition of his figure, enlarged by his overcoat and stationed on grass that the gloomy evening light had made vividly green, caused Magnolia to wonder why he wasn't nearer his van, unlocking the door and getting inside. He looked as if just previous to Magnolia's arrival he had been projected away from it by the fear that there might be a bomb inside, about to explode and scatter him to bits. His hands clenched his coat about him. His legs, planted apart on the green turf, seemed to be calling on the laws of gravity to save him from being cast into outer space.

For a brief moment, in Magnolia's eyes, he became a figure in a picture, its composition enhanced by the other six cars, disposed about him in artistic positions. Objects mute, unfeeling and stationary, whilst a gust of wind and a thin sheet of rain brought to life the lighter bodies of ice-cream cartons, tumbled them and raised a storm of minty papers to twirl, hover and descend about the portentous figure of Sydney Meyer, the beech woods behind him looming on his solitude. Sydney raised his arms in a gesture which, displaying the wide, black sleeves of his coat, enlarged his size, and dashed forward to strike his forehead and his fists on the bonnet of his car.

The Bowl of Roses

As SOON AS they entered the room Reggie saw the bowl of roses on the console table under the Chippendale mirror. The woman from the village who cleaned the house three days a week had not come that day and he knew that the roses had been picked by Frank who had arranged them as a gift to Reggie. Not only a gift, but a message full of mischief and playfulness because it was meant to remind Reggie, as it immediately did, of their conversation about mirrors and keeping flowers out of doors.

Conscious that Clive was watching him, he did not dare look too long at the roses, but it needed only a glance to confirm that Frank had chosen the finest blooms of his favourite rose. Big yellow heads with a touch of pink in the centre spreading out through the open petals. Frank had told him that the rose was called 'Peace', and when he looked at the roses, a feeling of peace fell upon him, but only for a moment, because it had to be kept from Clive and put away out of sight.

'What delightful roses,' said Clive. 'Unfortunately their perfume does not overpower the stench of sweat.' He wandered about the room, sniffing. 'Couldn't you drop a delicate hint and suggest that he take a bath every now and again, or, better still, keep him outside, where sweat belongs.'

'That creature,' said Reggie, 'with whom you were holding such an absorbing conversation today – the checky one with the carnation – was it he who detained you for two weeks when you disappeared to London in July?'

It was the remark of a jealous man and Reggie told himself he was not jealous, but still suffering from the shock of not having been preferred, he could not help saying what he had said.

Clive, in his favourite chair opposite the Chippendale mirror, sipped his drink, keeping his eyes on his own reflection. It struck Reggie that there might have been only two people in the room. Clive and his reflection. Once he smiled at it and the reflection smiled back. Reggie wondered what Clive thought about it. There didn't seem to be any exchange of admiration or affection between Clive and his reflection. At the most an understanding, a bond in conspiracy. Otherwise they regarded one another coldly. Once Clive lifted his glass and the reflection lifted its glass in reply. Reggie was reminded of scenes in old films when two crooks came to precarious terms and settled an agreement with one another.

Once Clive looked up with narrowed eyes, but was obliged to open his eyes so that he could regard himself with deeper concentration. He missed out on that look, thought Reggie, also detached and removed from affection.

Clive smiled and having concluded his negotiations with his reflection, leaned back in his chair and closed his eyes.

Guy and Irene

THE SUN WAS low and getting lower. You could almost watch it move. But still bright after a shower which had freshened things up and made the grass look so green. Irene liked the open landscape around the nursing home, that wasn't too hilly and oppressed with looming woods, like Thawle. A clump of Michaelmas daisies dropped long shadows on the lawn. The spaniels dashed about snuffling and smelling. What a wonderful life. No cares. But the old woman with the biscuits wasn't there. They snuffled around the place where her chair ought to be, looking up and wrinkling the skin between their eyes. Distressed, because the smell was still there but the old lady and the biscuits had gone. Even dogs care, thought Irene. Most of the older people had gone indoors and Guy wore a jacket.

'I couldn't get here earlier,' said Irene. 'They didn't go till after five and the cars blocked the drive. I couldn't bring you a pie because I couldn't get into the kitchen.'

'I ought to have been there,' said Guy.

'You wouldn't have liked it,' said Irene. 'I shut myself up with my irregular verbs.' Then because Guy looked puzzled and had forgotten, she reminded him. 'I'm learning French so I can read the books in Lord Frederick's library that your mother left me. She said in her Will that she was leaving me the books by a French lady called Marie de Sevigné. It's a whole shelf, and she said she was leaving them to me because of my love of literature, but I think it was a sort of condition that I ought to learn French. It's difficult because I don't know about grammar. I didn't know that English had grammar until I found out that we've got subjunctives too. But I'm getting the hang of it. I hope you don't mind but Giles sold a lot of vegetables in the Shepton Mallet market last Saturday to pay for my courses but I haven't touched the money that Mr Tippett gave me for expenses. It's accumulating.'

'You're a good sister to me,' said Guy. Quiet on that day and so subdued. Irene liked it better when he was cruel and hated her. His eyes looked at far away things. There didn't seem to be any fight left in him.

Guy looked up. 'They didn't sell Percy?'

'Of course not. I promised. We locked the door.'

'I'm glad,' said Guy. 'Our little son will love Percy.'

Irene held her breath. She felt that something beautiful and perfect but as fragile as a seed of thistledown had descended from heaven and was hovering before her eyes. She felt that the slightest movement of her body would condemn its loveliness to dust and blow it away.

'Mummy put me on Percy,' said Guy, 'when I was three years old. I might have been four. She put my feet in the stirrups and the reins in my hands and then she gave him a push and showed me how I could make him gallop, leaning forward over his neck and then leaning back. Sometimes I held the reins and sometimes I held his mane. I loved the smell of his mane and I used to tie it in plaits. When I untied the plaits it was all crinkly and I put my head in it and smelt the smell.'

'I didn't have a rocking horse,' said Irene, sad because the thistledown had blown away.

'Will you give her this letter?' said Guy, putting a letter to his mother in Irene's hand.

A Four-Course Lunch at Lyons Corner House

THERE WOULDN'T have been room for a rocking horse in the three rooms of the semi-detached that her mother rented.

In Irene's bedroom there was only space for a bed and a chest of drawers. When she wanted to open the bottom drawer of the chest of drawers, she had to shift the bed. Her dresses hung on hooks in the passage and, later, she put up shelves out there for her grandmother's books, which impeded the entrance to the toilet, but you could manage to get in by going past the door, then opening it and then going in.

Her mother needed the parlour for her gentlemen and had a really nice big bedroom with a double bed and red curtains that were nearly always kept closed so that the room looked pink like the strawberries on the barrow down the road outside. But there was always a wobbly crack in the curtains where the light came in. Her mother needed privacy and Irene wasn't allowed in the room except on Sundays which was her mother's day off. Irene loved Sundays when she could watch the sunlight, if there was any, coming through the wobbly crack, making the brass knobs on the bed shine like gold and falling into a long mirror with such a dazzle you could hardly look into it.

Her mother would lie on her bed, smoking cigarettes,

sipping from a glass and resting, while Irene tried on her dresses. Irene had always liked dressing up.

'Keep your shoulders back,' her mother would say. 'You won't have much of a bust by the look of you so make the most of it.'

When the sun had left the mirror so that she could look into it and not be dazzled by the light, Irene would watch herself in the mirror, walking barefoot, because her feet shuffled around in her mother's high shoes. She would walk into the mirror and out of it, or stand with her head turned over her shoulder to see the effect. Her mother gave her instructions but Irene did not feel that they were the sort of advice she wanted to follow. She wanted to be a lady.

The dresses didn't fit her, because she was only twelve, though tall for her age. But Irene loved the feeling that came over her when she put on her mother's dresses. They made her feel grown-up, experienced and dignified in the way she was going to be when she was older.

Sometimes her mother said she didn't know how she could pay the rent, but sometimes she seemed to have a lot of money and when she was affluent she took Irene on a spree. They went to see 'Puss in Boots' on the 17th December, which was Irene's birthday, and a week later 'Peter Pan' for Christmas. Next year her mother entertained a German gentleman who gave her two tickets for 'Hamlet'. Her mother was bored by 'Hamlet' but said it was a pity to waste the tickets. She was more interested in the audience, but Irene felt she would never forget 'Hamlet' until the day she died.

When she was fourteen which was the year after her uncle pulled her into the bushes on that day when they had all gone off for a picnic in the woods near Richmond Park, her mother had a stroke of luck. She bought herself a new dress and a dress for Irene and they went off together in their finery for a four-course lunch at Lyons Corner House. The one on the corner of Tottenham Court Road. They went by Tube, but her mother had a bottle of wine with lunch and they went back home by taxi. They ordered soup, fish with a foreign name which was just like her mother did it, lamb chops with peas and fruit salad.

'I can't believe my eyes,' said Irene's mother.

Irene had been staring about her entranced by the people, all dressed up and able to afford four-course lunches. By the white tablecloths, the sparkle of forks and spoons and the way the waiters swooped about holding trays they didn't drop, as if they were superior to everyone.

'I'd know him anywhere,' said Irene's mother. 'That's Lord Guy de Boissy.'

Irene felt that Lord Guy de Boissy was a wonderful name like the names of the heroes in her books. He was seated alone at the next table, eating a piece of fish. He had a beautiful face and a lot of hair. There were pieces of grey in his hair which meant that he might be forty, but his face wasn't so old as his hair. His clothes were rather shabby and there was dirt in his fingernails. But that was in order, because if you are an aristocrat you are above everyone and don't care what other people think of you. There was a look in his big dark eyes that made Irene feel he wanted someone to look after him.

Then her mother told her about his mother, Lady Evelyn, and his father who was dead, and how there had been a sale at their house in Somerset and the family had fallen on hard times. Her mother knew a lot about the aristocracy and followed their fortunes in the papers and *The Tatler* which she bought for 3d. a copy from the second-hand bookshop down near the World's End, which had a cheap 3d. stall outside for old books and magazines. Irene had found her copy of *The Rocks of Valpré* on that stall with an inscription on the front page in beautiful writing, saying 'To my dearest Dora, with love from Hubert'. Her mother liked the *Tatlers*. One of her gentlemen had been an Honourable and she had kept in touch, but she didn't know where the big house was. There were gaps in her knowledge.

Irene went to Fulham Library and asked if they had a book which would tell her about aristocratic families and their houses. The librarian gave her a copy of Debrett's *Peerage, Baronetage, Knightage and Companionage.* She wasn't allowed to take it home but the book fascinated her and night after night she went to the library and read it till closing time.

Two years later her mother died. Irene was sixteen and had a job in an all-night café. She didn't make enough money to pay the rent. Then she discovered that even the furniture hadn't belonged to her mother. Only the clothes. Some of her gentlemen had given her presents but she had to sell them when she came on hard times, which often happened, because she didn't look so young any more and the hard life she had led was beginning to show. Some of the presents, bracelets, brooches and strings of pearls, had looked expensive, but when they were sold they hadn't been worth very much. She had kept a watch from better days in the past and told Irene that a jeweller had told her it was real gold and worth £50, but when Irene looked for it after her mother died, she couldn't find it. She was convinced that the landlady had taken it one night when she was visiting the hospital.

The landlady lived downstairs in the other half of the semi-detached. She told Irene that she couldn't stay, but she let her off some of the rent, probably because of the watch. She wasn't given to generosity.

Irene felt numb. She couldn't think, but she didn't have to. She had done all the thinking two years ago and there wasn't any need to do any more. She packed a suitcase and the books in cartons that the man in the off-licence gave her for nothing because her mother had been such a good customer. She got five pounds for her mother's clothes and two pounds ten for a silver-backed mirror and brush that one of her mother's gentlemen had given her, and she found five pounds in a stocking in the top drawer of her mother's dressing-table before the men came to take the furniture away. More than enough to get her to Paddington in a taxi because of the books, a single ticket to Bath and then a bus down to

Thawle. Even so, there was a long walk, carrying her suitcase, but it wasn't raining.

She felt very tired when she came to the gates of Thawle and had to go on walking up the long drive. When the drive took a turn and she saw the house in front of her, she wanted to run towards it, but couldn't, because of her suitcase. When she was inside the house she was trembling all over and had a hard time composing herself. It hadn't been because she was afraid of Lady Evelyn and what she would say when she read the letter. She had never had any doubts that Lady Evelyn would take her in because that was the kind of person she was. But she hadn't known there would be woods so close to the house. She hadn't anticipated them and they were a disadvantage. But she also knew there were disadvantages to every situation, and that having come so far in pursuit of her destiny, it was no time to give up, because of the woods. She would have to learn to live with them, and perhaps at some time find a way of defeating them.

The Woods

A YEAR PASSED before she could muster the courage to walk into the woods. She chose a sunny morning with a clear sky. She couldn't have faced them if the sky had been overcast, but with everything looking so bright and the leaves flashing in the sun, there didn't seem to be anything to be afraid of. She followed the path along which, so often, she had watched Guy riding off on Rolling Home. But as she walked on, the heavy green overhead shut out the sky. The sunlight only came through in spots and flashes and there was a mist on the ground that the sunlight never reached. Without her having noticed, the path had turned a little, so that when she looked back the house had disappeared. The woods were in front and behind, closing in, and once again, in a dreadful way, she felt shock and pain. Even more dreadful than when it happened because that had been only a particular moment and this sort of shock and pain might go on for ever. At first she could hardly move. She wanted to cry for help but no sound came because of his hand over her mouth. Then somehow she was able to move and turned and ran back. But for long moments, safe in the hall, she trembled and couldn't collect her thoughts. Just like that day when she first arrived, saw the woods and couldn't hurry because of her suitcase. But fortunately she had had time to compose herself because it must have been ten minutes before anyone knew she was there and Guy had appeared, asking who she was and what she wanted.

She never tried the woods again, preferring her suite and Lady Evelyn's rooms which were so happy and friendly; the Library with all the books, and the kitchen with its warm used air smelling of apple-pie, wet dogs and wood, which was kept in a copper cauldron alongside the range and which she liked to keep polished because when you opened the door of the range the flames inside made it sparkle and gleam in a cheerful way.

In the woods the air, which had been so pure and fresh it might have been extracted from the stars, had made Irene think of death, because her uncle had put his hands on her throat and whispered in her ear, 'I'll kill you if you tell.'

She hadn't told – not even her mother – until she told Lady Evelyn. Lady Evelyn had told, because, she explained to Irene, it was better to tell in order to bring it outside instead of keeping it shut in.

Irene felt that Lady Evelyn had been right, as she almost always was, because driving back to Thawle from the nursing home she felt she was beginning to like the countryside. The view from the road was so long, it was easy to imagine the sea at the end of it. And on the other side of the sea was France where the de Boissys had come from and where Madame de Sévigné had written her letters. She even thought she would try the woods again, but taking precautions. Accompanied by the spaniels who would protect her. Or Giles. Or even Guy, who although he had given her another letter from his mother had also said, 'Our little son will love Percy.'

Magnolia, Alfie and Syd

'THE RING,' said Magnolia, after she had settled herself into a chair facing her favourite picture of the Houses of Parliament fitted with Big Ben, illuminated and striking the quarters, 'slashed all four of Syd's tyres today.'

Alfie lived alongside his warehouse in a cottage comprising a living-room, kitchen and two bedrooms. When his wife took exception to his having a bit of fun with the girl who held the fort when he was up in Birmingham – (who turned out to be light-fingered always with a hand in the till) and took the kids with her, and the opportunity to go off with Carlo from a three-star Italian restaurant in Wells, Alfie knocked down a wall to enlarge the living-room.

Even so, the living-room, commodious as it was, had contracted to its centre, where a sofa and two armchairs crowded about a table displaying a vase of artificial flowers and ashtrays that had found their way into Alfie's possession from local pubs. The contraction to the centre of the room and inward thrust, threatening sofa, chairs and table, had been brought about by the need to accommodate three Regina disc musical boxes in large cabinets, four polyphon disc musical boxes – two of German origin and consequently larger and heavier than the others – and a symphonium disc musical box, narrow, but deep and tall. On a table in the corner reserved for their display were two 'Sublime Harmonie' musical boxes, one two-comb with 120 teeth and six airs, the other two-comb with 125 teeth and eight airs. On the walls, three pictures painted in oils and fitted with clocks argumentatively announced the time every thirty minutes or so.

But in spite of the heavy cabinets, the profusion of dark wood and the brown roses on the Axminster carpet, it was a harmonious and happy room. The central chandelier, four candlesticks dripping with rigid wax, cast a festive light upon the circular and semi-circular perforated discs of Regina Polyphon musical boxes, which in their turn cast light across the room into the discs of other musical boxes situated against the opposite wall. The silence was continually and unpredictably enlivened by tinkling chimes.

'I've brought him here, Alfie,' said Magnolia, 'because he's in a spot with his car waiting for the AA to cart it back to Bristol. I've brought an extra pie but I forgot that he couldn't eat pork because of his religion.'

'A bit of bread and cheese would do,' said Syd, standing apologetically, and still wearing his overcoat.

Alfie retired to the kitchen and returned with a tin of pork and beans.

'Alfie,' said Magnolia. 'Pork's the problem.'

But an examination of the label disclosed that the tin only laid claim to beans in tomato sauce.

'No mention of pork,' Magnolia reassured Sydney, 'and believe me if there were a vestige of pork it would have been mentioned.'

'That'll do nicely,' said Syd.

After he had rung his mother to say he'd be late home if he got home at all, and she had told him he was always late for meals and never gave a thought to his poor old mother who, what with her rheumatism, couldn't get to the stove to make a cup of tea, and after he had rung the neighbours in the flat above to ask them if they would make her a pot of tea, Sydney consumed his beans, warmed up, and Alfie and Magnolia ate their pies.

Alfie said, 'Why did they slash your tyres, Syd? What did they do that for?' He had opened a bottle of beer.

'It's the Vicky sofa,' said Syd. 'I want that Vicky sofa

and I'm prepared to pay for it even though it's going to cost a fortune getting it recovered. The horsehair is bursting out and it's stuffed with newspapers. But they didn't want to go to my bid. And I want the Alkens which are not, as they've spread the word around, cut out of *Country Life*, but genuine, down to the walnut frames. But there's a long history, Alfie, to this Gestapo vendetta and these Trade Union tactics. In the beginning I played along a bit. I didn't have any choice, but it was a mistake because once you're in they won't let you go. And when we bought the flat in Bristol in a very nice area up on the hill, and my old mother was installed I got fed up. It was after that Dorset sale last year. I stuck out for a private individual bid on two credenzas with marble tops and two sword fish, beautiful blue with splendid fins, all the way from Honolulu. And there were twelve ruby wineglasses and six Bristol paperweights with silver flowers. This is the second lot of tyres in twelve months and where will it end? I wish I could get to London. There's so much stuff up there they leave you alone.'

He had taken off his coat and for the first time Magnolia saw what a tiny frame he had. Braces, pulling into his shoulders and crossed at the back, held together the frail collection of bones that constituted the structure of his chest, and gripped the buttons of wide black pants which, without their aid, would certainly have fallen off.

Magnolia had never felt a strong affection for any human being, including her mother and father, her energies after she had started trading at the age of fourteen on a capital of three pounds being directed to the need to survive and prosper. Her feelings for her fellow men comprised respect, contempt, trust, distrust, loathing, indifference and on rare occasions admiration. But her allegiance, once won, was more staunchly unflinching than the fickle and idiosyncratic moods of passion. She burned with fury over the injustice done to Syd, especially now that she had seen how small he was.

'They don't worry me,' said Alfie, pouring beer. 'They

can't be bothered with the hard work in rags and feathers.'

'Just you wait,' said Syd, 'till they realize that you're selling your pine chests for four quid apiece to London Trade that's flogging them for thirty quid in Portobello and just you wait till they find out that every Chelsea mews has iron bedsteads with brass knobs like you've got stacked at the back of your premises.'

'They leave me alone,' said Alfie, standing up to display his six-foot body, thrusting out his muscles and shaking his black curls and the gold rings in his ears.

'There's a lot of them,' said Syd, 'Gestapos that they are, and there's only one of you, big and strong as you have just demonstrated. Just wait until they get around to realizing that this collection you have here of musical instruments, which with great foresight you bought at the bottom of the market, will find its way to Sotheby's any day now. Then you won't have it all your own way, Alfie.'

'Have you heard my bird?' asked Alfie, pouring beer. 'Have you ever listened to the beautiful song of my nightingale that Ozzie David's had his eye on for the past five years, but he isn't getting it not over my dead body.'

'I have not,' said Sydney, 'seeing as this is the first time you have invited me into this treasure house.'

Magnolia, losing charity with every passing minute, waved her hand before her face to clear the smoke and fumes of beer. Just like a pub.

When Alfie had fetched the nightingale from next door and the nightingale had finished singing, Sydney said. 'You ought to get your bird re-feathered.'

'My bird,' said Alfie, 'is period with original feathers. If I re-feathered it, it wouldn't be original. Here, let me top that up.'

'When I have a Vicky chair,' said Syd, 'thank you, Alfie, that has one wormy leg, I take a good leg off another Vicky chair that has three wormy legs and one good leg. And I do not say to myself that the Vicky chair to which I have attached a good Vicky leg is no longer original. I say to myself that I have done my duty to a good Vicky chair.'

'But I haven't got another bird,' said Alfie, 'with which I can re-feather my nightingale and it wouldn't be period if I reconditioned it with modern feathers.'

'Why don't you collect the feathers in the bottom of the cage and replace them?'

'I do that,' said Alfie. 'Have another cigar.'

Magnolia rose to her feet. 'I'm going now because I want to have a good night's rest and a clear head unclouded by the fumes of alcohol and tobacco. But before I go, Alfie, I want to say that I'm going for those blue plates in the greenhouses.'

'I'm going for them too,' said Alfie. 'I fancy them.'

'Fifty-fifty,' said Magnolia, 'but I want the two small ones with the fish in the bottom. I can flog them to Mrs Carter for her cat.'

'I want the garden ornaments,' said Alfie. 'I fancy those horses and the tortoises, only I don't know why anyone painted them white like that. If you leave cement out in the rain it gets an antique look and a nice bit of green mould. They don't look weathered. They don't look period to me.'

'I'll keep off them,' said Magnolia. 'They're not my line, but I want the geraniums for the Taunton market. They go with the blue plates and you can bid, Alfie, I won't have room in my van.'

'I want the Vicky sofa,' said Syd, 'and there's a bed that looks Queen Anne to me. Very short. In Queen Anne's day nobody grew over five foot tall. I left my bid with Eddie King so they won't know and I can't get to the sale with my car in that condition.'

'You doss down here,' said Alfie, 'and come along with me. I was going for the Vicky sofa too but I'll hold off seeing as you've had your troubles with the Ring. Here, let me top that up.'

'I admire that girl,' said Alfie, after Magnolia had departed. 'There's not a better trader in the West Country. But puritanical what with her objections to a glass of beer and a smoke. And you can't get your hands on her.'

'Do you want to?' Sydney enquired.

'Sometimes, when she's sitting in that chair which she prefers, with her legs apart, the idea does occur to me.'

'You wouldn't get anywhere,' said Syd.

'I know,' said Alfie. 'And I don't care except in a passing way. Let me top that up while I play you my Orchestral Regina with automatic tune-changing device and long-running movement, priced at the time of its manufacture at £90. It has two combs with 172 tongues and is tuned in chromatic scale with seven octaves.'

'How do you know all that?' asked Syd, dropping ash from his second cigar on Alfie's Axminster.

'There was a paper inside, very brown, from an old magazine with a picture and full description of that selfsame instrument and the words of the songs.'

'I thought you didn't read so well.'

'Magnolia is always ready to oblige and once she's read me something I never forget. It's engraved on my memory.'

He approached the instrument in question, a tall cabinet, its disc perforated with small incisions of differing size, elaborate carving on the woodwork above and on the top a balustrade such as, executed in stone, finished the terraces of country houses. Two wooden urns provided dignity to the corners and at the side two handles suggested to Sydney's mind draught beer in London pubs.

> Oh poor Mary Ann, when she got to the top,
> Her heart went flippity flop
> The wheel began to stop
> The man in the moon was laughing at her
> And she began to squeal
> She lost her situation through the great big wheel.

The discs of the polyphon threw flashes of happy light into Syd's beer.

When Alfie had finished singing 'She wore a wreath of roses', 'Oft in the stilly night', and 'Ta-ra-ra-boom-de-ay', he said, 'I love this music, Syd. It's reliable. I've got no time for those amateurs on the piano at the Dance Hall. Pianos are prone to human error. They go fast, they go slow. They hit the wrong note. When you sing to my music you know just where to come in but if you try singing to a piano it starts before you're ready or after you've begun. My music never makes a mistake and it never lets you down because every time you play it, it's just the same.'

'I think I'd prefer it if it wasn't always the same,' said Sydney. 'It's a matter of taste,' he added, because he was a guest in Alfie's house.

Alfie overlooked this difference of opinion because Syd had been an appreciative audience, and on top of the world with beer and success, Alfie said, 'You haven't seen the piece der resistance of my collection. Here, let me fill up your glass and come outside.'

The sky was overcast and Syd collided into a dustbin, kicking up a din.

'Shsh,' said Alfie. 'The neighbours,' as the brat next door woke up and started howling.

A dark, large shape loomed in the centre of the yard at the back, almost as big as a building, but Syd, attempting to focus his gaze upon it, knew it couldn't be a building. More like a tent. Round, with a sort of roof with sloping sides and a pointed top. Alfie turned a switch and a spotlight attached under the gutter on the back wall, brought it closer, sparkling and glittering out of the dark. Sydney, opening and shutting his eyes, saw galloping horses with heads out-thrust, and horses with arched necks and tossing white manes; twisted silver poles, blue and gold saddles and mirrors around the top that were dim and speckled because they were old and had caught the reflections of so many fairgrounds and the shining faces of so many children.

'It's a merry-go-round,' said Syd, identifying it at last and impressed.

'I came on it last year,' said Alfie, towering with pride, 'very broken down, very dilapidated, but I got it going and now it works like a treat. I went over the horses, cleaning them up and doing a bit of repainting. Fifteen horses and not one the same. Just you look. That one's got his ears back and his mouth open. He's a bad-tempered brute and that one with the rose on his bridle has got his ears forward and one foot up. The one with the red saddle is called 'Dancer' because he's got it written on a ribbon round his neck, and the blue one has got a man's face on his saddle which is an interesting point, Syd, if you are a collector.'

'It certainly is,' said Syd. 'Who is he?'

'I don't know,' said Alfie, 'but it's my guess it's the man who carved the horses. Just look at that carving. Just look at that mane floating in the wind and the head of that brute with his ears back and his mouth open showing all those teeth. It's got an organ that plays a treat. It's a right one. Absolutely genuine and when I saw it stuck away in that junk yard in such condition I'll tell you, Syd, I trembled all over like a child.'

'What do you do with it?' asked Syd, who thought it was a large thing to collect.

'I take it to fairs and the kids love it. I'm taking it next week to Torquay for the fair. I've always wanted one, Syd. It's been my life's ambition. But it's a funny thing about ambition. It leads you on, and now I'm thinking about vintage cars. Do you know what my ambition is?'

He put his questions with seriousness, followed by a long pause requiring an answer.

'What is your ambition, Alfie?' asked Syd.

'I want to go to India and buy all those Silver Clouds from the maharajahs.'

'I want to get back to London,' said Syd. 'I'm a Londoner, Alfie. Out here in the West Country with all the fresh air around me I feel sort of stifled. I could spread my wings in London. I'd like to open a place in Kensington Church Street with a stall in Portobello. I like the foreign element. The French, the German and the London talk. I'm a Jew, Alfie.'

'Are you?' said Alfie, surprised.

'And Jews, as you must know, have no country, but they own the world. Bits of the world belong to other nations, but the world, if you can get my point, belongs to the Jews. It's a positive point of view you may be thinking but I like to be positive. Here in the West Country with its villages and its Rings I feel hemmed in.'

'Why don't you go to London?' asked Alfie, suddenly wanting to go to bed.

'Money,' said Syd. 'I'd need a shop with accommodation above for my old mother. Here we can live cheap, but I'm an exile in Bristol and being an exile has always been our problem. I'm a fish out of water in Bristol and ever since I left London I've been wanting to get back.'

'What we need,' said Alfie, waking up, 'is more beer.'

Back in the house, Alfie said, 'I wish I had the money to set you up in London, Syd. If I had it I'd willingly give it to you.'

Syd said, 'And if I had the money I'd willingly give it to you so you could go to India and further your ambitions by buying those Silver Clouds from the maharajahs.'

The Furniture

DURING THE viewing the furniture that was to be sold from the downstairs rooms had been left untouched in the positions it had occupied for so many years. Edward King rightly understood that its situation enhanced its beauty and therefore its value. But in the evening, after the viewing was over, it was removed to the main hall and arranged along the walls, shedding in the process of transference, most of its beauty and all of its dignity.

A high-backed, heavy-armed Jacobean chair diminished into insignificance a delicate Sheraton satinwood table standing beside it. Or, if one bestowed one's sympathy on the Sheraton table, the Jacobean chair looked loutish and coarse, good for nothing but a pot-bellied cavalier with one hand up the skirts of the innkeeper's daughter and the other brandishing a tankard of ale. A walnut Queen Anne bookcase struggled for some recognition of its proportions with a chubby Elizabethan armchair. A Sheraton commode, next in the line, made the Elizabethan armchair look as if it had survived from prehistoric times and the Sheraton commode, put out of countenance by its proximity to an object of such gloomy antiquity, looked modern and frivolous.

The pieces of furniture had been crammed together along the walls of the hall, side by side, so that when Edward King read out the lot numbers, one of the porters could pass from piece to piece touching it with his hand. Regimentation, submission and obedience to the command of an officer might have been the impression received by some minds given to attaching human qualities to inanimate objects. Others would have been conscious of a quarrelsome riot of styles and of fashion and taste that took a firm stand and a few years later turned about-face and outlawed their origins.

So argumentative were the various objects in the room, so bent upon denigrating one another, some people asked themselves whether the de Boissys had had any taste at all, disregarding the evidence before them that what had mortified the furniture, leaving it humbled and adrift in Time, was the loss of a harmony the de Boissy family had imposed upon it – a tolerance and composure which had been outraged when the white-coated porters of Boothby & Wigg hauled it from its long-considered, long-occupied positions and set it up in the hall, took the rugs from the floors and hung them up in place of the family portraits (not for sale and all removed), and then arranged rows of chairs in the centre of the hall, making it look like a cinema.

The First Day of the Sale

REGGIE DID quite well on the first day of the sale. He particularly wanted lot no. 15, the Queen Anne walnut bureau bookcase, and waited while two private bidders, confident that they were the only people interested in it, ran one another up to round twenty-five per cent of its market value. One dropped out; the other, soothed into complacency by a long silence during which Edward King searched the assembled faces for some sign of interest, sat secure in the certainty that he had acquired the bookcase, not for nothing but certainly far below the price he would have to pay in an antique shop. Four bids later, having been carried on against his judgement into dangerous excesses, he thankfully retired, leaving Reggie bidding against Ian Matheson.

Reggie knew that Ian's heart wasn't in Queen Anne walnut and that unless he was bidding on commission he would probably save his restricted means for the Jacobean oak. Ian retired and Reggie confronted a more formidable opponent, Anthony Hare.

Anthony had entered the antique business long after Reggie, but charm and connexions had helped to obscure deficiencies in his knowledge. He opened a small shop in Knightsbridge, now extended, and although he derived his keenest enjoyment from acting the part of a dealer in fine antiques who collected them because he loved them and sold them only to people he loved who would treasure them, he was as honest and conscientious as could be expected in the circumstances. Reggie and Anthony were business colleagues and friends of a sort. They bought and sold to and from one another and exchanged pieces that had been sitting around too long, to create an impression of movement and brisk trade. When Reggie stayed a night in London he often exchanged gossip with Anthony in a Chelsea pub. Anthony had twice Reggie's money to spend and occasionally paid frivolous prices for something that caught his fancy. Reggie knew that the Queen Anne walnut bureau bookcase was the kind of item which might catch Anthony's fancy and that if he pursued his own ardent desire to possess it, he also would have to pay a frivolous price. A difficult decision to make at the beginning of a sale. But Edward was on his side. For Anthony had made the mistake of bidding with his eyebrows and Edward had no time for such subtleties as eyebrows lifting up and down, twitching mouths and fingers pulling at the lobe of the left ear. He required a raised hand, or a catalogue flapping like a flag. Once his attention had been attracted, he would settle for a series of nods, but if the nods were not strongly and dramatically executed, he abandoned them for more urgent signals. From a front-row reserved seat, Anthony had come into the bidding with an uplifted forefinger, but when he slipped back into bidding with his eyebrows, Edward ignored him and knocked the bookcase down to Reggie. Anthony, who had been too well brought up to create a scene, made no protest.

Later in the morning, Reggie was in possession of a pair of spider-back chairs, a pair of Hepplewhite torchères, a Chippendale commode, one of the Library bookcases and a pair of George II armchairs with oval backs. He dropped out regretfully from a Sheraton mahogany rent table from Lord Charles's office, having decided to hold himself in reserve for the Fabergé.

The Fabergé came up around two-thirty and a French jeweller got the best of it. Reggie paid what he knew to be too high a price for a jasper dormouse with platinum whiskers and dropped out on a rock-crystal hippopotamus which he didn't care for but ran up out of pique and which sold for the same price as the much superior dormouse. Half an hour later he bid for a bombé cabinet which was not to his taste but which, during one of those curious lulls in a sale when everyone's attention wanders, was knocked down to him at a price which would more than justify his extravagant bid on the dormouse.

In the late afternoon Reggie, with nothing more marked

on his catalogue but curious to know what things would be going for, looked about him and was arrested by the face of a fashionably dressed woman seated in the same row but on the other side of the hall. He felt he might know her and kept looking back at her, searching for some memory that might tell him where he had met her before. She did not attract him. Though handsome, she was not beautiful, for beauty, in Reggie's opinion, could only be accorded to a woman who expressed some degree of animation. The carefully tended skin drawn tight over her excellent features looked so thick and inelastic as to prohibit any escape of feeling from her mind or heart within. If any feeling there were, which Reggie doubted. But he kept looking at her. She seemed to have some special importance and relevance to the occasion.

Suddenly, on lot no. 294 – a long Chippendale stool covered with fine, faded needlework – she raised her catalogue, bidding with an air of implacable determination that Reggie recognised when he referred it to himself. She was going to buy the stool at any cost. Reggie watched her with deepening interest. Her appearance and dress were rich and urban, and he guessed that she had probably come from London. The thought came to Reggie that she had attended the sale for no other reason than to bid for the Chippendale stool, and he continued to cast glances in her direction, searching for something that he thought for a moment he had recognised in her blank, unreflective face.

The Chippendale Stool

MRS STEPHEN DARCY, ex-Mrs Andrew Brentwood, *née* Georgina Bray, on hearing of the much publicised de Boissy sale had acquired a catalogue and studied it, trying to identify items that would strike a chord in her memory. The trouble

172

was that, in those days, although she had been entranced by an atmosphere of wealth and beauty all about her, she had paid little attention to details and had been less interested in the furniture than in the impression that she herself was making, in the young men who were enthusiastically responding to the impression she was making, and for a short disastrous interlude, in Lord Charles. But when she came to lot no. 294, a Chippendale mahogany stool with claw and ball feet, upholstered in needlework, she was immediately visited by a recollection of herself wearing a pale yellow chiffon evening gown, seated upon this very same stool in the Peacock Room, when, after dinner, the other guests having retired to the terrace to enjoy the warm summer night, Guy de Boissy had proposed to her.

'There I was sitting,' she told a number of her friends on a number of occasions, 'and it was so unexpected. I mean he was so good-looking and terribly sweet. But I think I was taken in by the whole *thing*. The house, the horses – I was simply mad about horses – Lord Charles and Lady Evelyn. I can't begin to tell you – there was something magical about them. Isn't it funny that two such remarkable people could produce such an ordinary child? And the trouble was he didn't know he was ordinary. He didn't make any particular effort to be charming like Lord Charles, or develop any aptitude for conversation. He was twenty-five, and, you wouldn't believe it, he still collected feathers and expected me to be interested in his feather collection. I don't mean he was retarded. He was simply absorbed in himself. He never thought about *me*. It never occurred to him to give me presents. I mean jewellery or anything like that. He gave me flowers, and I suppose *he* thought his flowers were presents, but he never gave me a bunch. He never *paid* for them. He just picked them from the garden and gave me one at a time. Or he'd give me a feather. He used to walk in the woods looking for a feather some bird had dropped and if he already had a good one in his feather collection he'd give the spare one to me. Once he gave me a twig, would you believe it, a dead twig without any leaves on it. Of course I was terribly flattered when he proposed to me, but after the first fine careless rapture he would have bored me to death. Thank heaven that young as I was I realised just in time, because it would have been an absolute disaster.'

As the sale continued, punctuated by smacking noises from Edward King's hammer, Georgina looked about her assessing the magnitude of the disaster from which she had been rescued in the nick of time. A huge shell of a house that after the sale would be practically stripped of its contents and perishingly cold. No money. There would still be crippling taxes because the sale after Lord Charles's death and the current sale following Lady Evelyn's death were only episodes in the procedure of cutting a noble family down to size.

Nevertheless, the past exuded a special aroma which had drawn her from London to rescue and treasure for herself a tiny part of it. And the Chippendale stool would look well under the Munnings in her drawing-room, and would provide an excellent subject for conversation.

'I've always felt a fondness for him. I mean, doesn't one? It must have been awful for him when I broke the engagement off because I was the love of his life. He never asked anyone else, which is why I made that silly sentimental gesture of driving all the way to Thawle to buy my stool at a hideous price, absolutely hideous.'

Continuing to look about her and still taking account of her good fortune in being married to Stephen Darcy, banker, who maintained her luxuriously in London and never questioned what she did, provided she did it with discretion, her eyes alighted on the handsome profile of a man seated in the same row but on the other side of the hall. Georgina, struck with an indefinable but confident sense of recognition, searched through the faces of the people who had passed lightly and trivially through her life. She would probably not have recognised him anywhere else. But Thawle placed him, because he belonged to Thawle.

After the sale Reggie came up to her. 'Isn't it Georgina?'

'Of course it's Georgina. And you're Reggie Thring.' She brushed her cheek on his. 'Reggie, isn't it so ridiculous that we've never kept in touch. I mean England is so small. But the world is so wide.'

Reggie didn't think it ridiculous at all as they had only met on half a dozen occasions. But he felt drawn to her, not because she appealed to him – quite the contrary – but because she had bothered to come to the sale and something told Reggie that coming to the sale had been a bother for Georgina, involving her in according to the sale precedence over more immediate pleasures, and that in doing so she had expressed an appreciation of what Thawle had once been and what she owed to it. Or had she returned in search of her youth and qualities in her character she had since discarded as uneconomical and impractical? He wondered what had happened to her over the intervening years to convert a high-spirited girl, who had given him the impression of playing about spontaneously and rather rashly on the fringes of convention, into a woman who looked to have been cast in a mould and polished up on a lathe.

'It's ridiculous,' said Georgina, 'and you'll laugh at me, but I've just paid the most exorbitant price for a stool.'

'It was a high price,' said Reggie. 'I noticed. But if you have the money and wanted it, then the price doesn't matter.' He was about to say, 'it will appreciate and next year it will be twice that price', but stopped himself in time, realising that this wasn't the reason why Georgina had bought the stool.

'You'll never guess why I bought it,' said Georgina. 'You'll think me a sentimental fool. I was sitting on that stool when Guy proposed to me. It was after dinner and I was wearing a yellow chiffon dress. We didn't marry, as you know, and it would have been a mistake because we didn't have anything in common except horses, and we never met again after Charles died, but I've always remembered Guy with such affection. And now poor darling, hasn't he had some sort of nervous breakdown or other?'

'After his mother's death,' said Reggie. 'He was devoted to his mother.'

'Weren't we all? Dear, dear Lady Evelyn.'

They fell silent. Public, dealers, and Boothby & Wigg porters swarmed around them. Suddenly Reggie wanted to tell her that Guy still kept her photograph in his bedroom. Had they met in other circumstances he would never have been tempted to expose to public view the privileged glimpse he had been allowed into Guy's private life. For certainly it would become public once he had disclosed it to Georgina who would not scruple to use it to her advantage. Moreover he knew there was no need to bolster up her ego which had every appearance of being robust and well nurtured. But meeting her after so many years against the background of Thawle, the sale, and the Chippendale stool, had generated in Reggie's spirit rich emotions demanding some form of expression.

'Come over here where there aren't so many people.' Installed between a console table and a clock, Reggie said, 'I thought you might like to know that Guy still has your photograph in his bedroom.'

Georgina clasped her hands and her inelastic face broke into a smile. Not radiant exactly, but fully extended. 'The darling! Isn't that so like him. I'm so glad you told me, Reggie. I'm very very glad.'

'I remember,' said Reggie, 'that evening when you showed me the feather he'd given you and you told me about his feather collection. It's still there, in his room, and I think he still keeps it up.'

'You see,' said Georgina, and her smile now attempted wistfulness. 'He never grew up. It wouldn't have worked and yet I still feel guilty because he must have been terribly hurt when I broke it off. I mean, he never asked anyone else.'

Driving back home Reggie regretted having told Georgina about the photograph and the feather collection, keeping at bay a deeper feeling that had he taken a close look at it, he would have recognised as shame. He knew that in some way he had betrayed Guy. But when a human being departs from normality, the world withdraws from him his right to privacy. Family and friends no longer gather about to cherish and protect him, but fall back, leaving him a subject for open discussion. The need for secrecy is instinctive to him, for he knows that once his abnormality has been detected he will be scattered to the four winds, without respect or mercy. Guy had not only surrendered his right to privacy but had left his secrets lying about unguarded. So Reggie excused his betrayal of Guy by telling himself that Guy would never know, or if he should come to know, was incapable of caring.

In betraying Guy, he shed his nostalgic attachment to Thawle and was restored to himself. An antique dealer, ex-Charterhouse, with a talent for making money honestly and a love of fine furniture which he would search for and buy wherever he could find it. The events that followed Guy's return to Thawle generated only temporary shock and thereafter, Clare, Clive, Georgina and the de Boissy family, who had all in some way become entangled, imposed diminishing claims upon his memories and ceased to trouble him.

The Second Day

ON THE MORNING of the second day the hall became turbulent with the excitement and anger of Iranians, Jews and Pakistanis who had come for the rugs. Much of the anger was directed towards a tall, blonde Danish woman, who arriving at the last moment wearing a mink-coloured suede coat and large-brimmed hat to match, practically scooped the lot. The afternoon took the sale upstairs.

Edward King had instigated the removal of the downstairs furniture into the hall because the smaller rooms, such as

Lord Charles's study and the breakfast-room, would not have contained a fraction of the expected dealers and wealthy private buyers who would object to being jostled and crammed into small rooms. But when it came to the upstairs rooms which would be of interest only to small-fry dealers, shippers and private buyers of moderate means, Edward didn't care how much jostling there would be. So the public – private and Trade – shoving, pushing and sometimes frozen immobile by a blockage in the traffic ahead, struggled up narrow stairways to nurseries and attics in pursuit of Edward King.

People unaccustomed to shouting in public could not make their bids heard and Edward's voice failed to reach the fringe of the crowd pushing up from the bottom of the stairs. Mistakes were made which Boothby & Wigg refused to rectify. One local pensioner of humble means, believing she had acquired a mahogany chest for £15, found herself in possession of a dented coal-scuttle.

Ozzie bid up to three pounds on the trunk. Magnolia, standing beside him to keep an eye on her interests, noted that the Ring, represented by Bill Thompson and Harry Scale, did not bid, so the trunk would certainly go to Ozzie. The underbidder, an ancient native, who wanted the trunk for storing blankets, dropped out at two pounds seventeen and six, but Edward went on up to three pounds two and six, taking his bid from a horse, stretching to the lead in one of the Alken prints on the wall. Ozzie, who had dropped out at three pounds, examined his fingernails while Edward scratched for another bid to get himself out of difficulties.

'Who will bid me three pounds five? Going for three pounds two and six. Who will bid me three pounds five?'

Magnolia, feeling that Ozzie was skating on thin ice, gave him a nudge. Ozzie continued to regard his fingernails, murmuring, 'Let him stew, Magnolia. Let him stew.'

'Three pounds two and six,' said Edward. 'For the last time. This fine trunk, so useful for all those little extras you don't know where to put but you don't want to part with, is going for the ridiculous price of three pounds two and six. Who will bid me three pounds five?'

With the air of being bored to death but prepared to make sacrifices, Ozzie waved his catalogue, and Edward, relieved, knocked down the lot at three pounds five.

Reggie, Clive, Frank and Clare

ON THE MORNING of the third day, at breakfast, Clive told Reggie that he wanted to go to the sale which was to finish at noon in the greenhouses.

'What on earth for?' asked Reggie.

Clive smiled briefly and tightly into his coffee cup. 'Do I have to account to you for my every whim and for every minute of my time? If you must know I thought I'd buy you some pots for your garden. You've suddenly become so interested in the garden and I have been thinking that I haven't shown sufficient interest in your interest in the garden.'

Reggie asked himself why he didn't want Clive to go to the sale and what association of ideas influenced him to remember the old man in the Bahamas who had accused Clive of unnatural sexual practices and betraying a confidence. At the time the accusation was made, Reggie had been so riveted with alarm by the mention of unnatural sexual practices, he had brushed aside the betrayal of a confidence. But having long since learned to accord justice to the first accusation he had begun to look more closely at the second. For how had Clive managed to equip himself with a £100 suit and to take trips to London and Europe costing a great deal more than his declared income and the support that Reggie provided? Whatever life he had been leading he had been able to pursue only under the aegis of Reggie's patronage, and there were days and nights, particularly nights, when Reggie was visited by a sense that for years insidious forces had been eating into his existence and that at any moment his house, his garden, his professional status as a dealer in fine antiques and his social status amongst friends who trusted him was on the point of falling into ruins. There were other days – fine and sunny – when he told himself that the old man in the Bahamas had seized on some trivial incident and exaggerated it out of all proportion because of his prejudice against unnatural sexual practices. But after a quiet day during which his fears had been put to rest he would awake at three o'clock in the morning to recall that Clive had made a tentative move to blackmail him over his valuation of the de Boissy estate.

Since that day nothing more had been said about the Empress Alexandra Feodorovna's coronation coach and Clive had become less confiding and more unpredictable. Why, for instance, did he want to go to the last day of the de Boissy sale, which would end up with the local people and the junk dealers buying ladders, spades, pot plants and garden ornaments in the greenhouses? The more enigmatic Clive became, the more Reggie feared him. But by now he was so afraid of him he did not dare refuse him the use of his car, particularly as he had said that he would stay at home that morning because he intended going to Thawle in the afternoon to settle his account with the auctioneers and arrange the transport of his furniture.

He accompanied Clive to the car as he always had in the past and keeping up old habits, entered upon in happier days unclouded by suspicions, seemed to be the only way of warding off threatening and frightening change.

While Clive backed the car out of the garage, Reggie looked down into the valley where Frank had just appeared from his cottage door. Reggie watched him close the door, and with a jacket thrown over his shoulder, because the evenings were getting chill, start walking towards the bridge on his way to the house. He came to a tall clump of grass, or maybe reeds, growing near the stream and, pausing, bent down to pick a flower. He smelt the flower and Reggie wasn't sure, but he thought that Frank smiled as he tucked it inside the neck of his shirt. He knew that Frank was unaware of being watched and was moved because he felt that Frank was bringing him a gift. He wouldn't actually give it to him, but he would show it to him and tell him what it was called and where it came from. As Reggie anticipated Frank's discourse on the origins of his flower, which would be wilted and crushed by his warm, moist chest and his shirt, his expression became tender with expectation and gratitude.

Clive put his foot on the accelerator and roared the engine. His hands clenched the wheel and his teeth clenched. His cheeks throbbed and his lips had disappeared. The withdrawal of blood from his face and generosity from his eyes struck Reggie, who had been startled out of his reverie, with foreboding. For several seconds – sufficient for the dreaming of a long dream – he was thrown back into the past and his life with Clare. A time so little regretted or remembered, but remembered more of late. There had been days when he could not recall what she looked like – the shape of her hands or the colour of her eyes – but now he saw her vividly. A woman who looked like a boy, her small head dressed with short, feathery hair; narrow hips and a flat belly. Hardly any breasts at all. He could not imagine them inflated with milk or sagging in a disgusting way. She hadn't been wearing a brassière that morning at Thawle when she had returned after her ride in the woods with Lord Charles. Perhaps she had stuffed the brassière into the pocket of her riding breeches. Her breasts were so small they had hardly moved when she walked into the Morning Room, but her nipples had been hard knobs pushing into her shirt. There had been a green smudge on her sleeve and a twig in her hair.

The car began to move. The land sloped from the house to the gate and Reggie and Clive always drove slowly down the drive in low gear. But Clive changed gear and accelerated.

'Look out!' cried Reggie.

But the car shot ahead, gathering speed, and suddenly Reggie knew that Clive was using it as a weapon to storm the bridge. At the same time understanding rushed into his mind, so that Clive, Clare and Reggie himself were suddenly torn from that comfortable version of events that he had needed to accept for his own peace of mind and rearranged into the grim but authentic relationships he had never dared to allow them. Recognising in another intended victim the calculated arrangement of Clare's death, he shouted and ran, shouting, after the car and down to the bridge where Frank stood beside the stream, holding the gate open.

The Afternoon of the Third Day

THE SALE finished at midday, after which the buyers lined up to settle their accounts with the auctioneers.

Alfie loaded the blue dishes from the greenhouses, beds, mattresses, eiderdowns, linoleum, pillows, a stair carpet, twelve saucepans of considerable age, two ladders, three spades and sundry garden ornaments into the back of his van.

Magnolia loaded her van with two footstools – wormy and the beads were coming off but could be replaced – a hatstand, four walking-sticks (one with a silver top), an Ugly Child, fourteen pots of geraniums and three cartons containing cups and saucers from the kitchen (one early Spode), a Mason's ironstone tureen, four ostrich-feather fans, twelve hats – around 1920 – a jug and basin with two soap dishes to match and the two blue dishes with the fish in the middle, from the greenhouses.

Whilst so engaged she encountered Ozzie pushing the trunk into the back of his car, alongside which she had been careful to park her van.

'What did you get it for, Ozzie?'

'They ran me up to ten quid.'

'Here's your five,' said Magnolia.

'Later, Magnolia, when we settle up. Could you just put those lusty country muscles of yours to work and give that corner a shove. Thank you, my dear.'

'Let's get it over,' said Magnolia. 'Why don't we sort it out here on the spot.'

'It'll take time,' said Ozzie. 'If we take turn by turn which is our arrangement I shall be at a disadvantage because you know what's in it and I don't. So I shall need time to look it over and consider. In your presence, of course. Taking this into account I have made up my mind not to return to London tonight and have booked myself at the Crown at Shepton where they do a very good steak-and-kidney pudding. So let us go back to your shop and we'll sort it out in peace and comfort.'

The word 'comfort' disturbed Magnolia. 'Just a minute, Ozzie.' But Alfie said he couldn't join her to defend her from Ozzie because he had to look over a cottage he'd been asked to clear. Magnolia, deciding that she could probably count on the Staff and keeping all the doors and windows open, returned to her van, but Ozzie had departed.

He was not waiting for her in her shop. He did not arrive later in the afternoon and when at seven o'clock she rang the Crown at Shepton it was not known that he had booked in there. Magnolia felt temporarily uneasy, but the excitement she had experienced when Ozzie had told her he had got the trunk from the Ring for ten quid was not to be readily allayed. Magnolia clung to the find of a lifetime and turned her mind against doubts and fears.

She unloaded her van and with all the stuff still on the pavement immediately sold one of the blue plates to Mrs Carter who fancied it for her kitty. Because of the fish. Magnolia, who believed in a quick turnover, took a small, but reasonable profit and felt satisfied.

When she had finished her tea of two boiled eggs and two cream buns and had turned on the pebble-polishing machines, she watered the magnolia tree, brought in the herbs and ticked off the kids from Church Lane who were careering about on roller skates, dragging a half-dead mangy puppy on a piece of string.

When peace reigned, Magnolia returned to her living-room to take another look at her purchases. She examined the blue dish, which was almost identical, but not quite identical, to the blue dish she had sold to Mrs Carter.

She knew nothing about it and had no idea where and when it was made. The fact of its having been used to support a pot of geraniums in a greenhouse had influenced her into supposing that it had been made by an English factory in order to support a pot of geraniums. But she had learned lessons from her years of trading which she now applied to the dish in her hand.

The Fish Dish

SHE OBSERVED that unlike factory-made plates it had an individual look. You wouldn't find another plate exactly like it, and therefore it might have been made by an artist potter. The foot rim showed marks made by some not very sophisticated instrument and in the bowl of the dish there was a glaze bubble and a small brown spot, but instead of spoiling it, the bubble and the brown spot added to its beauty, and the longer Magnolia looked at it the more she became aware of its beauty. Not only to look at, but to touch. She turned it in her hands. Again and again. It felt greasy, as if it had been dipped in butter, and when she put it down and rubbed her hands together she felt as if the butter had rubbed off and softened her finger tips. Moreover it was not, as she discovered, when she inadvertently struck the rim with a fork, whilst putting away the tableware she had used for her tea, pottery at all, as she had supposed, but porcelain. No Staffordshire blue and white plate rang with such a pure, sweet note. Magnolia began to question her first surmise that it had been made by an English potter. The blue colour, verging into green, she had never encountered in English pottery or porcelain. Nor the fish. In spite of being a maritime nation, islands surrounded by sea, the ceramic designers of Great Britain had neglected fish. Yet here were two fish, heads, fins, scales, tails, faithfully swimming about under the blue in the bottom of the dish. Dominating the dish, as though they were the whole point of the dish. So what was it? French, German, Austrian? Calling these countries to mind, Magnolia envisaged shepherds and shepherdesses, flowers, lambs, cows, courtiers in knee-breeches and black tricorn hats, playing flutes. But not a thick blue glaze that felt like butter rubbing off in your hand. And never fish. All she had discovered about the dish, after having scrutinised it for something like half an hour, was that it was mysterious and beautiful.

Magnolia rang up Reggie Thring who was the only dealer she knew with any knowledge of Chinese porcelain.

Her call was answered by a friend of Reggie's, an Edinburgh dealer whom she had encountered once or twice at Bath sales and whose almost unintelligible Scottish accent she immediately recognized.

'Hullo, Mr Matheson. May I speak to Reggie, please?'

'Is that you, Magnolia,' said Ian Matheson, immediately recognizing Magnolia's almost unintelligible Somerset accent. 'Reggie's not here. He's at the hospital in Bath.'

'What's the matter?'

'There's been a terrible accident,' said Ian Matheson. 'Clive St John has been killed. He was setting off down the drive and something must have gone wrong with the brakes or the steering because the car crashed over the bridge into the stream.'

'Good God,' said Magnolia, elated by a disaster that carried no grief. 'What's Reggie doing at the Bath hospital?'

'Someone was hurt. One of the men from the village. He had opened the gate and the car crashed into him and tipped him into the stream. Four broken ribs, but we think he'll be all right.'

Obviously it was not an appropriate time to pick Reggie's brains about Chinese porcelain. Magnolia rang Alfie.

'I'm going to London tomorrow to chase up Ozzie and my trunk. And, Alfie, don't part with those blue plates until I get back. Not over your dead body.'

Magnolia and Ozzie

OzzIE DAVID had established himself in the Portobello market some years before when most of the traders were genuine dealers and authentic spivs and crooks. The street entertainers had been pulling their concertinas on the London pavements most of their lives, and all that could be had to sustain hunger and thirst were cups of tea, beer and sandwiches.

Ozzie's shop with a flat above had been situated on the periphery of the market, but in the course of years, out-of-work actors, the sons and daughters of middle- and even upper-class families, bored with their own kind, Germans, French, Indians, Pakistanis, Iranians and American homosexuals, had extended the geography of Portobello; up the hill, down the hill, sideways and underground. Ozzie's shop had been engulfed, and now situated in the centre of the market, he could hardly fail to make a fortune.

But Thursday was not a busy day at Portobello and Ozzie was alone, sitting in what he called his office at the back, where, screened from the public by a curtain, he could fiddle his books and take a nip or two.

Magnolia, who was not on any account going behind that curtain, called him forth. Even so, the shop was not commodious. A phonograph with a large black convolvulus-shaped speaker, the head of a stag, a pianola, a Georgian flap table supporting four apothecary's jars, two paintings of Ugly Children and a stuffed pheasant occupying a glass case dressed with rock, stream, flower and fern-like objects assembled to suggest the landscape of its habitat, all crowded Magnolia into an unpleasing proximity with Ozzie's large, warm body.

'What a very pleasant surprise, Magnolia Tree,' said Ozzie, exuding from those repulsive fleshy lips a gust of cigar smoke flavoured with whisky fumes, which was not, in Magnolia's view, the consequence of a last quick swig and inhalation behind the curtain, so much as a residue that had settled in Ozzie's lungs and stomach from years of drinking and smoking in small bars, rigorously protected from any intrusion of fresh air.

Magnolia backed into the pheasant and waved her hand before her face. 'I've come about the trunk.'

'What trunk would you be talking about?' asked Ozzie. Which words were sufficient to inform Magnolia of the outcome of her dealings with Ozzie, but she saw the scene out.

'The trunk from the Thawle sale. Here's my five quid for my half-share.'

'Have you anything in writing?' asked Ozzie.

'In this profession,' said Magnolia, 'gentlemen's agreements between legitimate dealers are as binding as oaths sworn on the Bible.'

'Let us forget the Bible,' said Ozzie, 'in so much as we differ there. As to agreements between legitimate dealers, you know as well as I do that rings are illegal organisations, and should it be known that you and I have formed a ring, we could be accused of conniving to defraud the de Boissy estate.'

'A ring,' said Magnolia, 'is a circle, and it takes more than two people to make a circle. The distance between two people is a straight line. A straight, honest-to-God, honourable line that binds two people together in an agreement on which they have shaken hands like gentlemen. Now I would like to see the contents of that trunk.'

'I'm an honest trader,' said Ozzie, 'not one of those traders that keeps their best pieces for themselves. When I have sorted out the trunk you will be welcome to buy what you want in the way, I might say, that I am not able to buy in your shop.'

'Everything,' said Magnolia, 'in my shop is for sale.'

'Good. Good, Magnolia. Here is five pounds and next time I come your way I'll collect your "Pinkie" programme.'

'I'm sorry,' said Magnolia, 'but the way things are going, I put my prices up this morning. The "Pinkie" programme is ten pounds to Trade.' After which she told Ozzie what she thought of him. Ozzie listened, nodded, smiled, and when Magnolia had finished, opened the door and bowed her out into the street.

A cup of tea and fish and chips in Notting Hill revived Magnolia. An hour spent at Sotheby's revived her further. Setting off for home she felt on top of the world. 'I'll send the Staff,' she informed the boats on the Thames, the cows in the fields and the kids in the school playgrounds. 'I won't go myself. I'll send the Staff. Or Reggie. I'll buy the lot and I'll plaster them all over the window of my shop.'

The Danish Woman and the Chinese Porcelain Expert

MAGNOLIA HAD only twice previously visited Sotheby's sale rooms. On the first occasion she had hoped to establish the authenticity of what she perfectly well knew to be a piece of Gallé glass, but unsigned, they said, and therefore difficult. But they had been polite and had given her all the attention she deserved. Magnolia had felt free to browse amongst fashionably dressed women and weirdly dressed men wearing bits of velvet on the collars of their coats and talking foreign languages. She had deplored the shocking condition of the oriental rugs that muffled the tread of her forthright feet, and many of the paintings were no better than Alfie was selling for ten bob in his Gallery. On her second visit she had been told that twentieth-century English pottery was coming up but wasn't up yet, and though her plate might be by William de Morgan, on the other hand it might not. Again she browsed around. Some of the Tibetan tankas were so dark you could hardly see the hideous six-armed monsters sitting on lotus flowers, but she had been awed by a collection of Italian Renaissance jewellery.

On the present occasion – her third visit – she did not know where to go, because Sotheby's, like the supermarkets, kept changing around, so she mounted the stairs that precipitously rose from the main Bond Street entrance to the room at the top, which was crammed with drawings and water colours. The cabinets against the walls displayed Persian pottery, all broken, Magnolia noted, not being informed on Persian pottery and unaware that it is almost always broken. But she had studied, observed and handled many objects of varying age and origin since her first visit with the Gallé glass and knew that the rugs on the floor, showing soft colours that slid into one another and capricious departures from formal designs, were not to be despised. Nevertheless, Magnolia urgently needed to despise something. She chose a sketch by Augustus John and told herself she could have done better.

A sale had just finished and as she hesitated, considering her destination, a hoard of black coats and dark faces that had featured at the Thawle sale surged from an adjoining room. Shouting and gesticulating, the rug lot poured around Magnolia and disappeared down the stairs. Suddenly the room was empty, but after a moment of total silence a tall blonde woman wearing a mink-coloured suede coat and a large-brimmed suede hat to match serenely came out of the room. A chain bracelet dangled from her mink-coloured suede glove and her shoes were so designed

as to bring to mind the impossibly narrow feet supporting scraggy, elongated models in *Vogue* and *Harper's
Bazaar*.

Magnolia calculated that apart from her jewellery, she
was wearing well over £1,000, a supposition supported by
the expression on the woman's face, which was reserved and
a little vague, as though her thoughts were already settling
back into Copenhagen. Not young, but not old; not beautiful,
but noticeable; the corners of her mouth tilted in a discreet
smile, suggesting that whatever had happened at the sale
had fallen to her advantage.

Magnolia looked down at her stub-toed, lace-up shoes and
the practical ankles above them, for the first time in her
life admitting to a faint, though profitless desire to look as
that woman had looked and to know the secret of her de-
portment. To be able to sail triumphantly out of a scramble
of Pakistanis, Iranians and Jews, across the room and down
the stairs – no red rash on her neck, her confidence unshaken
and not one feather of her plumage ruffled.

Magnolia had never lacked confidence but to maintain it
she felt impelled to talk about it whenever an opportunity
allowed. The Danish rug buyer had carried with her an aura
of Arctic silence that was infinitely more impressive, because,
as there is no answer to silence, no one could refute it.
Magnolia considered emulating her example, but something
told her that if she stopped talking, nobody would notice
her. It wouldn't work.

Why not? But as her thoughts were leading her in directions which might result in the undermining of her confidence, she abandoned them. She approached a porter and
was told to go downstairs.

At a long desk where three girls and two young men were
answering telephones and scrutinising prints, miniatures and
general junk by the look of it, Magnolia awaited the arrival
of the Chinese porcelain expert. Men and girls kept coming
out of doors and disappearing into adjacent offices. Magnolia
hitched in her buttocks to avoid an enormous oil painting

of a storm at sea, showing boats in distress and sailors drowning, which two porters were transporting past the desk and along the passage ahead.

After having waited for five minutes going on for ten, Magnolia allowed herself the pleasure of indignation, for this was the territory of the snobs and the rich, and having taken one look at her lace-up shoes and her hand-knitted sweater, that girl behind the counter had said to herself here's someone we can keep waiting.

But the Chinese porcelain expert, when he eventually arrived, proved to be a youngish man wearing an anxious appearance of wanting to be pleasant. Politeness, integrity, knowledge and intelligence radiated from his face through a skin too fine and pale to hold anything back. Magnolia warmed to him. He smiled at her in a way that was little different from the smile the English porcelain expert, standing beside him, was bestowing on an overdressed Knightsbridge tart polluting the air with French perfume.

'They're rather late,' the English porcelain expert was saying, 'and they are extensively repaired.'

'This is a lovely piece,' said the Chinese porcelain expert, his eyes alight, possibly with greed, but also with obvious appreciation of Magnolia's blue dish.

He stared at the two fish, head to tail in the bottom of the dish, turned the dish over and examined the foot. His hands were as white as wax candles, and his fingertips, branching out a little from long, thin bones interspersed with knobbly knuckles, were flat and square. These fingertips, endowed with tactile intelligence, tenderly followed the circle of the foot rim and roamed about over the dish. They thought; they considered; they made up their minds.

'A beautiful specimen,' he said, 'in first-class condition. Sung.'

'English blue and white and art nouveau glass are my speciality,' said Magnolia, 'but I can spot quality when I see it. Sung is early, isn't it?'

'This plate could have been made around 1100,' said the Chinese porcelain expert, 'but you mustn't assume that early Chinese porcelain is necessarily valuable. There is really quite a lot of it around. It is a matter of quality and this is a fine-quality piece. The colour is superb and the fish exceptionally finely moulded. I think you could put a reserve on it of £300.'

Magnolia pulled a hard rein on her racing thoughts which had careered off to the twelve blue dishes, half of them hers, in the back of Alfie's van, to the shop she would buy in the main street when she had sold her present premises, the Ford Cortina she would buy when she had sold her van and the twice-a-year trips she would make to the States to establish contacts for the disposal of her ginger-ale bottles. And Ozzie David's entire theatre programme collection, mounted as a special exhibition in Bath and attracting London Trade, collectors and Princess Margaret.

While she signed a form and her trade name, Magnolia Tree Antiques, which allowed her a reduction in auction costs, she became aware that she and the Chinese porcelain expert, who was still lovingly fondling her dish, were not alone. Drawn by the realisation that eyes were upon her, her glance fell upon the sleeve of a jacket, ostentatiously checked, and extending from the cuff, a hand which was also engaged in filling out a form.

Dave Dawes, a small cog in the machinery of the Ring and stooge to Bill Thompson and Harry Scale, stood beside her, stinking of beer, Magnolia observed, though she had not smelt the beer until she recognized him and knew he would certainly stink of beer. Recalling Syd's slashed tyres, Magnolia declared in a ringing voice, 'In this trade it isn't numbers, power and intimidation that pay off in the end. It's taste, knowledge and expertise. The crooks in this trade, after a quick buck, are too stupid to realise that if they did some homework and invested the money they squander on beer and cigarettes on a good reference library they'd be a lot better off.'

But the latter part of this declaration fell upon the innocent and uncomprehending Chinese porcelain expert, Dave Dawes having swiftly departed.

Magnolia's Answering Service

AT SIX-THIRTY, Alfie, expecting that Magnolia would by now have returned from London, rang her up.

'This is Magnolia Tree,' a voice replied, 'specialist in fairings, English blue and white, Victorian and art nouveau glass, early postcards and theatre programmes. At the moment I am absent on business and if you have any transaction you wish to discuss with me please leave your name and telephone number and state the nature of your business. I am not interested in postcards that do not have some social or historical significance, or in theatre programmes after 1930, so please do not waste my time by bringing me the programmes of plays you attended last month at the Bristol Old Vic or the Bath Repertory. I do not give free valuations and I am not interested in damaged pieces of porcelain, apart from famille rose. Your reply will be recorded and, providing your request for my time and opinion is not irresponsible, I will call you back. I receive Trade only on Saturdays.'

Alfie was forever awed by this discourse and always heard it through because you had to if you wanted to get a word in. 'Magnolia,' he said, 'It's me, Alfie. When you get back give me a ring.'

Mrs Carter's Kitty

ON HER RETURN, Magnolia set in motion the pebble-polishing machines, took in the potted herbs and set off to visit Mrs Carter, three doors down the street. Four of Mrs Carter's illegitimate kids were dashing about creating a nuisance outside Magnolia's shop where they always congregated because the pavement was wider there. Magnolia ticked them off and the kids fell silent, waiting until Magnolia was admitted to Mrs Carter's cottage before they started up again.

Mrs Carter was seated in front of the telly, and the Staff, his huge feet hooked over the bottom rung of one of Alfie's five-bob wormy chairs, looked just about as intelligent as he was with his eyes about to drop out, but very deft with his hands when wrapping up a parcel so there must be a brain somewhere to get the message to the hands.

Magnolia, considering the delicacy of her mission, refrained from telling him to keep his mouth shut when stuffing himself with potato chips and bread and butter. She had to wait for 'Coronation Street' to finish before it was possible to talk.

'Mrs Carter. I've come to discuss with you that plate you bought from me yesterday. I have discovered that it is worth quite a lot of money. So I suggest that you let me take it to London and put it up for auction at Sotheby's.'

Mrs Carter deferred her reply while she made a pot of tea. She poured herself a cup, omitting to offer one to Magnolia, perhaps inadvertently, being immersed in thought.

Magnolia said, 'Do you know who Sotheby's are?'

'Of course,' said Mrs Carter. 'They're on the telly.' She sipped her tea and thought. 'How much is it worth?'

'They say it could be worth £300.'

'Either it is or it isn't,' said Mrs Carter, evincing no signs of shock and stirring her tea.

'At auction,' said Magnolia, 'you can't calculate on a fixed price. It might go for more and it might go for less.'

'How much more?' asked Mrs Carter.

'I don't know.'

'Didn't you ask them?'

'They don't know either. I've explained to you. Nobody can tell what something will bring in auction.'

'If they don't know,' said Mrs Carter, 'how is anyone to know? It's their job.'

'But it all depends on the bidding. There might be a couple of ignorant fools running it up, but the auctioneers don't know that. All they can do is give an estimate which is based on their knowledge and experience, and what I am suggesting to you is that you let me take your plate to Sotheby's and put it up for auction. You will get the money, less my commission.'

'What do you mean your commission?'

'Ten per cent for handling the transaction, for my time, wear and tear on my car and my expertise in finding out that your plate is worth a lot of money.'

'What is ten per cent of £300?' asked Mrs Carter, after a long pause for thought.

'£30,' said Magnolia.

Mrs Carter put down her cup with a force that rattled the spoon in the saucer. 'Magnolia Tree, I haven't got £30 and if I had why should I give it to you?'

'But you will have when you've sold your plate. It might go for more and it might go for less and I am asking you to let me handle the transaction on the basis of a ten per cent commission.'

'Now you're saying it's less than £300,' observed Mrs Carter. 'How much less?'

Magnolia wished she were dealing with honest Trade like Alfie who would have gone fifty-fifty. 'Nobody knows what it will go for. It might go for £500.'

'So now you're confessing to me that it's worth £500,' said Mrs Carter. 'You've been holding things back.'

'I don't know what it will sell for,' said Magnolia, 'but it's certainly worth more than the ten bob you paid me and it's stupid to leave it on your kitchen floor for someone to trip over when you might be able to sell it for quite a bit of money.'

'You said £300,' said Mrs Carter. 'Then you said £500. Then you got cagey and you said less than £300, but you didn't say how much less. Why don't I take it to some other auction where it will bring more than £300? It might bring £600. And why do I have to pay you £30? There won't be anything left.' Mrs Carter poured herself another cup of tea and with a trembling hand spilled the sugar.

'Mrs Carter,' said Magnolia, her anger becoming evident in the rash that was breaking out on her neck. 'Suppose I had come here and said that I'd buy back your plate for five quid after having sold it to you for ten bob. What would you have said? I could have bought it back, put it up to auction and kept the £300 for myself.'

'£500,' said Mrs Carter. 'You put it up. You said £500.'

'What would you have said?' Magnolia insisted.

After some thought Mrs Carter replied, 'Kitty likes it.'

'Be honest. What would you have done?'

Mrs Carter considered, but in the face of the information Magnolia had supplied her found it difficult to be honest. 'I think,' she said, her eyes roving about the pine-dresser, teacups hanging on hooks, a pile of dirty dishes in the sink and the Staff, goggle-eyed, stuffing down the last of the potato chips – and only passing over Magnolia as if she didn't exist, 'I think I would like to keep the plate because of kitty. Because of the fish.'

'You would have sold it back to me,' said Magnolia, 'for five quid if I hadn't told you what it was worth.'

'But you did, didn't you?' said Mrs Carter.

'Mrs Carter, after I sold you that plate I closed down my business which means a loss of income to say nothing of petrol and wear and tear on the car and my return ticket from Bath to London all in order to go to Sotheby's in London to confirm an opinion I had about your plate, and my opinion has been formed over many years of research and the expenditure of a great deal of money on an extensive reference library. If I were a lawyer or a doctor, for the information and expertise that I am providing you I could send you a bill for twenty quid.'

'But you won't, will you,' said Mrs Carter, 'because you

aren't. And I don't see why I can't go up to Sotheby's on my own. With that £500 I could put in a bathroom and have a holiday.'

'You know perfectly well you haven't been up to London in your life. Do you imagine you are ever going to muster the courage to go to Sotheby's and tackle all that lot?'

'I went up to London with Fred,' said Mrs Carter, 'for the Festival of Britain.'

'And since then I'll bet you haven't even been to Bath. You need an agent to handle your affairs. Up in London, handling a delicate transaction like selling your plate, you'd be smashed to pieces. You'd be ground underfoot. Whereas I have had long years of experience with the London auction rooms. They respect me. I can handle them.'

'I can handle my own affairs,' said Mrs Carter, 'and if my plate is worth £500 in Sotheby's I'll take it to London myself, so thank you very much, Magnolia Tree, but I'm not going to be talked out of what is rightfully mine.'

'Suppose I hadn't told you about the plate. I didn't have to tell you. I put my cards on the table.'

'But you did, didn't you?' said Mrs Carter. 'And if you hadn't told me, kitty could have had it. Kitty likes it because of the fish. And what's more, Magnolia Tree, Timmy won't be working for you any more. He's worn to a shred and he's got his lessons.'

Back home, Magnolia sloshed cold water on her face to bring down the rash, made a cup of tea and turned on the answering service.

Alfie and the French Butchers

THEY CROWDED into the narrow passage that wound through Alfie's warehouse from the street to the Gallery and the yard outside, and which, like a river threading its way through a deep ravine, was darkly enclosed by banks of wardrobes, bedsteads piled to the ceiling, chairs, also piled to the ceiling all in a tangle, and mattresses smelling of wet sheep. On the marble top of a chiffonier they put down hats, raincoats and a large saw.

'There were six of them,' Alfie told Magnolia, 'and you're just a fool if you take on six, especially if three of them happens to be Bill Thompson, Morry Fleet and Harry Scale. It's that Harry Scale that won't use his fists that worries me. It was Morry Fleet that did the talking. Bill Thompson didn't say a word. Just stood aloof, sort of lost in thought. "We've come to buy your plates," says Morry, "that you bought from the Thawle greenhouses. You paid ten quid for those plates and we'll give you fifteen quid which shows you a decent fifty per cent profit for a quick turnover." Well, what with that and after what you said I got the message and I said, "I don't want to sell those plates. Not at the present moment. I've got them on reserve for a customer."

'I've done business with Morry Fleet,' Alfie went on, 'and I've flogged him some chiffoniers and chests for his shipments and he's always paid cash from his pocket but I never liked the look of him. Every time he comes here I see him casting his eyes around. Summing things up. "Alfie," he said, "you've built up a very good business in rags and feathers. And you've gone up in the world into brass bedsteads and pine chests. You've made a lot of money, because the word gets around and aren't you the proud owner of four houses down Church Lane where you are exacting exorbitant rents from poor old people who can't afford what you're asking with no bathrooms, and no amenities, exploiting the needs of the poor." My blood rose in indignation, Magnolia, because only last month I did up No. 3 and put in that gas stove we got out of Rose Cottage, and for that amenity I didn't put up the rent one penny. Not one penny. "So, Alfie," Morry goes on, "you're doing very well and we don't interfere with you so we expect you not to interfere with us." "I don't interfere with anyone," I said. "We even," he says, "leave you alone with your tweet-tweet and your tinkle-tinkle," which is his way of referring in an insulting manner to my bird and my musical collection. "So, Alfie," he goes on, "you have got to respect our territory which is high-quality goods like Chinese porcelain. Unless you like to join us and bring us in on your rags and feathers and your tinkle-tinkle and your tweet-tweet-tweet." '

'What did you say to that, Alfie?' Magnolia asked.

'I didn't say nothing,' said Alfie. 'I folded my arms and I sneered. Then Harry Scale took out a knife and began to sharpen it on that sofa and careless as you might say, turned the blade.'

Magnolia regarded the upholstery of the sofa.

'I could have stood that,' said Alfie, 'but there were six of them and they said they'd have a go at my horses. Morry said that the Irish ship their old horses to France and in France there are butchers' shops with horses' heads painted all in gold and they eat horses. Is that true, Magnolia? Do they eat horses in France?'

'I wouldn't put it past them,' said Magnolia. 'Next to the Blacks, the Yids, the Pakistanis, the Irish, the Scots and the Spanish, the French are the worst.'

'That's the best merry-go-round in the West,' said Alfie. 'I pass my evenings polishing it up, washing down the horses and putting on a bit of paint where it's flaked off. But out they all went to the back. Then Morry says to Harry Scale, "Go and get that saw. What we want is some good heads for those French butchers." And he wanders about, feeling them over and looking for the best head. Then he stops in front of the one I like best that's called "Dancer" with a floating mane. "A coat of gold paint," he says, "and you couldn't find a better head for a French butcher." Then Harry Scale came back with the saw. They started on his neck, Magnolia. Just come and have a look.'

Out in the backyard he showed her the marks of the saw on 'Dancer's' neck. 'I couldn't let it go on, Magnolia. I couldn't let them have a go at my horses. And I'm sorry after what happened to you today with Ozzie David, but I couldn't let them have a go at my horses.'

Alfie delivered a hard kick at one of the garden ornaments he had brought back from the Thawle sale. One of a pair of cement tortoises. White paint, disturbed by Alfie's kick, flew off in flakes. Alfie nursed his foot.

Magnolia leant down to rub her finger on the glossy, milk-white material displayed beneath the coat of paint on the tortoise. She scraped off more paint and felt again.

'Don't sell those tortoises, Alfie,' she said, 'and hide them somewhere.'

'I'm not moving them again,' said Alfie. 'They're as heavy as lead.'

'Cover them up,' said Magnolia. 'Put all those sacks on them and that load of wood. Don't let anyone see them.' After which, Magnolia returned to Magnolia Tree Antiques to consult her reference library.

The Jungle and the Elephants

'I'M SORRY about the greenhouses,' said Irene. 'I had to tell Mr Tippett you wanted to clear them out because Mr St John told me if I didn't he'd tell what you did to the pictures and you'd be put in gaol. I think Mr St John was going to buy the ponies and the tortoises, but he was killed and he never got to the sale. I didn't know till it was too late and I couldn't have done anything because I haven't got the authority. I thought I'd find out who bought them and get them back, but I knew I couldn't because I haven't got any money. I'm truly sorry. But they didn't get the Chun bowls. I took them up to my room.'

Guy made no answer and Irene didn't know if he had understood. He sat, crouched in his chair, staring down at the lawn. Every now and again he clenched his hands.

Two of the nurses came out to collect the patients and take them back indoors. One of the nurses approached the old lady and hauled the spaniels off her feet where they had curled up on the end of her shawl. The old lady pushed out her arthritic neck, trying to raise her head, but managing to raise only her eyebrows and eyes. The nurse leaned over her, putting a hand on her arm. The old lady shook it off and Irene could see that she was angry.

What does it matter if she's cold? thought Irene. She loves the dogs and they love her. Why couldn't the nurse have brought a rug and left them alone together? No one ever visits her. She's old and perhaps they're all she's got. It's all for her own good, that nurse would say. What good does she want at her age? All she wants is to be happy. Like Dr Templeton saying it's the best place for him, when Irene last week had asked why he couldn't come home when the sale was over.

Irene knitted four more rows. Guy sat huddled in his chair, staring at the lawn and the clumps of grass with ants and beetles blundering through them.

It was dark in the forest. The parsley trees, drooping their branches over the sky, kept out the sun, making the air under their succulent trunks heavy and green. But near the pool where the vegetation thinned out and slopes of white sand slipped to the water, the light still came down because it was evening and the time for the elephants to come out of the forest for their bath. Guy was small and hid behind a pebble to watch the elephants. Beetles crawled about in the parsley trees. One of them fell with a crash on its back and waggled its legs, trying to turn over. Guy felt he ought to come to its aid but it frightened him. Its legs were metal tubes fitted together with joints. It looked like something clever made in a factory, except that it moved. He didn't feel it was human. Of course it wasn't, but he couldn't feel that it had ever been human or ever could be. It didn't have anything to do with mankind, and yet, if it didn't have anything to do with mankind, why did he receive from its struggling body such an impression of terror and suffering. He wanted to help it, but he couldn't because he was afraid of its claws that were like bunches of wire, waving and clutching for something to hook themselves on to. Then suddenly with a tremendous effort it turned itself over and waddled down to the pool. As big as a tortoise, but not so pleasant. The opal puppy came down to lap the water. The marks of his paws in the sand were the size of soup-plates and when he lapped he made waves in the water. He was twice the size of Guy. Guy hid behind the pebble.

The elephants came. First of all Claudius, so enormous that Guy shrank in terror behind the pebble. Mark trampled the ferns, breaking all the vegetation that had been provided for the elephants as a beautiful sanctuary for peaceful creatures. Instead of frolicking in the pool, blowing water out of their trunks and washing their backs, they charged one another, bellowed and roared. Claudius charged Mark and his tusks ripped a gash in Mark's side. The puppy dashed in and pulled off shreds of flesh. Elephants charged out of the jungle and hurled themselves into the pool, churning up mud, so that the water was brown. Then it was red.

Jimmy came, rose pink and twitching an ear. Here comes Jimmy, thought Guy, to save the day. But Jimmy's eyes, which when he was small were two tiny rose diamonds twinkling with fun, blazed like fiery lamps, angry and terrible. He stood, waving his head and flapping his ear. He was not interested in the other elephants. He had seen Guy and he charged the pebble. Lifting it in his tusks he tossed it over the parsley trees as though it had no more substance than a balloon. Guy, exposed to the stampede of the elephants, lay on the beach without any shelter and buried his head in the sand.

Guy sat huddled in his chair, his face in his hands. Irene put her hand on his arm and gently shook him. 'I have to go now,' she said. 'The nurse is coming to take you indoors.'

Guy looked up. Irene took his hand and pressed it because there was no look of recognition in his eyes. 'I have to go now,' she repeated. 'The nurse is coming.'

Guy put his hand in the pocket of his coat and gave her his letter. 'Would you give this to Mummy?'

In spite of the nurse, crossing the lawn and quite close, and Dr Templeton and Dr Gore, one of the best psychiatrists in England, and all their instructions telling her what she should say and what she shouldn't say, Irene bent over Guy and kissed him.

'Darling, she can't read your letter. She's dead.'

'I know,' said Guy, seizing her hands and crushing them till she thought he would break her fingers.

Letters to a Dead Mother

BUT HE HAD known before when he talked about Lord Robert's wreath at the funeral and wanting to keep the Morning Room where his mother had been young and beautiful and not her bedroom where she had been dying. The truth had flicked on and off like the neon signs in the shops across the road from her mother's lodgings. Driving back home, Irene thought it all over and although she couldn't have put it into words she knew that even if Guy came out of the darkness and solitude of the past months, he would have to be damaged, it stood to reason, and forever haunted by the places he had been.

Up in her room she changed into a 1924 pastel pink wool dress with long black points on the hem and onyx buttons, because Dr Templeton was coming at nine to collect Guy's letters to his mother.

There wasn't much room left in Irene's suite because of the furniture from Lady Evelyn's bedroom. It was almost as cramped as her room in Fulham Road and she had to push the bed around in order to sit down in front of Lady Evelyn's dressing-table.

Irene took a handful of hairpins out of the Chun bulb bowls, now containers for hairpins, combs, safety-pins and rubber-bands. Holding hairpins in her teeth, she pushed others into her hair. There was plenty of time and she wanted to look her best. She also needed time to think about the letters and referred her decision to the four lovely girls who had directed her life – not asking their advice, but rather because she was putting them to a test, as they had put her to tests over the years.

Katherine Bush. Intelligent, brave, but hard and ambitious. Never loving or compassionate. Katherine would have used the letters as she had used everything and everyone to further her own fortunes.

Lady Diana Mayo was hardly worth considering. She would have thrown them to the desert winds and galloped away over the sandhills on the most vicious and uncontrollable Arab stallion she could lay hands on.

Evangeline would have opened them, again to further her ambitions. Not for the same motives as Katherine Bush, but because, sitting in a black dress under a light that enhanced the dazzling splendour of her skin and driving Lord Robert wild, she was a minx, just a kitten, and would have read the letters for some clue to trap her man. But with no feeling of obligation to Guy or Lady Evelyn.

And Ambrosine . . . . Having arranged her hair, Irene descended to the kitchen. Ambrosine would have done what Irene was about to do now. She would have burnt the letters, as Irene was now burning them in the kitchen range, tearing them up and putting them into the fire. But not because this was the best thing to do for Guy and Lady Evelyn. Ambrosine would have burnt them as a point of honour, French honour, because she was Ambrosine Eustacie Marquise de Calincourt, and members of noble French families did not read other people's letters. They lost their heads to the guillotine.

When she had put the last of the letters into the fire, Irene continued to stare at the flames, turning the letters black and curling them up.

'Lady Evelyn,' she said, 'I'll look after him as I swore I would when I first saw him in Lyons Corner House in Tottenham Court Road. I made up my mind on that day and I never faltered. Uncle George raped me in the bushes but I kept myself pure for the man of my choice. Mother told me all about you. How you lived three doors down in Fulham Road and were in the front row of The Gaiety. She was only a little girl then, but she told me how beautiful you were and how she used to admire you. She told me how you were never stuck up and after you married Lord Charles you used to go back to the King's Arms and have a reunion with the Gaiety girls. Once a year, you used to make a special journey to London to see your old friends until they got married. One of them married a lord like you, but some of them dwindled away. Mother told me how you helped them when they fell on hard times though they never asked. And you still went up until there were only three of you left. So when Mother died and I didn't have a roof over my head, I packed my bags. I knew you wouldn't turn me away because, like you, I was up from Fulham Road. You took me in and we never talked about it because it wouldn't have been correct for us to talk. But we understood. You taught me how to walk and how to wear your dresses and you corrected my grammar. You prepared me, Lady Evelyn, but you died too soon and I'm not properly prepared. And now I'm going to have his baby. It might be a boy, but I hope it's a girl, just as sweet and beautiful as you. But I can't look after him if you keep interfering and won't let him go. Please, Lady Evelyn, please let him go.'

Irene closed the door of the kitchen range, and made final preparations for the arrival of Dr Templeton. She wasn't sure what wine she should offer him and what were the correct glasses. She knew that the wide flat-topped glasses were for wine with bubbles and the ones that were taller and shaped like a tulip kept in the smell. The smaller ones were for sherry. She wished she had the assurance of Lord Guy who being an aristocrat didn't care what he did and gave Dr Templeton wine in the jars they kept for jam after they had finished the peanut butter. Then she told herself that if Lord Guy gave Dr Templeton wine in peanut butter glasses it didn't matter what sort of glass she chose. Wine, champagne, sherry, brandy – it didn't matter. Who was Dr Templeton to criticise? He was her guest, and probably he knows more about wine than I do, thought Irene, but I know about other things. I know about my mother and her gentlemen and about Uncle pulling me into the bushes. Nothing like that ever happened to Dr Templeton. And I know about Guy and what's best for him, whatever Dr Templeton likes to say.

She received Dr Templeton in the Morning Room, seated in Lady Evelyn's favourite George II armchair of Virginia walnut. Reclining her back against the negro boy with the tasselled sunshade, she held her hands quiet in the lap of her dress.

'I burned them,' she said, in answer to Dr Templeton's question.

Dr Templeton was very angry. 'Dr Gore,' he said, 'believed, as indeed so did I, that those letters contained invaluable information and would have assisted him in treating Lord Guy's condition. You have done no service to Lord Guy.'

When he had finished admonishing her for the irresponsibility of her actions, Irene said, 'I would like you to discharge him from that place and bring him back home.'

Dr Templeton became yet more angry and went on talking for some time about Dr Gore, recounting his qualifications and successes in that firm confident voice that defeated the merest thought of contradiction.

When he paused for a moment, Irene said, 'There was an old woman in that place and she loved the spaniels, but she wasn't allowed to have them because it was time for her to go indoors. I don't expect she's got much longer to live and she would have preferred staying outside in the cold and dying with the spaniels.'

'I perfectly understand what you mean,' said Dr Templeton, 'but you are not taking into consideration the routine of a hospital and the hours worked by the nursing staff. Your argument is humane and understanding but in its application totally impracticable.'

'We don't have a routine here,' said Irene, 'or working hours.'

Dr Templeton found himself bereft of a reply.

'All I am saying,' said Irene, 'is that some people are sick so you try and make them better, but some people are old, and there isn't much you can do about that. And some people are different. Why can't you leave them alone and let them be happy? I don't believe that Lord Guy is sick in any way you can cure. He talks to Percy, he sees ghosts, he writes letters to his mother which are things that most people don't do, because he's different.'

'Guy,' said Dr Templeton, 'is suffering from a severe breakdown brought about by the death of his mother and his desperate attempt to preserve this estate. You know nothing about these matters.'

'You won't change him,' said Irene, 'because he's different. He's probably always talked to Percy, only you haven't noticed before. Sometimes he thinks I'm his mother. He gets people muddled up. So do I. So does everyone. He just does it more, so you notice. Why shouldn't he? What's it got to do with us? Just let him come back and be happy.'

Dr Templeton's thoughts were more forthright than his conversation. Who are you, you under-age bastard Cockney daughter of a prostitute with a bastard child in your belly, to tell me what I should and should not do and what is best for Guy? What right have you to set yourself up as mistress in this house?

Irene leaned forward and turning back the black velvet cuff of her dress, poured two glasses of wine. 'I don't know,' she said, 'whether this is the sort of wine to drink after

207

dinner, or whether it should be taken with dinner or may-be before, but it's a good wine and I know you like good wine.'

As she spoke Irene felt a confidence in herself she had never felt when Lady Evelyn was alive. Lady Evelyn had instructed her in all sorts of kind and delicate ways. Irene had been slow to learn because there hadn't been any back-ground and she had been very raw material. She saw that now. She had listened and imitated, but there was something about waiting around for instructions that kept you back-ward, so the instructions only really worked when you were left on your own. The instructions of Evangeline, Lady Diana Mayo, Katherine Bush and Ambrosine had carried her a long way, but they weren't of use any more. They hadn't been adequate to deal with her present situation. Just at the right moment Lady Evelyn had stepped in and Irene felt that she would follow Lady Evelyn's instructions for ever because they would never let her down, but would carry her along through happiness and disaster, gracefully, wisely and power-fully. One of the things that Lady Evelyn had told her was that breaking the rules of social behaviour didn't matter, providing you didn't make people feel uncomfortable. 'But never,' Lady Evelyn had said, 'get uppish about rules. Never break them on purpose just to make other people feel ill-at-ease. And never, never worry about them if you don't know exactly what they are because this is just another way of making people feel uncomfortable.'

'I have never had the opportunity to learn much about wine,' said Irene. 'Lord Guy used to open a bottle occasion-ally, but Lady Evelyn preferred Guinness or beer. I expect it was different when Lord Charles was alive and they had so many dinner parties, but all that has changed since I've been here.'

Her composure, her air of resolution and the unashamed way in which she had confessed her ignorance about the wine overpowered Dr Templeton and vanquished his anger.

As they drank the wine, they discussed the sale and the

death of Clive St John. Irene asked questions about Paris. The evening wore on until Dr Templeton, looking at his watch, saw how late it was. By the time he stood up to make his departure it had become clear to him that without money or position, unidentified and unplaced, unmarried and pregnant as she was, Irene had established a right to demand that Guy should be discharged from the nursing home and a right to preside over the future of Thawle. Not because these rights had been bequeathed to her or invested in her but because she had earned them and claimed them.

So Guy came home.

Sydney's Overcoat

I COULD BUY that, said Syd to himself, as unsteady with midday beer and knocked about by the push and shove of the crowds, he descended the hill to Portobello. Or that. A good-sized premises partitioned off inside into stalls selling maps, Japanese swords, books, jewellery, assorted junk, snuff bottles, watches, books, jewellery, and assorted junk. Or that. Not partitioned off. A self-contained shop selling quality oak and bits of treen. Or another good-sized shop next door selling pictures, with a real quality window showing only one exhibit, a large sand picture of a recumbent lion. Very nice. Living quarters above. I could buy them both, thought Syd, and put up two stalls outside. I could handle one shop myself and lease the other and the two stalls. I could live over one and make a nice flat for Mum in the other so I wouldn't have to listen to her grouching all the time and we could meet at meals.

But whatever he bought, one shop or two, with or without stalls, he could leave the claustrophobic fresh air of Somerset and come back to the Jews, the Cockney crooks, the out-of-work actors, the scramble of languages, the rush around in the morning for the real trading before the tourists arrived, sandwiches in cafés full of steam and smoke, cups of real strong tea, the tom-cats on the roofs, rotten oranges in the gutters, the queers, the street musicians, the monkey people and all the lovely muck of Portobello.

I could buy that, thought Syd, stopping in front of Ozzie David's shop. A fair-sized shop and Ozzie dressed a very presentable window. The musical box in the centre, labelled 'Sublime Harmonie – three combs, 127 teeth and eight airs', isolated to emphasise its importance. Two apothecary's jars on the right-hand side and a pheasant in a glass case on the left. A quality window, Syd had to admit, with only half a dozen theatre programmes cast about in front of the 'Sublime Harmonie', cluttering the effect.

Syd slipped into the pub next door for another beer. But the beer, instead of keeping him on top of the world, dampened his spirits and brought his mind back to the as yet unanswered problem as to how he was to reward Alfie and Magnolia for letting him have a free go on the Vicky sofa. Of course they hadn't known about the drawings, but neither had he until he got around to having it re-upholstered. So how did you pay off an obligation like that? Sydney had never faced such a problem and didn't know how to deal with it.

Suppose he split £200,000 three ways so that Alfie could go to India to buy those Silver Clouds from the maharajahs and Magnolia could realise all her ambitions. Then Sydney would be left with little more than £60,000. Hardly enough to buy two shops with living quarters, one for himself and one for Mum. Then he'd have to put in bathrooms and do them up, probably put on new roofs, new plumbing, have them all rewired because nothing had been done to these slums since the war. Stock for two shops and two stalls outside. £60,000 would disappear into thin air with nothing to show for it.

If, on the other hand, he gave them only £10,000 each and they found out he had made £200,000 from the drawings in the Vicky sofa, they would think he was mean. Mean as a Jew.

Sydney decided it was no solution to give them a third share each or even £10,000 because they wouldn't accept it. Alfie would say, the Ring swiped my celadon plates that were worth a fortune and Magnolia would say, that crook Ozzie David cheated me out of my theatre programmes, but that's all in the game and good luck to you, Syd. We're glad you've put it over the Ring that slashed your tyres and we won't take a penny. Syd knew that was what they'd say because in their position it was what he would say himself. He'd feel unhappy taking their money. Under an obligation.

Back out in the street Sydney had another look at the 'Sublime Harmonie' in Ozzie's window. Being Saturday the street was crammed and people kept knocking into him. Somebody blew a trumpet and the monkeys in their striped knitted jackets jumped on the shoulders of tourists, while the people who owned the monkeys took photographs. Sydney felt positively miserable and almost wished he hadn't bought the Vicky sofa. On an impulse, he opened the door of Ozzie's shop which proved to be empty, until Ozzie appeared from behind the curtain.

'I've come,' said Syd, 'to buy that musical box.'

'I didn't know,' said Ozzie, 'as you were interested in musical boxes.'

'I've got a customer,' said Syd.

'I can't give you trade discount,' said Ozzie. 'It's under-priced.'

'Every legitimate dealer,' said Syd, 'gives discount to Trade.'

'It plays eight airs,' said Ozzie, 'and it's under-priced.'

'Why did you under-price it?' asked Syd. 'An experienced trader like you who knows you ought to allow ten per cent to Trade?'

'That is a collector's piece,' said Ozzie, 'and I'm not particularly interested in selling it to Trade.'

'I didn't think you were,' said Syd, wishing, as he fished out a bundle of notes from the top inside pocket of his overcoat and counting out £35, that his hands wouldn't shake. Because it wasn't that he was mean and didn't like paying out money. There was nothing he enjoyed more. And shaking was probably hereditary.

It was when he put the thirty-five quid into Ozzie's outstretched hand and avoiding Ozzie's eye, because of his embarrassment over shaking, that he saw to one side of Ozzie's shop the trunk from the attic at Thawle which had contained the theatre programmes so ardently desired by Magnolia Tree.

'I'd like it carefully packed,' said Syd, 'in a carton.'

Ozzie took the musical box out of the window and departed with it behind his curtain. Syd, alone in the shop, approached the trunk. He lifted the lid. Reaching inside, he grabbed a handful of the contents and thrust them into the left-hand bottom pocket of his overcoat. Reaching in once more he filled the right-hand bottom pocket. He filled all the pockets, the two big ones outside and the four bigger inside ones. A good deal remained in the trunk but there was a limit to the capacity of his overcoat. He squashed it down and put in some more. When this had been squashed down he retired to the window to pretend he was looking at the apothecary's jars. He felt enormous and very hot. He trembled all over. Not just his hands.

He'd never pinched a thing in his life, though he wouldn't go so far as to say he never would if he and his mother were starving, because they'd never starved. But there were things you could do for other people that you couldn't do for yourself. Perhaps you passed on the guilt. But that couldn't be so because Magnolia wasn't going to feel guilty. She wouldn't have done it for herself, but she wouldn't feel guilty. Maybe the guilt would drop off somewhere in the gutter with the ice-cream cartons and all the rubbish up on the way to Notting Hill. Or even if he kept it intact for Magnolia it would wither away before he passed it over because she hadn't pinched the theatre programmes. The decision had been his and he didn't feel guilty because although he'd filled his pockets for the first time in his life he hadn't done it for himself but for Magnolia Tree who was an honest trader that had had a rotten deal and, in spite of her anti-Jewish prejudices, had helped him when he needed help.

Ozzie appeared with the musical box in a carton and Syd, carrying it in both hands, walked to the top of the street and hailed a taxi for Paddington.

He put the musical box on the seat beside him and fished in a pocket for a handkerchief to wipe the sweat from his face. But with all those programmes he couldn't find a handkerchief and wiped his face on his sleeve instead. Another man would have opened the taxi window for fresh air to dry himself off, but not Sydney, who was thankfully saying goodbye to fresh air for ever.

The Octagonal Room

ONE FINE NIGHT in late autumn when Irene was entering into the eighth month of her pregnancy, Guy, around midnight, awoke with an urgent sense that something needed to be done. Controlling his agitation and moving quietly so as not to disturb Irene, he dressed and descended by the back stairs to the Octagonal Room. The tables and mirrors were too cumbersome for him to manage without assistance and he didn't want to wake Giles because of the need for secrecy, but he carried out the twelve Adam chairs, two at a time and piled them up on the front terrace.

He collected kindling from the copper cauldron alongside the kitchen range and set alight to the Adam chairs. Standing back, watching the flames and the smoke dimming the sparkle of the stars, Guy experienced an exhilarating sense of achievement and told Irene when she woke up in the morning that he had dealt with at least one of the problems which would confront their son, who was to be called Wilfred.

But for the next few days he became very quiet and Irene knew that he was reconsidering and perhaps regretting his hasty decision about the Adam chairs. Later he suggested that they might try to recover some of the treasures of Thawle. They couldn't trace the Victorian sofa in which he had installed some of the French drawings, because four Victorian sofas had gone in the sale and Edward King told them that they had been bought by the Ring so heaven alone knew where they had ended up. But Edward disclosed the name of the dealer who had bought the garden ornaments.

Alfie wasn't in his shop and they talked to a girl who wasn't very bright in Irene's opinion. At first she didn't remember anything about the ponies and the tortoises, but Irene felt that the reason why she couldn't remember was because she couldn't be bothered. Later, when they went on asking questions and describing the tortoises and the ponies she began to remember and then remembered quite clearly because Alfie had taken a day off to take them up to London and had asked her to stay in the shop which meant that she didn't even have time off to go home at twelve o'clock for her dinner. She didn't know who it was in London had bought the tortoises and the ponies from Alfie because she hadn't asked and she couldn't ask him now because he had gone to India. She didn't know when he'd be back.

At the time, Irene had had no doubts about the correctness of her decision to insist that Guy should leave the nursing home and come back to Thawle. Even when Dr Templeton had told her that she was taking a great responsibility on her shoulders, she had felt strong and sure and prepared for responsibilities. But during the weeks that followed she worried about Guy and became more aware of her responsibilities. Not at any stage would she have gone back on her decision, but she became more understanding of Dr Templeton and his point of view.

Sometimes at night after she had gone to bed in Lady Evelyn's bedroom which they had moved into because of the big bed, she heard Guy outside the door, talking to his mother. Sometimes when he embraced Irene he called her my darling Irene, or my darling wife. Sometimes he called her little sister and sometimes he called her dearest Mummy. Irene remained herself and did not know how to deal with her shifting identities. In the nursing home it had been a different matter when he got muddled because the fact of his being there meant he was sick, but when he was discharged from the nursing home Irene had believed he had recovered, not only because she herself had believed so but because she had persuaded Dr Templeton to allow him to return to Thawle. She had known that he would be damaged, but she hadn't really admitted that it might be for ever and that for ever she might have to shift her identities. She didn't know whether to correct him when he was wrong or to assume all the roles he asked her to play and learn to slide in and out of them without becoming too distressed. It was going to be a strain and there was the baby to think of.

Irene kept up her confidence because Guy never had any doubts about Wilfred. He knew Wilfred was his son. He was absolutely certain and Irene felt that if you had only one certainty in your life maybe it could radiate outwards and throw light on other mix-ups and confusions. She saw it like that – his certainty about Wilfred – as a small but constant sun that would slowly in time spread its light into the darker troubled places of his spirit.

The burning of the Adam chairs came as a shock because of the violence and the unexpectedness when until then he had been so gentle and seemed to have settled down. A feeling of danger came out of it and stayed for several days. She felt she had to keep a close watch on the danger so as to be ready for it if it ever broke out again. But it wasn't easy to predict where and how it would show itself because it was in Guy's mind, and she could never have foreseen that he would decide to burn the Adam chairs. She didn't tell

Dr Templeton about the Adam chairs and the feeling of danger because she knew if she did, Dr Templeton would send Guy back to the nursing home where he would be sick again, and unhappy. But a week or two later, entering into her ninth month, she came to the conclusion that the burning of the Adam chairs had been a blessing in disguise – a last outburst in which Guy had got something off his chest. He changed. He went back to old habits.

Getting up early in the morning he cleaned out the fireplace and lit a fire so that the room would be warm for Irene when she got up. When the fire was burning he departed for his morning ride on Rolling Home. Afterwards he brought her breakfast on a tray always decorated with something pretty that had caught his fancy. A leaf, an acorn, a sprig of holly or a feather. Irene realised that they were gifts and looked forward to them, wondering what he would bring her next time.

Sitting on the end of the bed he told her how he loved riding in the winter when the leaves had fallen and he could see the sky through the bare trees that had branches like the trunks of elephants. He told her how, when they came out of the woods, Rolling Home cantered to a white gate and stood with his head raised and his ears pricked, looking out on the long fields that had once belonged to Thawle but had to be sold to help pay the probate after Lord Charles died, and how, when Guy turned him back to the woods, Rolling Home shook his head in a stubborn way and fought the reins because he didn't want to leave the scenes of his childhood.

Listening to the stories Guy told her about his rides through the woods and looking closely for the first time at acorns and pieces of holly, Irene realised that because she was a Londoner she hadn't used her eyes to look at country things and determined that after Wilfred was born she would tackle the woods again and wouldn't be afraid if Guy went with her.

After she had finished her breakfast Guy took her tray

down to the kitchen, changed from his riding clothes and went out to the orchard and the vegetable garden.

Irene was happy.

Wilfred

WHEN THE TIME came Guy drove Irene to the hospital in Bath. Irene had wanted to have her baby at Thawle because she said she wanted to keep an eye on things. Dr Templeton might have understood what she meant but he had passed her on to Dr Mount who told her that because she had a narrow pelvis and several other anatomical deficiencies, she ought to be delivered of the baby in hospital. Guy also wanted her to go to Bath where she would have expert attention and every care.

Wilfred was born at five o'clock in the evening. Guy wanted to watch the birth, but on being told that although this was sometimes allowed it wasn't allowed in that particular hospital, he waited outside in the corridor. There were no complications. In spite of her narrow pelvis, Irene's body performed naturally and there was no need for an anaesthetic. As soon as she was returned to her room, Guy was allowed to visit her and to see his child. Few newborn babies are particularly attractive and Wilfred was no exception. What most moved Guy about Wilfred were his fingers which felt like small moist pink caterpillars. He sat by Irene's bed, holding her hand and looking lovingly into her face. But she was tired and because he wouldn't stop kissing her and telling her how much he loved her, he was told that he had to go and could return in the morning.

Guy drove back to Thawle with joy in his heart different in kind to any joy he had known before. Giles had cooked roast beef and they dined together in the kitchen with a bottle of wine, toasting Wilfred and Irene.

Around midnight Guy woke up and lay calmly enclosed in an atmosphere that filled the room with peace and which seemed to emanate from his own happiness. He thought about Wilfred, but there wasn't a great deal that anyone could think about a child only eight hours old with a red crumpled face and tiny hands with fingers like caterpillars. The only possible thoughts that could come to mind about such a new, unformed creature were thoughts of what it might become and what might be in store for it. At first Guy allowed his mind to dwell on the resolve that as soon as Wilfred was old enough he would put him on the back of Percy, put the reins in his hands, his feet in the stirrups and show him how to make Percy gallop. When Wilfred was older he would put him on the back of Rolling Home, for Rolling Home was only eighteen and many a horse had lived to be thirty-five. Every summer he would take Irene and Wilfred to Trouville where Wilfred would ride a donkey. Irene, a sunshade tilted over her head, would hold the bridle and Guy would take a photograph.

Later, he allowed his thoughts to venture further and stumbled upon the fact that he was forty-two and that his mother had been forty-two when he was born. If he lived to be the same age as his mother, Wilfred would be forty-two on the day of his death. Wilfred, when he was forty-two, might be lying in the very bed where Guy was now lying, grieving for his father, just as he Guy had grieved for his mother. There seemed to Guy to be something harmonious about the way the years had fallen into shape.

But just before he was carried back to sleep on that sense of harmony and the correctness of the years, a doubt, a presentiment, came to him and threatened his expectations. Suppose he did not live to be eighty-four. Suppose he died next year. Wilfred would still be a baby, unable to walk or talk. Or suppose he died when he was fifty. Wilfred would be eight. Just a boy and too young to deal with the problems that would confront him.

Because he was tired, Guy went to sleep but with the

impression that just before sleep took him away into unconsciousness, a spike had been driven through his brain and
that he was bleeding. He didn't know how long he slept.
Perhaps only a few minutes, but long enough for his sleeping
mind to form a resolution which when he awoke possessed
him with such power he did not pause to question the
necessity for what had to be done.

He got up and dressed. In the attic he found the box in
which he had installed the elephants, buried under the walnut tree and dug up again after he returned from the nursing
home.

In the Library he opened the oyster-wood cabinet and put
the elephants back into the box along with the other birds
and animals. Outside in the orchard he buried the box in
the same spot, under the walnut tree.

In the kitchen he woke up the spaniels which since Lady
Evelyn's death had slept on a mat in front of the range. When
the spaniels had been sent outside he filled four baskets with
the kindling in the copper cauldron. He was very meticulous
about putting the same amount of kindling into each basket.
At first he put too much into one basket and had to take
some of it out to fill up the others. The wood was soft and
brittle because of the long dry summer, but it would need
paper to start it off. Newspapers rarely found their way to
Thawle, except the *Somerset Gazette* which Giles bought
every Saturday and Guy knew that there was a pile of *Somerset Gazettes* under Giles's bed, but he did not want to disturb
Giles. Because of the need for secrecy.

Searching in vain for paper, he thought of the Library
where Lord Frederick's books had been returned to the
bookcases. But because one of the bookcases had been sold,
some of the books were piled up on the floor, because, at
the time, there hadn't been anywhere else to put them. Guy
tore pages from the books on the floor, gathered them in his
arms and dividing them into three parts, heaped them up
under the Spanish curtains in the Morning Room.

Regarding the piles of paper and noting that one pile

was larger than the other two, he took some of the paper off the big pile and put it on the smaller ones so that the paper was evenly distributed. Then he put the kindling on top of the paper, arranging it carefully. Over the top of each pile he draped the end of a Spanish curtain.

When the Morning Room was ready, he returned to the Library. He put the covers of the books on one side and every now and again paused to look into them. Flashes of pleasure crossed his features as he browsed in a world of winding streams, feathers and pebbles set in gold cement. In a book that he could not remember having looked at before he came upon patterns that reminded him of the beech leaves, flattened by rain that had covered the path in the high woods when he had last taken his morning ride on Rolling Home. He piled the covers neatly in a corner and arranged kindling on the pages. In case of mishap he returned to the kitchen for three tins of paraffin which he bought in bulk because it was cheaper.

When the flames had climbed the Spanish curtains in the Morning Room and smoke gushed through the Library window, Giles woke up. It was the smell of smoke rather than the rush of sound and glare of flames that penetrated a heavy sleep induced by a surfeit of roast beef and red wine. The room seemed to be shifting and dancing around him. Bridles, saddles, spurs, and the green and white silks of the de Boissy stables flashed and sparkled in the bounding light. Images of flames, so vivid and close they looked like flames themselves licked over the polished sides of Lord Charles's racing trophies.

Still close to sleep, Giles struggled to understand where he was and what had happened to fill the quiet dark of his room with the menacing reflection of a projected disaster. For a moment he believed that he was on the point of being consumed by the fire that had towered over the orchard walls when the German bomber had crashed in 1943. Throwing on a coat, he stumbled out to the terrace to stand appalled, and for a split second entranced, by the awe-inspiring sight that filled his gaze. Flames from the windows of Thawle lit the belly of the smoke. Above, the smoke rolled in blue and white formations pierced by leaping sparks that died at their brightest moment. There was nothing else. The woods blotted out; the sky filled up. Only Thawle burning majestically. The night roared and crackled. Rolling Home, his eyes filled with flames, kicked in panic at his stall.

Giles came to his senses, freed the terrified horse and ran to the kitchen calling, 'Lord Guy! Lord Guy!'

The fire had not yet attacked the west wing and in the kitchen there was an extension to the telephone. But the line was dead. Giles opened the door leading through a passage to the hall. A wall of smoke swayed towards him. He was loyal and brave, but he was old and not heroic. Where in that multitude of rooms, stairways and attics would he find Guy? He rushed back to the terrace calling, 'Lord Guy! Lord Guy!'

Guy, who had been watching the fire from the front terrace, had gone back into the house to rescue Percy.

He ran through the hall, half-blinded by smoke and smacking at his hair to put out the sparks that were setting it alight. It was difficult getting Percy through the narrow door of the attic, but when he had managed the attic stairs it was easy shoving him along the passage. Smoke rose to meet him from the hall below and moved about beautifully, like the mists hanging over the Rustle in the valley. But it wasn't just a matter of getting Percy through the smoke. Flames were consuming the family portraits and the heat was so intense he doubted whether he would be able to get Percy through to the main door. There would be no time to stop and put out the smaller fires that were breaking out on his clothes and on Percy's mane.

He decided to take Percy down the stairs leading to the Octagonal Room. Here the fire he had lit and encouraged with paraffin hadn't been a success and had fizzled out. So he was able to manoeuvre Percy down the stairs and along a passage to an outside door behind the kitchens.

The fire, before it attacked the west wing, turned and

burnt out. Perhaps there had been a change in the wind. Giles felt it was a mystery and a small compensation for which one ought to feel gratitude. For there was still plenty of accommodation in the servants' quarters above the kitchen for Lord Guy de Boissy, Lady Irene, and their son, Wilfred.